Brutal Capture

All the naked soldiers were dead and dying.

Only the one upriver was unscathed, and he was firing his pistol. Once, twice, three times the gun fired. The enemy pistol exploded a fourth and fifth time at others, then the soldier aimed it at Crow Feather.

Crow Feather gritted his teeth and nudged his mount with alternating knees so the horse followed a crooked path toward the soldier.

Bang!

Crow Feather smiled. The sixth shot had missed. Now he would count coup upon the soldier. Feats of bravery were many among the Comanche, but not even killing and scalping an enemy warrior could compare with touching a live enemy.

Crow Feather charged the soldier. He was a brave man, for he did not run. . . . The soldier never flinched, even though he was almost a dead man. Behind the bluecoat, Crow Feather saw the warriors of his band watching. Crow feather saw no fear in his enemy's eyes. He saw only courage.

The two men stared at each other.

Then Crow Feather screamed.

Instantly the warriors who weren't taking scalps converged on the brave soldier. Five warriors jumped from their horses and swarmed to him.

"What shall we do with him?" Gives Gifts asked.

"Stake him to the ground," Crow Feather said. "Later we shall torture him."

TONY HILLERMAN'S FRONTIER

People of the Plains
The Tribes
The Soldiers
Battle Cry
Brothers in Blood
Cold Justice
Comanche Trail

Published by HarperPaperbacks

TONY HILLERMAN'S

FRONTIER

COMANCHE TRAIL

Will Camp

HarperPaperbacks
A Division of HarperCollins*Publishers*

HarperPaperbacks
A Division of Harper Collins*Publishers*
10 East 53rd Street, New York, NY 10022-5299

ISBN 0-06-101293-9

First printing: May 1999

Printed in the United States of America

❖10 9 8 7 6 5 4 3 2 1

For Jessica Lichtenstein,
with thanks

COMANCHE TRAIL

1

Santa Fe, Spring 1859

Captain Jean Francois Xavier Benoit answered the knock at the door of his spartan Army quarters. In the dying light of day, he saw Sergeant Hamilton Phipps waving a letter in his hand.

"General Smedley asked that I bring this to you."

"Another letter from Senator Couvillion?" Benoit asked, anger simmering in his voice.

Phipps nodded.

Benoit cursed silently as his jaw tightened. He made no effort to accept the letter or to invite Phipps inside.

The sergeant stood awkwardly a moment, his hand slowly falling. "Wish it was a letter from your wife, Captain."

Benoit realized his anger at Couvillion had made him forget his manners. He motioned for Phipps to enter.

Phipps lifted his right foot, displaying his muddy boot. "Don't want to track up your room."

"Can't hurt a hard-packed dirt floor like this, Sergeant."

"Won't do it no good either."

Benoit looked at his candlelit room, taking in the cot,

the table and stool where he managed his correspondence, a trunk for his clothing, a small corner fireplace, and a washbasin on a washstand in the opposite corner. "These adobe quarters aren't exactly palaces, Sergeant."

"Better than enlisted men's quarters, sir, and besides, Lieutenant Coker's giving a concert in a half hour and I need to get over there soon to get a good seat."

"I'd forgotten about that, Sergeant." Benoit took the letter from Phipps. "Thank you for reminding me."

Phipps nodded sympathetically. "You're anxious for them to get here, aren't you, your wife and daughters?"

"Wouldn't you be, if you'd never seen your twin daughters?"

"Army's a hard life for families, Captain. Lieutenant Coker hasn't seen his wife and girls for eighteen months."

"I don't know whether it's tougher on a man never having seen his daughters, like me, or being like Lieutenant Coker, separated from them." Benoit ran his fingers through his dark hair.

"Sir, I must be going if I'm to get a seat at the Governor's Palace for the concert."

"So they moved the piano from the saloon?"

"Yes, sir! You know Lieutenant Coker, as straight as they come. He wouldn't play where there was sin." Phipps grinned and saluted, then spun about and strode away, his boots making slurping noises as he escaped down the muddy street.

Benoit shut the door softly and walked to the table that served as his desk. He sat on the stool, fingering the letter a moment, then reached for a bundle of letters tied together with twine. He loosened the twine, slid the letter beneath the string and retied it. He didn't have to count to know that the bundle held seven letters, each from Couvillion, each unopened and each unanswered.

He tossed the bundle aside, picked up the top letter from another bundle, and reread the most recent missive from his wife, Inge, marooned by winter at Fort Laramie, his previous post.

Winter had seemed to linger forever in Santa Fe to Captain Jean Francois Xavier Benoit because of his separation from his family. When winter finally did break, spring came in a rush. One day it had been unbearably cold and the streets of the territorial capital were carpeted with an inch of snow as pure as a virgin's sheets. But by the following day, the sun had muscled through the low-hanging clouds. The snow, crisscrossed with the tracks of men, animals, and wooden wheels, and smudged with the pinyon smoke that settled like a gray veil upon the winter precipitation, had turned the streets and paths of Santa Fe into mush. The warmth of the days increased, and the chill of each passing night diminished.

The abundant snows in the mountains began their annual melt, first with a trickle, then with a gush that filled the stream beds that ultimately fed the mighty Rio Grande River as it roiled southward toward Texas and Mexico, providing the very boundary that separated them.

The land was the tawny color of a doe's skin, splotched with the gray of rocks shouldering their way through and the green of plants vying for precious moisture plentiful in the spring, scarce the remainder of the year. The pinyon pine with their dark green needles, and the juniper bushes with their needlelike leaves, were hardy but not colorful. The scattered cacti were efficient collectors of water but certainly not ostentatious in appearance.

Inge was like the desert cacti, Benoit thought. She was not the prettiest woman he had ever met, but she was the best. She was practical, dependable, and so loving that her daughters, like their father, would never want for affection. He had never seen Colleen and Ellen, but Inge had sent him a lock of hair from each. No treasure could mean more to him. Benoit unfolded the sheet of paper in which Inge had secured each lock of hair with a drop of candle wax. Beneath each she had written the daughter's name. Softly, Benoit stroked each lock of hair with his finger. An angel's hair could not have been softer. He touched the soft hair a final time, then returned the treasure to its envelope.

He knew he had his best friend to thank for his two daughters. First Lieutenant Jason "Jace" Caldwell Dobbs had been post surgeon at Fort Laramie while Benoit was stationed there. The babies had been premature, and only Dobbs's medical skills saved them. It had been Inge's idea to name one girl Colleen, for Dobbs's late wife, and the other Ellen, for the woman Dobbs had planned to marry at Fort Laramie before her tragic death.

Benoit arose from his stool, tucked his Army blouse in his pants, then grabbed his hat and blew out the candle on the table. The glowing coals from the corner fireplace warmed the room and illuminated it with a soft light.

Benoit placed his hat atop his head, then stepped out the door and into the muddy street. Though officially stationed at Fort Marcy, few soldiers actually lived on the fort proper on the outskirts of town. Instead, most lived in quarters near the compound that was headquarters for the Ninth Military District, which oversaw eleven forts in New Mexico Territory. Benoit, a captain years before his time because of Senator Couvillion's distant manipulations, was aide-de-camp for Brigadier General Arnold Smedley, commander of the Ninth Military District. As aide-de-camp, Benoit was in the perfect position to know the Army's vulnerability in New Mexico Territory. This vulnerability could give the South a doorway to the West and the mining riches to finance the war that nearly everyone feared was inevitable, as the United States grappled with slavery, states' rights, King Cotton, and the myriad other issues driving a wedge between North and South.

As he walked two blocks down the street toward the Governor's Palace, he treaded between low-slung adobe buildings with tiny windows and thick plank doors. He turned at the plaza and glanced toward the outline of the adobe parish church, its crenellated bell towers standing as holy bookends to a cross that rose majestically between them. The cross seemed to glow white against the darkening sky, which was fading from the rich maroon of a priest's vestment to the pitch-black of the devil's soul.

Other people were converging on the Governor's Palace, a long adobe building that housed the territorial government and fronted the north side of the plaza where the Santa Fe Trail ended. Except for community socializing on those rare pleasant days of winter, the plaza had been almost lifeless since late November, when the last of the caravans from Missouri arrived. The trade would resume shortly; several caravans were likely on the trail already, each hoping to reach Santa Fe first in the spring so they could get top dollar for goods the locals had been unable to acquire for four months.

Benoit stepped upon the plank walk beneath the narrow portico that provided a functional adornment to the sorely misnamed Governor's Palace. As he stomped his boots to clear the mud, he saw his commanding officer approaching.

In the dim light that escaped from the palace's small windows, Benoit made out the general's thin frame and wide handlebar mustache, which hung from the corners of his mouth like cavern stalactites. His uniform was as crisp as military regulations demanded, and his boots, despite the mud, seemed spotless.

Benoit saluted sharply, and the general answered with a crisp salute and a question.

"Another letter from Senator Couvillion?"

Benoit nodded.

"How many does that make, Captain?"

"Seven."

"Have you answered any?"

"No, sir. I haven't even opened them."

The general nodded. "I pledged to help you with this unfortunate intrusion into your military affairs."

"You know he wants information detrimental to the United States Army, sir, should war come."

"I do, Captain. And, I also know you are a man of honor who takes his oath of allegiance to protect and defend the Constitution of the United States much more seriously than does the senator. If you do not respond, he could make matters worse for you. You haven't forgotten your time in the stockade at Fort Fillmore, have you?"

Benoit shook his head. How could he forget being imprisoned for killing a scalp hunter in self-defense and then being threatened with a court-martial until he had agreed to gather intelligence for Couvillion? When

Benoit returned to Santa Fe, he confessed his agreement to General Smedley, his new commander. The general, a man who also took his oath of allegiance seriously, had promised to assist him.

"Bring the letters to my office tomorrow, Captain," the general told Benoit now, "and we'll make the senator happy without giving him any information of value."

"Thank you, sir."

Smedley reached out and put his hand on Benoit's shoulder. "The politicians are ruining this country because so few are men of honor. Men of honor are more often drawn to the military. It is both an inherent strength and weakness of a democracy."

"May I ask you a question, sir?"

"Certainly, Captain."

"If war comes, how will you side? With your state or with your country?"

"I have taken an oath to the United States, not to Mississippi."

Benoit, who was also a southerner, nodded. "That is how I feel."

Smedley dropped his hand from Benoit's shoulder and paused, as if he had something more to say.

"It is not an easy choice, is it, General?"

"No, sir," Smedley replied, "not when Jefferson Davis is your cousin and all your kin are Mississippi bred."

Benoit had known that Senator Jefferson Davis, one of the South's leading firebrands, was Smedley's third cousin.

The general turned and walked away. For a moment, Benoit thought he noticed a sag in Smedley's straight shoulders as people crowded around him to get into the Governor's Palace.

Benoit finished scraping off his boots, then moved toward the double door of the palace. Just as he was about to enter, a man with a wide-brimmed hat stepped in front of him.

"*Buenas noches*," the man greeted him, touching the brim of his hat with an index finger, his face hidden beneath the wide hat.

Benoit knew of but one man in Santa Fe who wore a hat that wide: Alejandro Frederico Valentin Valencia Ortiz, son of a landed father in Mora Valley northeast of Santa Fe.

"*¡Alejo, que milagro verte aqui!*" Benoit answered.

"It's great to be here, Jean, and your Spanish is improving."

"I've had plenty of time to work on it this winter, but my Spanish will never be as perfect as your English," Benoit answered, recalling that Ortiz had spent several years attending a Jesuit school in St. Louis. The two had met the previous year when Benoit was new to Santa Fe and had wandered down a street into the Barrio de Analco, a neighborhood of Mexican Indians who despised the American soldiers. When several young men had attacked Benoit, Ortiz had rushed to his aid and extricated him from the thugs.

"I have come to hear the concert," Ortiz said. "I hear Lieutenant Coker is quite good. I have not heard good piano since I last left St. Louis, and that has been seven years ago now."

The two men fell in beside each other and entered the Governor's Palace, being swept with the tide to the building's largest room, crammed with rows of finished and rough-hewn benches.

Benoit removed his hat like all the other men, save Ortiz.

The Hispano pointed to a bench along the back wall. "Can we sit together, Jean?"

"I prefer to be nearer the piano."

"It is better for me to sit near the back. When I remove my hat, many people find my scars repulsive. I prefer to prevent them—and me—the pain."

"Then the back it is." As Benoit turned he saw Lieutenant Frank Coker pacing back and forth beside the piano. Benoit tried to catch his eye, but the lieutenant was intently focused on the program.

Benoit trailed Ortiz to the back row. They seated themselves.

"Music," Ortiz said, lowering his head so the brim screened him from a pair of young children, "is the only art that the blind man can truly enjoy. Perhaps he enjoys it even more than the man with all his senses."

"You should talk to my friend Jace Dobbs of Fort Laramie, because that's the kind of question he would love."

"But not a question you'd give much thought to?" Ortiz asked, lifting his head again to make sure no children were watching.

Benoit smiled. Ortiz was known as "El Disfigurao," the Disfigured One, among the Hispanos. Captured by a Comanche band led by the great warrior Buffalo Hump, Ortiz had been tortured and hung over a fire so that his head might roast. A cavalry patrol had arrived in time to save his life, if not his appearance. Between the scars, his face was red and peeling from jawline to the top of his bald head. He had no eyebrows, eyelashes, or facial hair, and his eyelids closed only with great effort. Before the torture, Ortiz had likely been a handsome man, but afterward, even his own father could not stand to look at him, and in fact had expelled him from the family's lands in the Mora Valley. Ortiz now ran the freighting business which had made his father a wealthy man.

"Tell me about Lieutenant Coker," Ortiz asked.

"As good an officer as you will find, a Pennsylvanian by birth, Bellefonte, as I recall. Plays the piano and plays it well. Misses his wife and daughters back East. A moral man of strong principles."

Ortiz laughed. "There are no principles in the freighting business."

Benoit pointed to the door as a short man in a priest's garb entered. "The archbishop himself is joining us."

Ortiz crossed himself. "Why is it when I talk of no principles in the freighting business, the priest arrives? To remind me I must go to confession."

Archbishop Joseph P. Machebeuf stood but four inches over five feet tall. He carried in his right hand a Bible well-worn, and well-read through the silver-rimmed spectacles that enlarged his eyes. A silver cross dangled from the chain around his neck. He gazed across the room as a shepherd observes his flock, then moved to the front.

"As short as he is, Alejo, he'll be like your blind man and unable to see unless he sits in the front row."

"As long as he doesn't sit near me and ask for my tithe, I will be happy."

Both men laughed, though Ortiz's chuckle died suddenly.

Benoit saw his friend stiffen on the bench. "*¿Que es eso?*" he asked.

Ortiz pointed to a man just entering the room. "That is Eduardo Crespin, a despicable Comanchero who trades with the Comanches. He sells them guns and powder and lead and liquor, and they terrorize New

Mexico and Texas and Mexico. No man is more despicable. He trades goods for captives to sell as slaves."

A swarthy man with dark eyes and a black, untrimmed mustache, Crespin wore a sombrero and a red serape draped across his chest. He swaggered into the room, stood staring at the crowd, then picked out a spot he wanted. He stepped to the bench and motioned for two men to make room. One hesitated. Crespin grabbed him by the throat and squeezed his neck. The man quickly abandoned his claim to the seat.

"Between Archbishop Machebeuf and Crespin is the best and worst of New Mexico Territory," Ortiz said, "or maybe even the world."

Before Benoit could answer, Lieutenant Coker stepped before the audience and held up his hands. As the audience quieted, Benoit estimated there were a hundred fifty people packed into the room.

Ortiz removed his hat, and the man beside him grimaced, arose, then tried to slip discreetly away. No one moved to claim the empty spot on the bench.

"Thank you for coming this evening," Coker announced. "We are all anxious for spring to arrive for good, so I would like to begin with 'Spring Song' by Felix Mendelssohn. I hope you enjoy it."

Coker turned to face the piano, wriggled his fingers, then seated himself on the stool. He lifted his hands, then pounced upon the ivory keys.

The moment the music arose from the piano, the people became as one noiseless body soaking up the melodic strains that permeated the room. Benoit closed his eyes and relaxed, letting his thoughts be swept away by his imagination. He saw Inge running in a mountain meadow of spring flowers. She was carrying a bundle in each arm, and when he ran to meet her, the bundles were his daughters, Colleen and Ellen, their laughter as reassuring as the music itself.

When the song ended, Benoit opened his eyes and clapped exuberantly with the rest of the audience. Next, Coker played a minuet by Luigi Boccherini, a serenade by Joseph Haydn, then a suite by George Frederic Handel.

When he completed the Handel selection, the audience broke into sustained applause. Coker stood and acknowledged their praise with a bow. After the applause died, Coker spoke.

"I prefer the classics because they capture the full range of emotion that great music can inspire. Then there is music by Stephen Foster."

The crowd applauded.

"I'd like to play 'Camptown Races,' 'Oh! Susanna,' and 'My Old Kentucky Home.' Then I want you to hear a new song, just four years old, called 'Listen to the Mockingbird.' After that I will play a song I learned when the Army had me in Tennessee. It's a haunting melody called 'Sandy River Belle.'"

Coker returned to the piano and sat down. He attacked the keys as exuberantly as before. The audience turned raucous, the Anglos and the Hispanos who knew English singing the words to "Camptown Races," while those who spoke no English bobbed their heads to the music. "Oh! Susanna" received a similar boisterous reception, before "My Old Kentucky Home" calmed the audience. The lieutenant ended with "Sandy River Belle."

When Coker finished, the audience burst into applause, then stood and stomped their feet on the floor. Coker returned to the piano and played "Sandy River Belle" one more time, then stood up and took a final bow, receiving thunderous applause.

But loud as the applause was, Coker could not be tempted back to the keyboard once again, and people began to file out of the room.

Ortiz pulled his hat down snugly on his head and nodded to Benoit. "Your friend is very good. I should like to invite you and he to La Estrella for drinks and some games of chance."

"*Gracias*, Alejo, *gracias*, but Lieutenant Coker does not drink or gamble."

"Then at least let me congratulate him on a fine performance."

"Certainly."

The two men made their way to Coker. The lieutenant grinned widely and stepped toward Benoit.

"Jean, I'm so glad you came." He smiled warmly.

"It was delightful, Frank," he said. "The Army is a waste of your talents."

Coker's face darkened for an instant.

"Frank," Benoit continued, "I'd like you to meet Alejandro Frederico Valentin Valencia Ortiz. Alejo for short."

Ortiz took Coker's hand and shook it warmly. "A pleasure to meet you, sir. Your music was beautiful, and please forgive me for not taking off my hat. I am a difficult one to look at, thanks to the Comanche."

"I am flattered by your kind words," Coker replied.

"You will have to do it again, soon," Benoit suggested.

Coker frowned.

Benoit realized something was amiss.

"There won't be a next time, Jean." Coker looked around the room, confirming that it was empty. "I plan to resign my commission from the United States Army tomorrow."

"But why, Frank? You're a fine officer, the kind the Army needs, especially now with the country in such turmoil."

"My family needs me more."

"Send for them."

"Sara Ann wants roots, and we both know the Army is a rootless existence. I'm going back home to be with her and my girls. You'll understand once you see your twins."

"But what will you do, Frank?"

"There's been a new university created four years ago. The Pennsylvania State University, it's called. They need teachers, and my experience at the Military Academy qualifies me to teach. So I'll be teaching mathematics, possibly even Latin."

"Congratulations, though I can't say I ever figured you for a college teacher. Even so, I'm sure gonna miss you."

Coker smiled. "I plan to tell General Smedley in the morning. I should be gone in two weeks."

"I can't forget you're the one who brought me the letter informing me I was a papa. It was the best news ever delivered to me."

"The honor was mine." Coker turned to Ortiz. "It was a pleasure to meet you, Senor Ortiz."

"Alejo, *por favor*."

"Alejo, then. I am flattered that you liked my music, and I am sorry that I will not have the opportunity to get to know you. Any man worthy enough to be a friend of Jean Benoit is my friend also."

"*¡Gracias!*"

Benoit sensed that Coker wanted to be left alone. "I'll visit you more tomorrow."

Coker nodded, then turned and walked to the piano. "I want to play a few songs for myself."

As Benoit accompanied Ortiz out the door, they heard the results of Coker's supple fingers on the keyboard.

Once outside, Ortiz repeated his earlier offer. "The invitation to La Estrella still stands. I'll buy the drinks."

"*Gracias,*" Benoit said, thinking a drink might counter Coker's news.

Benoit moved with Ortiz along the muddy streets and backways that led to La Estrella, another low-slung, windowless adobe building, though larger than most in Santa Fe, and the premier gambling hall in New Mexico Territory. No sign identified the building, and nothing indicated that the thick plank door facing the street opened into the gambling den. The thick adobe walls muffled the noise so well that Benoit heard nothing until he was within reach of the door, where he made out the din of men gambling, drinking, and whoring.

Ortiz pushed open the door and stepped in, Benoit behind him. The dim illumination from the wall sconces and crude candle chandeliers hanging low from the ceilings showed a crowded, smoke-filled room that reeked of cigars, tobacco juice, cheap liquor, and unwashed bodies.

The front room was for monte, a simple card game that infatuated the Hispanos, while one back room conducted poker and another provided two billiard tables. Any man with money, no matter how much or how little, was welcome to lose it at La Estrella.

Ortiz started toward Doña Rosalia's monte table, then stopped in his tracks and grabbed Benoit by the arm. "Scoundrel," he growled, then pointed to the monte table.

There sat Eduardo Crespin, the Comanchero.

"You despise him, Alejo. Why?"

Ortiz yanked his hat from his head, then pointed to the scars and pulp. "That is why." He flopped his hat back on his head and grimaced. "He bought his goods from my father's competitor in freighting, which is his right, yes. But when he learned that I was returning from the university in St. Louis with some of my father's wagons, the Comanche attacked. I cannot prove it, but I know he sent them to attack the wagons, for the Comanche do not normally travel as far north as the Cimarron cutoff. Some say he was with them and even bragged about watching me roast. I did not see him. You don't look for acquaintances when you're being cooked. One day, I'll return the favor, but not tonight."

He turned toward the door. "I've lost my appetite for gaming and drink, my friend. Would you mind if we left?"

"Not at all," Benoit said. "I must meet with General Smedley first thing in the morning, and it would be best if tonight's drink did not dull my senses."

Benoit followed Ortiz toward the door, squeezing between the men jammed around the monte tables and the rouged women vying for their attention and their money.

Benoit was almost to the door when he felt a hand close around his arm. He spun around, his fist doubling instinctively.

Instantly, he was barraged with an Irish brogue. "Cap'n Benoit, it's good to be seein' ya."

"Well, Tim McManus, how have you been doing?" Benoit replied, studying the scout who had led him on a failed expedition against the Apache back in the fall.

McManus wore a grin as wide as a barrel stave.

"Been doin' grand, winnin' money 'nuff at the monte table to keep me in drink but not 'nuff to keep me drunk. Means I can walk home without fallin' in the mud. Beats chasin' 'Paches 'cross the territory."

"You giving up scouting?"

"Been thinkin' 'bout goin' up to Coloradi, see if I can uncover some of that gold they keep findin' 'round Pike's Peak. I hear, yes I do, that they be findin' gold nuggets the size of washtubs." He lifted a bottle of whiskey. "Care for a nip?" The mouth of the bottle disappeared in the full beard framing a bronzed face, shaded by the brim of the high-crowned slouch hat that made him appear taller than his five and a half feet.

"Not tonight," Benoit replied, looking over his shoulder and seeing Ortiz waiting for him at the door.

McManus pulled the bottle from his lips and laughed. "May not be any tomorrow night, if me luck sours."

"I'll risk it."

"Cap'n, I admire a man who lives dangerously."

"We'll visit when you're sober." Benoit turned for the door.

"That could be summer, unless'n I find one of them washtub nuggets, and then it'd be never," McManus called after him.

Ortiz opened the door at Benoit's approach and both men emerged into the night air, which was cool and fresh compared to the stuffiness and smoke of La Estrella.

"Another time," Benoit said.

"Indeed," Ortiz replied, "when Eduardo Crespin is not around."

Benoit reached the headquarters of the Ninth Military District early, arriving well before Sergeant Phipps, but not before Lieutenant Frank Coker, whose voice he heard coming through the cracked door into General Smedley's office.

Benoit retreated to his small office down the hall and tossed the bundle of letters from Senator Couvillion on his desk. He filled out requisitions until he heard the general's door swing fully open and the voices of Smedley and Coker.

"Like I said, Lieutenant, I'm sorry to lose you. Your resignation will be a loss to the Army, but you must do what's right for yourself and your family."

"Thank you, General."

Benoit picked up the letters and stepped into the hall.

"Morning, Captain," Smedley called. The general pinched the bridge of his nose between his thumb and forefinger, then shook his head at Coker. "There may come a day when we all have to decide our future with the Army. Maybe you're right to get out now."

"If it comes to war, General, it'll catch up with us all, regardless of whether or not we're in the Army," Coker answered.

"Perhaps you're right, Lieutenant, perhaps you're right." He grabbed Coker's hand and shook it. "Good luck to you."

Coker saluted the general, turned about and marched outside.

No sooner had he slipped away than Sergeant Hamilton Phipps entered. He saluted Smedley and Benoit.

"Lieutenant Coker's turned in his resignation," Smedley said.

Phipps cursed. "He's a good officer and a good piano player. We'll miss him and his music."

Smedley turned to Benoit. "I suppose you brought the correspondence from Senator Couvillion."

Benoit nodded.

Smedley pointed to his office and waited for Benoit to enter, then followed him inside and closed the door. He motioned for Benoit to take a seat.

Benoit obliged, then offered the bundled letters to Smedley.

Smedley waved them away. "You haven't opened them?"

"No, sir. They'll only bring more misery."

"If you don't answer them, he'll likely make your life even more miserable. I want you to read the letters. Then I'll read them. Together we'll decide how to answer them."

"I am grateful, General." Benoit ripped open the end of the first letter and pulled it from the envelope. In the letter, the senator reminded him of his pledge to spy on the Army in New Mexico, and further demanded that Benoit spy on General Smedley as well.

"Sir," Benoit said, "let me read you this section."

"Go ahead."

Benoit cleared his throat. "'There are times that I question whether it was wise to use my influence to get General Arnold Smedley appointed as commander of the Ninth Military District. Though he is a third cousin to Jefferson Davis, the great senator from Mississippi and former Secretary of War, his blood does not boil with the same fervor as that of his cousin, a true patriot to the U.S. Constitution.

"'We cannot win a war without true believers in our cause. You must observe General Smedley carefully and make sure he is a true son of the South, a son who can be counted on.'"

Smedley growled. "Son of a bitch. How dare he talk about true patriots when he's plotting treason."

Benoit finished the letter, then passed it on to the general, who snatched it from his hand. Smedley stepped to the window and began to read. Benoit saw the general's face redden in anger.

Tearing the end off the next letter—the thickest of the seven—Benoit pulled it free, then unfolded the nine pages.

The letter, written three months before, spoke not of the Army, but of national politics:

Jean,

These are bad times for this nation. Perhaps you do not realize that, being isolated from news in New Mexico Territory, but the time is approaching when we must destroy the evil that seeks to keep white men from living by the Constitution as it was written. There is a misinformed upstart lawyer in Illinois who has taken it upon himself to be the lapdog of the abolitionists. He challenged that state's fine Senator Stephen Douglas, who has represented Illinois nobly since 1847. Abe Lincoln is this rabid dog's name and he debated Senator Douglas throughout the fall in Illinois.

When it came time to vote, the sensible people of Illinois saw fit to return the noble Senator Douglas back to office. But the press have seen fit to elevate this abolitionist cur as a potential candidate for the presidency in 1860.

The mere suggestion is a blasphemy upon the Constitution. Can you imagine a man such as him elected to the presidency? It would surely mean war. After all, the abolitionist papers are attributing to him many comments such as, "There is no reason in the world why the Negro is not entitled to all the natural rights enumerated in the Declaration of Independence—the right to life, liberty, and the pursuit of happiness. I hold that he is as much entitled to these as the white man."

This cannot be. The framers of the Declaration of Independence did not think of the Negro when they wrote that noble document. They thought only of white men, men of European birth and descent. Only they have equality among men, for only they have the intelligence and desire to fulfill their responsibility in a democracy.

Thomas Jefferson, who wrote that document, owned slaves from the day of his majority until the day of his death. He did not say or imply that his Negro slaves, which were little more than his property, were his equal under law created by divine inspiration in the minds of white men.

No man of sound mind can believe that the wise signers of the Declaration of Independence declared the Negroes as their equals. All the thirteen colonies had slaves at the time of the Declaration of Independence, and many if not all of the signers to that holy document had slaves. Not one of the signers emancipated his slaves after he signed the Declaration of Independence, so surely they did not perceive the slaves as their equals.

Even when they wrote the U.S. Constitution, which is now threatened by the abolitionists, they instructed that the census count the Negro as only three-fifths of a man. Three-fifths is not the equal of the whole, and the Negro is not the equal of the white man. To say otherwise is to accuse the signers of the Declaration of Independence and the authors of the Constitution of a hypocrisy without limit. I am not prepared to do that because it is the true treason of our age.

The founders of our republic made sure that the states should have the right to determine those issues for themselves. It is not for my beloved Louisiana to say what Massachusetts should do. If the citizens of that state decide to establish or abolish slavery, then I will not interfere.

Likewise, it is not for the citizens of Massachusetts to decide what the citizens of Louisiana should do. Louisiana has the right of self-determination. Should Louisiana lose that right, then all states will lose the right, and once the central authority takes it over, it will lead to oppression of the many by the few, and those few will reside now and forever in the District of Columbia.

The letter went on for eight more pages, listing Senator Couvillion's arguments for slavery and states' rights and against a strong central government.

Couvillion concluded,

The Army is the arm of that central government. Under such rabble-rousers as Abe Lincoln, that arm can easily be raised to strike the very citizens who believe in the ideals of our Declaration of Independence and our U.S. Constitution.

That is why you are so important to our cause, Jean. From within the Army you can see that it does not turn against the true patriots and that it strikes down miscreants like Abe Lincoln. By gathering information upon the Army, you can surely help the true patriots if the Army does attack the very people it is supposed to defend.

Benoit shook his head and passed the letter to Smedley. As the general started reading it, Benoit opened another. The letters were much the same, though the tone toward Benoit changed in the later letters from one of reason to one of threat if Benoit did not respond.

He read them all, then passed them to the general, whose anger was visible in his reddened face and the bulging veins in his neck. When Smedley was done, he tossed the last letter onto the desk.

"I will work with you to answer those letters in a manner that will keep you true to your oath," he said. "It is the rantings of men like Senator Couvillion that will bring a great sorrow upon this country."

2

Coahuila, Mexico, April 1859

On the north bank of the Rio Sabinas just before it received the waters of the Rio Nadadores eight-year-old Armando Sardinas stood chunking rocks into the river while his father and two brothers paused for a smoke. They rolled the tobacco in fine corn husks, then touched twigs to the dying embers of the fire that had warmed their lunch. When the fire took hold, the men transferred the flame to the tips of their cigarettes and inhaled. The dry corn husks flared up as the three sucked in the bitter smoke, then exhaled quickly. The corn husks burned quicker than the papers the mayordomo could afford for his cigarettes, but he was *muy rico* and could afford such luxuries, as well as fine cigars that burned sweeter than nectar.

When Armando saw his brothers, Miguel and Jesus, squatting around the fire with their cigarettes, he squatted too. Picking up a twig that he broke into the length of a cigarette, he poked it in the corner of his mouth like his father, Manuel Sardinas.

"Don't choke on your fine cigar," Miguel teased.

Armando could tolerate his brother's teasing because now he was of an age to help shear the sheep. He could consider himself a man. Miguel, barely twelve, was shearing sheep for his first season, and Armando had assumed his chores in the process. Jesus, at sixteen, had manned shears for four years and was getting as adroit as his father at snipping away the wool without cutting the pink flesh beneath it.

Beyond the men with their cigarettes, his father's sheep circled nervously under the watchful eye of their dog, Blanco, who skittered back and forth keeping the flock from escaping the makeshift pen. The men had driven stakes into the ground with their axes, then circled the stakes with their lariats tied together. The sheep could easily have jumped over the ropes or ducked beneath them were it not for Blanco, ever vigilant that no animal might escape. More than 230 sheep, half already sheared and the other half nervously waiting for their punishment for surviving the winter, milled about. The sheep bleated their protests and stamped their tiny hooves in anxiety but made no effort to escape, for they could not outrun Blanco.

Once the sheep were sheared and the wool bagged and delivered to the mayordomo's hacienda, Manuel Sardinas would receive his pay for a winter's work. The mayordomo would grow richer and have money for cigars, while Manuel Sardinas would barely have enough to make it until the fall. But at least they had mutton to eat and an occasional beef the mayordomo would slaughter for his shepherds and vaqueros to share with their families.

As the men smoked their cigarettes to nubs, Armando tossed the twig from his mouth into the river. He jumped from the bank to a large flat rock on the edge of the stream. He teetered for a moment before he found his balance, then quickly squatted and dipped his cupped hand into the water. The water was cool, and he splashed another handful on his cheeks for the work was hot and dusty. He looked at his reflection in the water. The river was a distorted mirror, and his eyes seemed to sparkle and dance like a candle flame. His black hair was matted to his forehead. He had never felt more tired nor more proud, for now he was surely a man. Even if he didn't shear the sheep like them, he treated the cuts where the sharp blades had nicked flesh instead of wool. He gathered the wool and put it in great sacks, stuffing as much inside as his aching muscles could before his father used his strength to compress it even more.

"Armando," his father called, "it is time to go to work."

Armando scooped up another handful of water and tossed it down his throat, splattering most of it on his face and shirt. He pounced off the rock, then bounded up the shallow bank and toward the shearing stations the men had set up in the soft shade of the cottonwoods clumped along the river.

Herding sheep was a poor man's occupation, requiring little equipment: shears and a whetstone for sharpening the blades regularly; axes for cutting wood for kindling or stakes for temporary fencing; a copper caldron for rendering tallow; knives for slaughtering sheep; poison for combatting wolves, coyotes, and other predators; and a well-trained dog. With a dog, a man didn't require a horse, for he could easily work the animals by foot.

Since Manuel Sardinas could not afford a flock of his own, he rented one from the mayordomo and shared the profits. He was proud that he had brought the flock through the winter without a loss to weather or predators. This would be his best year ever.

Manuel took up his shears and began to sharpen the blades until the metal was shiny. The shears were two blades joined by a U-shaped handle of the same metal. The handle was stiff, and squeezing it required a man's strength.

When his brother had gone to fetch his next sheep, Armando grabbed Miguel's shears and squeezed the handle. The spring action was stiff and required both his hands. One day, though, he knew he would be strong enough and he would shear more than his brothers.

Their father demanded that his sons produce by age. Jesus, being older, was expected to have sheared more sheep than Miguel. When each boy finished, he notched a broken limb he kept at his feet. At the end of the tally, his father would add up the totals and make sure they tallied with the sheep in the pen.

Armando watched his father walk in the narrow opening they had left between the two stakes that closed the circle. Manuel lunged for the nearest unsheared animal, grabbed its hind leg and dragged it out of the pen. The animal kicked, stamped, and tried to escape, all the while bleating, to no avail. Reaching the shade with his struggling ewe, he threw it on its side, jammed his knee against the animal's hindquarters, and wrapped his arm around the animal's neck, beginning to clip the greasy coat. The wool fell away in sheets.

Armando ran to the tree where he had left his bucket. It rested beside the musket the mayordomo had loaned them to protect against predators and, if the need be, against Comanches. He stood beside the gun, which was taller than him by a head, proud that he could actually reach out and touch the weapon.

"Armando," his father called. "Bring the bucket."

Heeding his father, Armando grabbed the bucket's

rope handle and raced to Manuel's side. Armando's job was to daub the cuts with a tarry concoction that looked black as night and smelled worse than anything short of death.

Armando grabbed the stick with its end wrapped in a cloth that was now saturated with the black goo. The stick made a popping sound as he pulled it from the disgusting salve. He swabbed the bleeding cut on the animal's shoulder, making sure that he completely covered the wound and its perimeter.

Proud though he was to be with his father and brothers, the job was boring and he was tired. He knew it would be at least four hours before his father quit for the day, and that would only happen when it got too dark to see or they finished the flock.

"Pay attention, Armando. Your job is the most important of all."

"How can it be, Papa?"

"You know that I made it through the winter without losing a single animal, not even a lamb."

"I know that, *sí*. You are a good herdsman."

"But each cut can destroy an animal."

Jesus called out, "Nick!"

Armando rushed from his father to his oldest brother and dabbed the tar upon the cut. Darting back to his father, he almost bumped into Miguel, who was dragging his next sheep to his station.

"If we do not dope the wounds, the blowflies will be drawn to the blood and will lay their eggs in the open wound. The eggs will become maggots, which will eat the flesh and kill the animal."

"Nick!" Miguel called, and Armando jumped to treat his animal before returning to his father.

"Maggots, Papa, what are they?"

"They are like the grubs you dig from the earth, like short fat worms. Have you ever seen a dead animal after a few days? It's swarming with flies and maggots."

Armando nodded.

"Sheep are God's best animal gift to man, my son."

"Why, Papa?"

"Because they give you wool and lambs. You must kill the cow to get his hide, but you can shear the sheep twice a year, just as we do in late March or early April and again in August. And the lambs come twice a year, in January and July. Even Jesus Christ was a shepherd, so the padre says."

As soon as his brothers released their animals, Armando gathered the wool and stuffed it in the bags. He was tired, but he enjoyed being a little man and learning from his father. And though his father never missed a beat of work while talking, he seemed to enjoy teaching his son what he knew.

His father, just finishing his animal, motioned for Armando to come to him and inspect the animal, daubing anything that looked like a scratch before turning the animal loose. Armando slapped the rag stick in the tar and pulled it out, then touched the animal in several spots.

Behind him, Armando heard Blanco growl, then start barking wildly. Blanco's excitement flustered the sheep, which fought harder.

Armando stabbed at the ewe with the tar, but the animal broke free from his father. That had not happened before. "Papa?" he said as he looked up at his father.

Manuel Sardinas had collapsed upon both knees, snapping the shears in his right hand. Armando did not understand. Then he saw the arrow.

Miguel screamed.

Armando looked at the arrow, staring at the feathers beneath the notch, then following with his gaze the slender wooden shaft that ended in his father's chest.

"Comanche!" Jesus cried.

Armando saw but did not understand.

Blanco was going crazy barking, and the sheep were bleating wildly. Suddenly, everything was noise and confusion. A half-dozen gunshots were followed by screams that seemed to be inspired by the devil himself.

Manuel Sardinas looked from Armando to the arrow in his chest, then back to Armando. Then his eyes rolled up.

"No, Papa, no!" he cried as his father began to pitch forward.

Armando dropped the bucket and threw his hands toward his father's shoulders, but the butt of the arrow jabbed him in the chest, and when he jumped aside, his father collapsed on his chest, driving the arrow through his back.

"Papa!" he cried. "Papa!"

But his father was dead. The only thing coming from his mouth was a trickle of blood.

"Comanches!" Miguel screamed. "Run, Armando, run!"

Instinctively, Armando spun about, grabbed the bucket of tar, and saw a dozen warriors charging on galloping horses.

Armando knew he must escape.

Jesus fled to the tree, grabbed the musket and cocked the lock. He pulled the trigger, but the musket did not respond.

"Run, Armando!" Jesus cried, grabbing the musket by the barrel and lifting it over his shoulder like a club.

Armando stood transfixed, as a Comanche warrior charged his brother.

The warrior, hanging by his legs over the side of his horse and holding a bow and arrow under his mount's neck, galloped past Jesus. When the animal and warrior cleared his older brother, Armando saw the musket slip from Jesus's hands and slide away. Jesus stood with an arrow through his neck, blood gushing out of the wound and a pink foam bubbling from his mouth.

Armando dashed for Jesus, who jerked at the arrow. Then his knees buckled and he leaned back against the tree and slid down until he sat on the ground in his own pool of blood.

"Jesus!" Armando cried.

His brother did not answer.

Armando turned and dashed for the river, so terrified that he did not release the bucket.

He caught a glimpse of Miguel running along the riverbank, then saw a warrior swoop out of nowhere and hack at him with a tomahawk. The force of the blow sent Miguel tumbling head over heels. Miguel crashed to the ground, dead.

And then Armando knew he was alone and about to die.

He heard pounding hooves and a growling behind him. He looked over his shoulder and saw three warriors slowing their horses, pointing and laughing.

Blanco ran to Armando, then spun around beside his legs. The dog planted his feet, growling and snarling at the warriors.

Drawing courage from Blanco's ferocity, Armando faced his enemies. He felt his hands and legs tremble.

The warriors stopped, not eight feet from Blanco. Their faces were painted with black and vermilion.

Blanco lunged for one of the horses, and the pinto danced away. Then its rider, his face painted black from the tip of his chin to the bottom of his ears, yanked an arrow from the quiver over his shoulder, notched the end over the bowstring, and in one fluid motion drew back the bowstring and released the dart. The arrow plowed through Blanco's head. The dog collapsed, its head pinned to the ground.

Armando dropped beside the lifeless dog as the warriors maneuvered their horses around him. Armando began to cry, the shock of what had happened finally penetrating his numbed mind.

Then rage suddenly surged through him, rushing like the Rio Sabinas behind him. He shot up from his dog's corpse, looked at the wooden bucket still in his hand, drew back his arm and swung the bucket for the pinto of the brave who had killed his dog. The horse shied away, but Armando charged at him, pounding the horse's chest and foreleg as he advanced.

The warrior yanked another arrow from its quill and slipped it over the bowstring. As he aimed the arrow at Armando, a warrior on a dappled gray horse yelled something, then rode toward Armando. Leaning over his horse, he scooped Armando from the ground and plopped him belly down in front of him.

Armando twisted around to stare at the warrior. He was terrified by the brave's dark eyes, made more frightening by the broad band of black war paint that spread from his nose across both cheeks. Armando swung the bucket feebly for the dappled gray's chest, and the warrior's grip tightened around his arm. Though Armando did not drop the bucket, he did not swing it again.

The warrior on the pinto rode back toward the shade of the trees where Armando's father and brothers had done the last chores they would ever do. Armando twisted his head and saw the warrior dismount. The warrior unsheathed his knife, grabbed Manuel by the hair, and yanked him upright. He sliced the skin over the forehead, then pulled the skin loose back over the head, the flesh crackling as it was torn from the skull. Then the warrior sliced the circle of flesh and hair where it joined the neck and hoisted his trophy high.

Armando closed his eyes and gritted his teeth. He had seen too much, and felt suddenly sick to his stomach. He knew the Comanches would do the same thing to Miguel, Jesus, and possibly to him as well. Then he lost consciousness.

When he awoke, the sun was barely a glowing ball about to kiss the western horizon. He was resting on a blanket, while the warriors were laughing and eating around the fire his father had built. As he stirred, he realized he still gripped the bucket's rope handle. He was hungry and confused, worried what his fate might be.

He saw the bloody wounds of his father and brother. He remembered his father's lesson about blowflies. He knew he could never bury his kin, so he arose slowly, uncertain what the Comanches might do, then stepped to his dead father.

He could tell by the inflection of the warriors' voices that they watched his movements with amusement. Armando, though, could not look at them because he had a job to do. Squatting by his father's body, he dipped the swab in the tarry concoction and lifted it to the bloodied mass. As his father watched him with open but lifeless eyes, he spread the tar over his head, carefully making sure he covered every bit of bloodied flesh so that maggots would not breed in his father. Then he daubed the tar around the arrow still protruding from his chest.

The Comanches did not interfere, so he moved to Jesus and covered his savaged head and the neck wound with the tar. He gagged at the gore, but promised himself he would not pass out like before. He owed this gesture to his father and brother. As he finished with Jesus, he marched toward the river for Miguel's body. As he worked he peeked at the warriors, still clumped around the fire. All watched him, but not a one made an effort to stop him.

Finishing with Miguel, he retreated to the spot where Blanco had made his stand. With what little tar was left in the bucket, Armando doctored the dog's wound, then dropped the bucket. He wanted to run, but knew it would be futile. And he was too tired, the exhaustion deeper than any he had ever experienced in his young life.

The warriors watched. The silence was overwhelming, not a single sound from the flock of sheep behind them. He started toward the flock beyond the warriors. None of the animals were standing, and at first he thought they had bedded down early, but they were too still. Then he realized all the animals were dead.

"I'm sorry, Papa," he said, fighting back the tears, "that today you lost all your sheep."

He retreated to the blanket and lay down, his back to the warriors. They resumed their conversation as the sunset cast a bloody veil across the evening sky.

Then he sensed an even greater darkness over him, and looked up to see the warrior who had captured him. The Comanche squatted beside him and offered him a strip of meat.

Armando's mind said he should reject the offer, but

his stomach spoke otherwise. The hunger in his stomach was stronger than the revulsion in his mind. He took the meat, a couple of ribs. They were hot and stung his hand, but he held onto them.

The Comanche said something that Armando did not understand.

Armando studied him. He was muscled, but stocky, both of torso and face. In the declining light his bronzed face and chest seemed even darker. His black hair was tied in two braids that hung past his shoulders, ornamented with glass beads and silver gewgaws. His expression was solemn but not savage.

Armando pulled the ribs to his mouth and bit off a hunk of meat.

The warrior nodded his approval, then returned to the fire. Armando gnawed at the meat, then fell asleep after the most horrible day of his life. But even sleep brought him little respite because he relived the terror in his dreams.

Crow Feather awoke with the others before sunlight. He moved to the remains of the fire and pulled a leg of mutton from the ashes. He bit through the charred sheath around the meat until his teeth sank into the sweetness of the moist mutton. The meat was fine, better than horse, but not as sweet as buffalo.

He carried the remainder to the young captive. Squatting beside the boy, Crow Feather dangled the meat before his nose until he stirred. Then he placed his hand upon the boy's shoulder and shook him. The boy came awake with a start, then whimpered.

"Get up. Here's meat. Eat plenty. The ride will be long."

The boy did not understand until Crow Feather

grabbed him by the arm and pulled him to a sitting position. He took the boy's hand and put the meat in it. When he released the meat, the captive's hand sagged under the weight.

"Eat," he commanded. "We are a day's hard ride from the others. If you show strength and bravery, you will live. If you whine or show weakness, you will die. Already Speaks Loudly wants to kill you, like he killed your dog."

Crow Feather knew the Mexican boy did not understand, but he would learn soon. Or he would die on the trail.

"From the sunrise of this day to the sunset of your life, you will be known as Paints the Dead," Crow Feather announced, then pulled the blanket from under him. The warrior went to his hobbled horse. He quickly removed the restraints and mounted. He pulled the rawhide reins and rode to another horse that he had stolen on this raid. Paints the Dead would ride on this horse.

Crow Feather led the extra horse to the rope pen where the dead sheep were beginning to stink. Leaning over the side of his dappled gray, he cut a length of rope as long as his arm span because he knew he must tie Paints the Dead to his mount. Mexicans who tended sheep were poor riders.

He returned to Paints the Dead, dropped gracefully from his pony and picked the captive up, quickly putting him astride the stolen horse. The boy ate the meat ravenously as he sat on the horse. Crow Feather tied one end of length of rope around Paints the Dead's ankle, then went around to the opposite side of the horse and pulled the rope beneath its belly. He yanked the rope snugly under the horse, then tied the end around Paints the Dead's other ankle.

He did not like to tie a rope so tightly under a horse's stomach, like the white man did with his saddles, because it affected a horse's wind and might slow him a bit. But Crow Feather had no choice, for if the boy fell from his horse, he would die; if not fatally injured in the fall, he would be killed by Speaks Loudly for delaying their progress.

Speaks Loudly wanted to kill the boy and scalp him so he could return to their band as though he had killed a great enemy instead of a boy. Crow Feather, though, thought Paint the Dead's feistiness might one day make him a great Comanche warrior.

When he was done securing Paints the Dead to the horse, he cut the excess rope and threw it aside. He grabbed the reins of the horse and handed them to the captive. Paints the Dead lowered the leg of meat from his mouth long enough to accept the reins, then continued to gnaw away at the food.

Crow Feather jumped upon his horse and motioned for Paints the Dead to follow him. The other warriors were mounting their horses and herding their fifteen stolen horses together for the hard ride back into the mountains to the north. There, another six warriors waited, keeping watch over 129 horses and mules they had stolen on their foray into Mexico.

Once they joined up with those warriors, the entire raiding party would return to the land of the Comanche. The journey would take a full moon, but when the warriors arrived, they would be greeted joyously, for their raids had garnered 144 animals and three captives, in addition to Paints the Dead.

As Crow Feather fell into line with the other warriors, Paints the Dead followed behind him, riding awkwardly astride the animal as if he had only ridden animals with saddles. At first, the band rode at a walk, giving their mounts time to warm up and loosen their muscles before they started running. But by the time the sun had chased the darkness behind every little rock and bush, the Comanches were galloping north toward the mountain rendezvous with the others.

Crow Feather kept a close watch on Paints the Dead. Initially, the boy had ridden stiffly on the horse, but gradually he loosened until his every movement seemed to be in concert with the strides of his mount. "You learn quickly," Crow Feather called over the pounding hooves.

Paints the Dead looked at him like he wished he understood.

The Comanches rode through the heat of the day. Crow Feather waited until the sun was at its hottest before he took a drink of water from the buffalo bladder he carried. Not once during the day had Paints the Dead complained or asked for water.

Crow Feather eased his horse beside Paints the Dead and offered him the container. The boy grabbed the bladder and put the mouth to his own. He drank greedily before Crow Feather pulled the water away and gave him his first lesson in becoming a Comanche warrior.

"Drink enough to wet your mouth but not to quench your thirst. The land of the Comanche is big and water is not always at hand. Drink as little as you can on the trail, and you can last longer than the enemies who follow you. The Comanche survives because he knows the land and does not waste its resources."

Paints the Dead watched him speak.

"The Comanche knows every water hole, every spring, every creek, and every river in his land. And when he must, he will kill a mule or horse to drink its blood. The white eyes will not do that because he does not understand survival, yet the white eyes will kill a buffalo and take only the tongue or hide, leaving everything else to rot beneath the sun. The Comanche uses every bone, tendon, horn, hoof, and hair of the buffalo. The buffalo has more uses than the white eyes can ever understand. If you remain brave, you can be as smart and wise as the Comanche."

Paints the Dead did not understand the words, Crow Feather knew, but the captive would learn. With time, he would come to accept the Comanche as his own people.

Armando had ridden for so long and so hard that he ached all over. By dusk the horsehair lariat that bound his feet had rubbed his ankles raw. As darkness began to swallow the earth, he wondered how much longer they would ride and where the trail would end. Already they had ridden into mountains taller than any he had ever seen, and yet they continued to ride hard as darkness made the trail more difficult to see. His horse merely followed the others, seeing by instinct.

In the distance he finally saw a large fire. He hoped it might be the Mexican Army waiting to save him, but he knew that the soldiers would never come to save a boy like him. He had heard the horrors of children captured by the Comanches, children never seen again, though he never thought that he might one day be one of them.

As they drew closer to the fire, the warriors eased their horses into a trot. Then the lead warrior screamed, his cry reminding Armando of the cries during the sudden attack upon his father and brothers. The other warriors around him began to shout. Armando trembled because the celebration brought back the savage memory of the previous day. Scared though he was, he would not let the Comanches defeat him.

Around the campfire, Armando saw another five or six Comanche men and a trio of captives, a boy who looked his size and a girl who seemed younger. The little girl clung to the boy like he was her big brother. As the horses passed, Armando saw the little girl's eyes, wide and terrified.

The third captive seemed even more horrified. She was a young woman; Armando could see her breasts through her tattered blouse. She did not look up, for her shame was great.

The mounted warriors chatted wildly with the six around the campfire as they rode by. The riders never stopped, and as Armando looked around, he got the sense that he was in a box canyon. Ahead, he heard the sound of milling horses.

Finally, he could make out the forms of the horses behind a makeshift fence that penned them into the canyon. The warriors dismounted quickly, and the one who had saved him untied the rope around his ankles. Armando slid off the horse, landing softly on the ground, his knees as limp as a willow branch.

As the Comanche warriors attended their mounts, Armando stood alone and confused. Shortly, he felt the iron grip of a hand that told him his captor had returned. The warrior led him to camp and toward the other captives. Armando was glad, for at least he would have someone to talk to. Stopping beside the other captives, the Comanche tied a rope around Armando's left ankle, then tied the rope to the ankle of the other boy.

Armando said nothing until his warrior had joined

the circle of warriors around the campfire. Armando sat down beside the boy, whose gaze bounced back and forth between him and the warriors.

"Did they kill your mama and papa?" the boy asked.

"My father and two brothers."

"Do you think they will kill us?" the boy asked.

The little girl began to cry.

The boy stroked her long matted hair. "No, no, Lupe. I didn't mean that. I was just trying to scare him."

Lupe did not believe him.

"My sister is scared," he said.

"They will not kill us," Armando said with as much conviction as he could muster. "What is your name?"

"Esteban, and my sister is Lupe."

Armando pointed to the older girl, who sat with her knees bunched up under her chin.

"Who is she?"

"I do not know," Esteban said. "She says nothing and cries much of the time. The Comanches take her away into the darkness a lot."

"But why would they do that?"

"I do not know," Esteban whispered as a warrior approached.

Armando did not look up, but the warrior grabbed his hand and put a strip of meat in it. The warrior also offered meat to Esteban and Lupe. The two children snatched it from his hand and ate greedily. The brave offered nothing to the other girl, but returned to the fire.

Armando watched him, then saw three braves waving scalps over their heads and bragging. He knew those were the scalps of his father and brothers. Suddenly, he did not feel at all hungry. He offered the meat to Lupe. She took it.

"*Gracias*," she said meekly.

Armando watched the Indians around the fire, taking note of the one who balanced a scalp on the tip of his arrow and laughed. That was the one who had scalped his father, the one who had shot his dog and had ridden the pinto that Armando had attacked with the bucket. Armando wanted to kill the brave, but what could a six-year-old do against a warrior? He knew he must do what the Comanche wanted so he could become a man. Then, when he became a man, he must kill the warrior.

Suddenly, the very warrior Armando vowed to kill jumped up. He shoved the arrow in the quill on his back and draped the scalp over the belt that held his knife. He turned from the fire and marched toward Armando, who trembled.

"Are you cold?" Esteban whispered.

Armando shook his head as the warrior neared.

The brave shouted gleefully, then grabbed the arm of the girl, who said nothing. He pulled her up, then bent and cut the rope that connected her to Lupe.

Armando sighed, then felt sorry for the girl, who began to sob.

The warrior took the girl deep into the darkness. Shortly, the girl began to scream and sob while the warrior grunted and groaned. Armando did not understand.

"This happens each night," Esteban said, "but the girl will not talk about it."

The girl's screams made Armando desire to help her, to stop whatever the warrior was doing to her, but he was just a boy and the last two days had brought enough bad memories for a lifetime.

He leaned over and rested on the ground, but could not stretch out fully because of the rope that bound him to Esteban. Then Lupe reached out and began to stroke Armando's cheek. Her soft fingers felt nice and reassuring. Her caress was the last thing he remembered before falling asleep.

After finishing a portion of his meat and giving the remainder to the three young captives, Crow Feather returned to the fire. Speaks Loudly bragged about his heroics in attacking the sheepherders and claiming a scalp for his own. He had waved the scalp on the tip of an arrow as though he had killed a great enemy rather than a man who tended sheep. Speaks Loudly was well-named.

Gives Gifts and Owl Eyes showed their scalps, but without embellishing their deeds. While Speaks Loudly arose to take the girl into the bush to spend his lust, Gives Gifts and Owl Eyes began to prepare their scalps.

They pulled out their knives and began to shave the flesh from the skin. Then each man produced a green twig he had cut from bushes while riding into the mountains. They bent the twigs and tied the ends with sinew, making a hoop just smaller than the cleaned scalp. Then, with buffalo sinew for thread and a cactus spine for a needle, they began to sew the scalp onto the hoops. They sewed the hoop, as custom called for, from east to south to west to north. When they were done, they greased the hair with fat from the meat they had consumed for supper. Then they hung the scalps from their bows so they would dry.

The process took more than an hour, and when both were finished, Speaks Loudly was still raping the girl, torturing her with his unsated lust.

Speaks Loudly should have prepared his scalp rather than attacking the girl, Crow Feather thought. Speaks Loudly was not a true warrior, but an imitator.

"When Speaks Loudly is done," Owl Eyes said, "I shall have the woman."

"If he gets done," Gives Gifts replied.

Crow Feather glanced at the other three captives and saw that Paints the Dead had fallen asleep. He took a blanket to cover the boy. The girl and the other boy looked frightened, but he motioned for them to lie down and he covered them all with the blanket.

Crow Feather returned to the fire where he told the warriors who had not been on the raid about Paints the Dead.

"The little one has a strong heart," Crow Feather said. "He will become a great warrior. He shall be known as Paints the Dead by all Comanche."

One of the others asked him to explain.

"After we killed the three who scalped the sheep with him, he went to each dead man and painted over the wound. The paint was black like the paint of war."

"Do you know why he did it?" Gives Gifts asked. "I saw him, but did not understand why. Or why he painted the dog that Speaks Loudly killed."

Crow Feather shrugged. "Maybe it is a ritual as common to the Mexican as scalping is to the Comanche."

"But I have never seen it done before," Owl Eyes answered.

"Maybe he wanted to show us that he had the makings of a warrior."

Yellow Dog, one who had stayed to guard the horses previously stolen, said, "The boy that we kept has the heart of a girl. His sister is stronger, though younger. He whines like a girl."

Crow Feather shook his head. "Inspect the ankles of Paints the Dead. They are cut and bloodied from being tied to the horse, but he never complained. He was uneasy at first astride the horse, but he quickly became a part of the horse, riding easily until he was so exhausted he almost fell off. Paints the Dead shows promise as a warrior."

Speaks Loudly returned to camp, the blade of his knife tainted with red.

"Where did you leave the girl?" Owl Eyes asked.

Speaks loudly pointed into the darkness.

Owl Eyes arose and disappeared in the night.

Speaks Loudly took his seat.

"You were gone long," Big Wolf said. "Did you not leave any for the rest of us? We have been long without a woman."

Speaks Loudly looked into the fire, not answering.

Then Owl Eyes stumbled back into camp. "Why did you kill the girl before the rest of us could use her?"

He lifted his head and leaned back, stretching his neck so that all could see the chunk of flesh that she had bitten from his shoulder. "She bit me like a cougar bites and I killed her," Speaks Loudly replied. "There will be others that we can capture for ourselves."

"But not tonight," Owl Eyes answered.

"There is the little girl. Take her."

"No," Crow Feather said.

"Go ahead, Owl Eyes," Speaks Loudly said.

"Any man that takes her," Crow Feather said, "will have to go through me first."

No one challenged Crow Feather.

3

Captain Jean Benoit watched Brigadier General Arnold Smedley lift his wineglass and study the deep red of the liquid inside. Then Benoit looked at the two dozen officers around the long table in the mess hall. The soldiers, resplendent in their dress uniforms, held their glasses high, awaiting the toast that would honor Frank Coker on his last night in the United States Army.

Coker cut a handsome figure in his double-breasted uniform jacket with the black leather belt that carried his sword.

Smedley stood ramrod straight, the squareness of his shoulders accentuated with the gold epaulets of his rank. The general, like all the men around the table, wore his black felt Hardee hat with its tapered crown and flat top. The right side of each hat was pinned to the top of the crown. A length of gold cord ending in acorn tips rested on the edge of the brim beneath the brass insignia of crossed swords. Army regulations required that an officer of Smedley's rank wear a plume of three black feathers pinned to the cord on the left side of the hat. The lesser officers around the table carried but two black feathers on their hats, the regulations of the War Department being quite specific.

"Let's toast," Smedley said, "the best piano player in New Mexico and perhaps in all of the Army."

The men shouted their approval in unison.

"Good luck, Lieutenant Coker, in Pennsylvania," Smedley continued. "May your life be long and prosperous, may your family be healthy and wise, and may you always look fondly upon these times."

The soldiers clinked their glasses with their neighbors then tossed back their heads and downed the red wine. When they lowered their chins, General Smedley asked each of the men to make a few remarks.

They spoke of Coker's piano playing and his sharp mathematical mind. They mentioned his kindness, and one even said he was too decent to be an Army officer. The other officers hissed and General Smedley laughed.

When it came Benoit's time, he took off his hat and held it over his heart. "Lieutenant Coker and I don't have much in common, him being from Pennsylvania and me from Louisiana, but we both have fine wives and two daughters.

"Last fall when I was sent to Fort Fillmore, I did not know that we had daughters in common and wouldn't have known for three months were it not for Frank's thoughtfulness. He knew Inge was pregnant, and when I received a letter from Fort Laramie after I had departed, he rode more than half a day to deliver the letter. I will never forget that act of kindness."

The remaining officers spoke of Coker's many qualities, then passed the bottle around to fill each glass again. When the last testimonial was finished, the officers chanted, "Speech, speech!"

Coker quieted them with his left hand, then looked

from man to man, answering the praise that had been heaped upon him with compliments of his own.

Reaching Benoit, he grinned. "As I recall, Captain Benoit wanted to have nothing in common with me, preferring sons to daughters."

The soldiers laughed, one slapping Benoit on the back.

"And," Coker continued, "I learned that not everyone from Louisiana had a little alligator in his blood."

"Yeah," answered another soldier, "but he's probably got some alligator in his stomach, the way those Cajuns eat crawfish and other strange varmints."

"They're called delicacies," Benoit shot back.

Coker lifted his hand for quiet. "And I should also say that I learned that men of honor can take stands on both sides of an issue."

Coker's words hung in the air a moment, the merriment suddenly stilled. Politics might eventually force every member of the U.S. Army to make a decision. It would be especially tough for the sons of the South. For the soldiers from the North, the decision might be less painful, but the ultimate result could be the same. Whatever choices were made, these men might have to face friends on the field of combat.

Coker raised his glass. "To you all, men, soldiers, and patriots, with admiration and respect for the decisions you each may be forced to make."

The men drank their toast, placed their glasses on the table, and congregated around Coker, extending him best wishes.

As Benoit moved toward Coker, Smedley motioned for him to step aside. Benoit quietly joined his commander in the corner.

"Captain," Smedley said, "I have learned some disturbing news today that will force us to consider the most appropriate way to respond to Senator Couvillion."

"What is it, sir?"

"Gold, Captain, gold!"

"Where?"

"Colorado, around Pike's Peak."

"We knew the senator had been considering this possibility."

Smedley shook his head. "The senator is evil, and now he'll be pressuring you even more for details on the Army in New Mexico Territory and how it can be turned to take those gold fields."

"What should I do?"

Stroking his chin, Smedley looked about the room. "I think," he whispered, "that you should inform him of this. Getting word to him before he learns it independently would reduce his doubts about you."

"It makes sense."

"Then see me in the morning, after Lieutenant Coker leaves, and we will draft a letter."

Benoit nodded, then walked across the room to visit with Coker. "Good luck, Frank. You will be missed, as all good men are."

Coker saluted sharply. "Thank you, sir, I have nothing but the greatest respect for you."

Benoit nodded. "And I for you."

While others tried to talk Coker into going to a saloon with them for more celebration, he waved the offer away and left with Benoit, the two men walking silently through the streets to their quarters, where they retired for the night.

Come morning, Benoit was up and waiting when Coker stepped from his room. Benoit had never seen him in civilian clothes. He looked strange out of uniform.

Coker smiled. "Of all the officers, I knew you would be the one here to see me off."

"I came to help you with your bags."

Coker shook his head. He had a traveling trunk in one hand and a leather satchel in the other. "Four years at West Point and seven years in the Army and this is all I've got to show for it."

"You've sent everything to your wife and girls." Benoit took the satchel from him and they fell in side by side as they walked toward the plaza where the stage would pick him up to begin the long journey to Pennsylvania.

"It'll be good to see Sara Ann and the girls. My one regret, Jean, is that I won't be here to see you with your family."

"Me, too, Frank."

They spoke of the good times they'd had and the strange course that had led their lives to intersect. In front of the Governor's Palace, they put down the bags and shook hands warmly, then hugged each other.

"Good luck, Frank."

Coker nodded.

"I hope you enjoy teaching, and that we meet again someday."

Coker smiled. "I would like that."

They left unsaid what was understood between them: that they wanted to meet as friends, not as enemies across a battlefield.

There being nothing else to say, they turned from each other, Coker looking for the stage and Benoit walking toward the headquarters of the Ninth Military District.

Benoit entered General Smedley's office. The general was waiting. "You see Lieutenant Coker off?"

"I left him waiting for the stage."

Smedley stood up from his desk and grabbed a sheet of paper. "I've written a response for you to Senator Couvillion. Read it and let me know if you are comfortable with it."

Benoit took the draft and began to read the general's handwriting:

Senator,

Your letters have been numerous, and their frequency have tended to raise suspicions among some officers who may disagree with your positions on some matters. Therefore I have been reluctant to respond more frequently for fear that the post might be intercepted by those who would do great harm to this country and the principles upon which it was founded.

Too, when I write, I want there to be significant news to make it worth the risk of an interception of our correspondence. This day, though, I have major news. It appears that long heard rumors of significant gold deposits in Colorado Territory are true. There are reports of major strikes in the Pike's Peak region.

I do not know how long this will remain unknown, but when it is found out, it will certainly stir the souls and passions of many men, and there may be a stampede for Pike's Peak. Men will likely flock to the Rocky Mountains just as they did the Sierra Madres when gold was found in California in '49.

There is but one good route from Santa Fe, and that is up and over Raton Pass. Any approach from the south must be made in this direction, and it is not always possible in the winter, when the snows can get too deep for man and beast.

There will be some value to New Mexico Territory if a conflict comes, but the scarcity of water, the hard terrain, and the physical distances between it and virtually everything else may not make the territory critical to our cause. These are things that matter for any army trying to do its duty.

General Smedley spends much of his time dealing with these matters and is loyal to the principles we hold dear. He seems sympathetic to what we know to be the real cause in this age. He does not know what I know, but does tend to favor officers of a like political persuasion.

I am checking on the strengths of the eleven forts under General Smedley's command. While they are adequate for defending against the Indians, they will not hold up to attack by a real army.

Please be patient; haste in addressing these matters will not bring the results that would be of greatest value to the cause we both hold dear.

I will write when I know more and have information I think of equal value.

Benoit looked up from the letter, nodding his approval.

Smedley spoke. "I hope I worded it so as not to give any information that would not already be known, and so it could in no way be construed as treason, because we both know Couvillion will keep the letters to use to his own benefit and your detriment."

"I think you've done an excellent job."

"Be certain of that, for it will have to be sent with

your name on it. Even though I have written it, I do not want you to sign anything that you fear might jeopardize your career or reputation. My draft is merely a starting point."

"Yes, sir."

"What I would like you to do, Captain, is take that back to your room, where there is no chance that it might be seen. Put it in your handwriting, making whatever changes you think it needs, and then we will post it."

"Thank you, sir, for helping me out of this predicament."

"Senator Couvillion makes many people uncomfortable."

Benoit took the draft and folded it.

"Take your time on the letter, Captain."

Benoit paused for a moment. "Sir, the more I think about what Lieutenant Coker did, the more I begin to wonder if it might not be better for me to just resign from the Army. I can find work in New Orleans. The Benoit name is a good name. There are many things I can do."

Smedley shook his head. "Next to war, the worst thing that could happen out of all of this trouble, Captain, is for the Army to lose its good men. An army, for all its might, is no better than its men. The army does not make the men, the men make the army. If we have a weak army, it is because we have weak leaders. Think about it, Captain, as there is much to consider before giving up a commission."

"Thank you, sir. I'll return after lunch with the letter."

"That will be fine, Captain."

Benoit saluted and exited the building, returning to his quarters. He copied the letter word for word as Smedley had written it. He added his signature and was pleased with the effort when he was done. Since he had his paper and pen at his desk, he started a letter to Inge, asking when she would be coming to Santa Fe, as he was anxious to see her and the girls. He asked about her mother and then inquired about her brother, who had been paralyzed from the waist down after being thrown from his horse in an attack by Crow warriors. He also told Inge how he missed Jason Dobbs, especially now that Frank Coker had resigned and departed for Pennsylvania.

When he was done, Benoit sealed the letter to Inge, then carried both letters to headquarters and poked his head in on General Smedley. "Care to see what I wrote, General? It's your words, word for word."

"Seal it and send it. By the way, I think you got a couple letters this morning after you left, and neither of them's from Couvillion."

"Thank you, sir."

"Check with Phipps, he has them."

"He must still be eating lunch, General, as he wasn't at his desk when he came in."

"Check his desk or yours. When you find the letters, get out of here and relax. I don't have anything for you to do."

"I've some reports to finish, sir."

"They can wait."

"Why're you doing this, sir?"

"I don't want to lose another good man like Coker. I've decided that giving you some time off will endear me to you."

Benoit laughed. "You're a carrot man and Couvillion's a stick man. That must make me a jackass, then."

Smedley laughed. "Couvillion's the jackass."

Benoit retreated from Smedley's doorway to Phipps's desk, checking it for letters, but not seeing any addressed to him. He went to his own desk and found the letters sitting on top. They were from Inge and from his brother, Theophile. Benoit forced himself to address an envelope for his letter to Couvillion. He folded the letter, inserted it in the envelope, then lit a candle and dripped wax over the flap to seal it. Blowing out the candle, he sat it back on the table, then hurried out the door and headed to his room, where he reclined on the bed. He opened his brother's letter first because he was worried that Theophile had let the senator poison his mind and his thinking.

Dear Jean:

In a matter of months I will graduate from the Naval Academy, fulfilling what I thought was a lifelong dream. However, I can't look forward to graduation with the same excitement because my country is going downhill.

From what I read in the newspapers, I understand the Republicans will have a 113–101 majority in the House of Representatives. All they have been talking about is abolition and a central government they'll use to trample upon all states' rights.

I have thought long and hard about the political situation and I can't see any improvement. Some people are even promoting Abraham Lincoln for president. That would create utter chaos in the United States. The man is no more fit to be president than one of the darkies he's so interested in saving.

Knowing that that kind of politician may well run the country and become my commander-in-chief makes it difficult for me to fully support this country and fulfill the oath I took when I joined the academy.

Many of us from the South have talked this over, and we are of split opinions. Some think it is wisest for us to stay in the academy and in the Navy afterward so we can take over from within, should secession or war come. Others—and I fall more closely in this camp—feel like they should resign. If they cannot abide by the oath that they swore to upon admission to the Naval Academy, then a resignation is the only honorable alternative.

Of course Cle Couvillion thinks I should stay, but I have become more and more uncomfortable with him. He seems devious and has begun to threaten me that he will ruin my career if I don't do what he says and when he says it.

Jean, I wanted to be in the Navy and defend our nation from attack, but now I am no longer sure what our nation is. Is it our state to which we owe allegiance? Or is it the nation made up of all the states? I cannot abide what the northern states would do, telling us what we can own and how we can act. It seems their real motivation is not to free the slaves, but to make the southern states and their citizens slave to their way of life and business. I do not care to be subjugated to their whims and avarice.

I need time to think and work this through. I value your advice and hope that Cle hasn't been trying to manipulate you as he has me. I know I wrote some unwise things to him in my earlier letters, things he has called treasonous, but I was rash and did not understand the depth of his evil.

I am sorry to burden you with my problems, but you have always been wise and a source of admiration for me. I await your wise counsel.

Your Brother,

Theo

For all of Theophile's problems, Benoit thought this was the first encouraging letter he had received from his brother in months. Theo at least now understood the evil ways of Senator Cle Couvillion. His brother had honor after all, and was grappling with it. Maybe there was hope that Theophile had not been snared in Couvillion's web of deceit.

There were many things he thought he should say to Theophile, but he knew he must choose his words carefully so that Theo would make his own decision the right decision. He would consider the proper response over the next few days and then write back.

With anticipation, Benoit opened the next letter. He hoped the news from Fort Laramie was as good as the news from Annapolis, Maryland.

He pulled the two pages out and began to read them.

Darling Jean:

The time is drawing nearer when we will be together as a family. Jace is making the arrangements so we can join you in Santa Fe as soon as possible. There is something about an Army caravan that will be heading south from Fort Laramie in May, and wagons are being provided for families.

Colleen and Ellen are growing almost by the day. They crawl around our room as if they are looking for their father. I know the day will come when we will be together again, but they do not seem to understand.

They are twins but they are so different in personality. When I feed them, they are so different. Colleen takes her time, liking to cuddle. She'll eat slowly and then when she is done go to sleep in my arms, but if I try to pull her away from my breast, she will begin to suckle again, so I know she wants to stay. Ellen wants to be done with eating so much that she gulps down her supper fast and hard, leaving me sore afterward. She seems much more impatient than Colleen. I guess she takes after me and Colleen after you.

There is so much more to tell you about the girls, but since it will only be a few weeks until we are together, I will wait so I can see your face when I share with you all the wonderful things I know about them.

I do not know if the girls and I will be accompanied by anyone or not. Erich still cannot walk, and I have about given up that he ever will. I should have more faith in my brother, but he is so depressed that it affects me too. Mama says she would take care of him as long as she could, but he doesn't want her to do that. It requires a lot of work. With two girls, I cannot take care of him, and he cannot take care of himself. I don't know what Mama will do if Erich decides to come with us. Jim Ashby has told her he will not leave Wyoming Territory, and a woman should not leave her husband. I think he feels he's at fault for the injury, leading Erich into becoming a mountain man and scout. So he has taken to drink more than normal. Our lives have taken so many turns, Jean, since we met on the wagon train heading west. Papa was killed, Mama injured and lost her leg, you and me getting married, Erich getting hurt, then the girls, now the separation. Lives are never simple, but few are more complicated than Erich's now.

His only bit of hope is a letter you wrote last year. You remember the one about the church where miracles occur? I do not believe in such things, nor does Jace. With his doctor knowledge, Jace says some damage was surely done to Erich's backbone. No doctor in the world can fix that, nor can any God.

There is more that I should write, but Colleen is crying and I am tired. I go to sleep each night thinking of you and waiting for the day when you will be in my arms.

Your Loving Wife,
Inge

Benoit finished the letter, then read it again. He felt sorry for Erich but didn't know what to do. He had so anticipated the joy of seeing his girls, that he hoped Erich would stay in Wyoming rather than diminish the excitement of seeing his twin girls. Then Benoit thought himself selfish and cruel for not worrying more about the brother of his wife. But miracles? A man should not travel from Fort Laramie to Santa Fe in hopes of a miracle that might never happen. He must write Erich, he decided, after he had talked to Father Machebeuf and heard what the priest had to say about the miracles. Machebeuf was of French extraction, so Benoit and the priest had hit it off magnificently when he presented himself to the archbishop upon his arrival in Santa Fe.

Benoit folded the letter and inserted it back in the envelope, then left his room and walked down the street toward the plaza. He told himself he was out for a stroll, but he knew he would wind up at the church. At the plaza, he turned toward the adobe building and walked through the doors into the sanctuary. He saw Father Machebeuf kneeling in front of the altar.

Benoit removed his hat and waited, but Father Machebeuf seemed frozen in prayer, so still that Benoit wondered if it were really the priest or a statue. Finally, Machebeuf crossed himself and stood up. He turned about and saw Benoit, apparently not recognizing him.

"Padre," he said softly, his word magnified in the room, "it is Jean Benoit."

"Ah, yes," Machebeuf cried as he started down the aisle to greet Benoit. Reaching him, Machebeuf shook his hand warmly and looked into his eyes. "Is there something wrong, Jean? You look troubled."

Benoit nodded. "Remember when we visited at the bishop's residence and you spoke of miracles?"

"Yes, at Chimayo." Machebeuf pointed to a pew. "Please, sit."

Benoit sat down and the priest slipped beside him onto the pew.

"Why this intense interest in miracles?"

"It's a matter of last resort, Padre."

Machebeuf wagged his finger at Benoit and smiled. "True miracles are a matter of faith. They are granted when the faith matches the expectation of God. That is why miracles do not occur every day, for few men have the faith demanded by God. If you are looking for a miracle, whatever it might be, you must be sustained in your faith in God's powers."

"It is not for myself, Padre, but for the brother of my sister. He may come with her when she joins me with my daughters."

"Ah, yes, your twin girls. You have not seen them yet."

"No, and I am anxious to."

"Jean Benoit, you are already responsible for two miracles in your daughters. Some miracles are so common that we accept them as a matter of life. Now what is it about your brother-in-law?"

"He cannot walk. He was thrown from his horse and paralyzed. Beneath his waist he has no feeling, no ability. After our first dinner together upon my arrival in Santa Fe, I wrote my wife of the miracles that seemed to occur at Chimayo."

Machebeuf nodded. "And now he wants to be healed there."

"He has no other options."

"It is not a matter of options, Jean, but a matter of faith, and faith can triumph anywhere, not just at Chimayo. Must I remind you that none of the so-called miracles at Chimayo have been certified by the Church? These miracles have to be put to a severe test. It is difficult to have faith in God when you can't have faith in the Church."

"I thought it would be the opposite, that you can't have faith in the Church when you don't have faith in God."

"Perhaps we are splitting hairs, Jean, but you know that I have had my worries about the activities at Chimayo, particularly the perverse doctrines of the Pentitentes, as we have discussed before. This sect craved religious teaching, but priests were scarce in this region, certainly not enough to meet the many needs of the people. Needing religious teachings, but with no one available who was familiar with the doctrine of the

Church, the Pentitentes developed their own rituals, which verge on paganism.

"Sure, there are certain similarities between the beliefs of the Church and the Pentitentes, but the Brotherhood, as it is called, is like a weed in the Church's garden. If it spreads, it will take over the garden and destroy the plants that have been cultivated for years with good effect.

"What the Brotherhood has done, without guidance from priests well-trained in the faith, is misinterpret our sacraments, especially penance. They have confused our doctrines, so as to make penance the preeminent sacrament and the sacrament around which all others revolve. That is a blatant misrepresentation of the teachings of the Church, because penance should not involve flagellation with whips and cactus branches and other tortures. Christ endured that torture on behalf of all mankind so that we should not have to endure it in the name of the Church and its beliefs, yet that is what they continue to do.

"That, Jean, is why I am hesitant to endorse the church at Chimayo. It has been influenced greatly by the Brotherhood, so whether its miracles are genuine or not cannot be confirmed."

Benoit scratched his head. "But if a man who cannot walk is cured, the cripple who can now walk needs no confirmation. It seems to me the confirmation impedes religion and faith."

"The world is full of charlatans, Jean, and the Church must be ever vigilant against them, for they undermine the very foundation of the Church."

"I should like to take my brother-in-law to Chimayo and see if he can be cured."

"I cannot stop you, nor will I try, Jean, but I believe

you should know my feelings and the feelings of the Church. Father Candid Zavala is the shepherd of the wayward flock at Sanctuario de Chimayo. I shall be glad to provide you a letter of introduction so that you can take your brother-in-law to see for himself, but you must always remember that miracles are not just an act of faith, but an act of God as well."

"Do you believe in miracles, Padre?"

"Indeed, but what we view as miracles may not be viewed by God as miracles. The challenge before us is to make sure we are doing His work in a Godly manner, and to maintain our faith no matter the challenges, no matter the tribulations."

Benoit nodded hesitantly.

"Do you have troubles with matters of God?"

"It is hard to believe that God would allow something so terrible to happen to someone so young as Erich. He may never ever walk again. He may never have children. He may not even be able to care for himself, much less find work."

"Faith, Jean Benoit, faith. You must have faith. We cannot see God's map for us individually. We can only see what He shows us. We know that Erich is crippled, but we do not know what else God has in mind for him."

"But what can a cripple do?"

"You ask the wrong question."

"What?"

"What can God do? That is the question, and only He has the answer, not you, not me, not even Erich. You must have faith that God will prevail with what is right for Erich."

Benoit pursed his lips.

"And for you, Jean, God will do what is right for you."

Benoit felt uncomfortable when the religion turned to him. He had doubts, or, as Machebeuf would say, a lack of faith. It was hard for him to put his faith in the unseen, the unknown, especially when he had seen so much turmoil and strife in his young Army career.

"I have a friend," Benoit said, "perhaps the best friend I have ever had, and the smartest. He would question the mere existence of God, saying that logic dictates that there is no God."

"Faith is not the domain of logic, otherwise it would not be called faith. Faith is the domain of the heart, not the brain. Your friend is doubtless interested in science and mathematics."

"He is a doctor."

"Then he is a scientist. There are some things that only science can cure, and other things only faith can cure."

"Like useless legs."

"Yes, like useless legs."

"I fear that I do not have the brain or the heart to cure Erich, so tell me about Chimayo."

Machebeuf nodded. "Chimayo itself sprang up near an Indian pueblo, in fact the name is Indian for 'flaking stone' or 'rock.' Nowhere in all of New Mexico Territory will you find better weavers than in Chimayo. They brought the traditions and the looms from Spain. Today they use a treadle loom and weave as fine and as tight a cloth as you will find anywhere in the world."

Machebeuf paused, "But you do not care for the history of the community, you want to know the story of the sanctuary, is that not correct?"

Benoit nodded.

"Now, about El Sanctuario de Chimayo, it is a simple church, and many miracles are said to have occurred there. As a result, many people believe the church has great curing powers. They forget that it is God who cures.

"The church was built in 1816 as a private shrine of the Abeyta family, and it was dedicated to Jesus Christ as Our Lord of Esquipulas, a Guatemalan town also known for its great cures and miracles.

"The sick and the weary from all over New Mexico Territory flock to Chimayo. They come as an act of faith and rub themselves with the holy earth from the floor."

"Why?"

"They believe the dirt has healing powers."

"Do you?"

"God has healing powers. Faith has healing powers. Without faith, the soil is merely dirt. Inside the church are the crutches and canes of many who came to Chimayo and say they left cured. Whether they are actual miracles or not, I cannot say."

"Padre, I do not mean to be disrespectful, but could I ask a question?"

"Indeed."

"Might your opinion of these miracles be influenced by your beliefs about the Pentitentes?"

Machebeuf cocked his head and rubbed his chin. "It is possible, but I am a cautious man in matters of the faith. I do not care for people's expectations to be raised and for them to be disappointed that their expectations or their faith was not met."

"Chimayo may be in Erich's mind his only hope."

"But hope and faith are two different things, Jean."

"Then why are there no easy answers?"

"Because God put us here to make choices. If man does not have choices, he cannot have faith."

"I am confused."

"Only faith can clear the confusion."

"But I want to be—"

Machebeuf lifted his hand and put it on Benoit's shoulder. "This is not a matter of what you want. It is not a matter even of what Erich wants, however much he may desire to walk again. It is a matter of what God wants.

"Remember that nothing of this earth is without God's purpose. Men go astray when they go counter to God's purpose. Even if your faith is weak, just believe that God's hand is in Erich's injury."

Benoit shook his head and sighed. "It is difficult."

"But you are strong."

Machebeuf arose. "I should love to visit with you more, but I must attend my bishop."

"I am sorry to have delayed you."

"Be not sorry, for you have challenged me to think and articulate my beliefs on the miracles of Chimayo. I learn from the faith of all, no matter how great nor how small the person or the faith." Machebeuf arose, bowed slightly, then stepped from the pew.

Benoit grabbed his hand and shook it. "Thank you."

"One day, we should have dinner again together, Jean. I enjoyed so much our visit after your arrival."

"I should like that. When my family arrives and we are settled in a new place, then I should like to invite you over for dinner as well, so you can meet my wife and see my children."

"That would be a delight, Jean."

Machebeuf turned toward the altar and walked away.

Benoit bowed his head, asking a silent prayer for Erich's well-being, then turned toward the door. He stepped quietly, but even the slightest sound was amplified in the sanctuary. As he reached the door, Machebeuf's voice carried across the room.

"And Jean . . ."

"Yes?" Jean turned around.

"One other thing . . . When your brother-in-law arrives, let me know. I will make arrangements to take you both to Chimayo."

4

May, Palo Duro Canyon, Texas Panhandle

Ribbons of brown, orange, red, and maroon rock alternated with stripes of yellow, gray, and white sediment as if a petrified rainbow had crashed and embedded itself in the earth, gashing out this great canyon and staining the walls, pinnacles, buttes, and mesas. Gnarly-barked cottonwoods adorned in spring leaves shaded the creek at every meandering twist through the canyon. The new spring grass, invigorated by recent rains, seemed too delicate to survive among the prickly pear, yucca, mesquite, and juniper.

After more than a moon on the trail, Crow Feather felt exhilarated to be so close to his village. Around the far bend in the creek would stand the village he had left almost three moons ago. As was the custom of successful raiding parties, he had timed his arrival for the middle of the morning.

He halted his pinto, then looked at the caravan behind him. Not only did his raiding party return with more than two hundred horses, some fifty mules, and a dozen cattle, they had brought back three young captives who—if they survived the cruel initiation to follow—might grow up Comanche. He had no doubt that Paints the Dead would survive, but he was less certain about the other boy, the one they had taken to calling Willow Leaf because he often trembled. His sister, though, was stronger and she had been named Stone Flower.

As the other warriors approached Crow Feather, he watched the awe—or fear—in the eyes of the three captives as they looked at the surroundings that would be their new home.

When all the warriors had gathered around him, Crow Feather spoke. "We have returned to our village with all who left. The celebration will be great."

Speaks Loudly nodded. "You are a great leader, and I should be honored to announce to the village your arrival."

Crow Feather shook his head. "That is the honor that goes to the youngest warrior, Owl Eyes."

"I counted more coup," Speaks Loudly said so all might hear.

"The captive girl you killed does not count as coup," Crow Feather retorted.

His nostrils flaring with anger, Speaks Loudly yanked the halter on his horse, spun the animal around and rode off with a war shriek.

Crow Feather ignored his own anger. "Go, Owl Eyes," he instructed. "Let the village know that we all return without wounds. And, we return with many horses for gifts to the people."

Owl Eyes nodded. "As you say, I will do." Nudging his horse with his knee, the young warrior trotted toward the creek bend.

No time was happier than the return of a victorious raiding party. Crow Feather was proud of his success as displayed by the many horses and mules he had to give as gifts to his people. Though Comanches counted their wealth in horses, no man was wealthier in spirit than the man who gave more horses away than he kept. Crow Feather understood that, as did Gives Gifts, who was known among many bands for his generosity.

Once Owl Eyes disappeared around the bend, Crow Feather turned to the others. "We must prepare for the celebration."

The warriors circled away from Crow Feather and took up positions along the string of horses and mules, which placidly grazed on the grasses at their feet. The warriors dismounted and began to pull clumps of grass to rub over their horses' hides, wiping away the trail dust and leaving the horse hair glossy and fine.

Crow Feather opened his war bag and pulled from it his war paint. He painted his face with the markings his enemies had seen on the raid. Then he greased his hair and placed his beaded headband over his forehead. He wanted to look fine, for he had not laid with Weasel, his wife, for three moons and he missed her sorely.

Shortly, Owl Eyes came riding back. He pulled up in front of Crow Feather, smiling widely.

"The people are coming to welcome us."

Crow Feather nodded. "Ready yourself and your horse so they will long remember your first raiding party."

Owl Eyes rode away. Crow Feather nudged his horse toward the gelding the three captives rode. He grabbed Paints the Dead under his shoulders, lifted him from his mount and dropped him to the ground. Paints the Dead landed nimbly on his feet. Then Crow Feather removed Willow Leaf and Stone Flower from the mount. Captives should not ride into camp like warriors, but should enter on foot like the slaves they would become until they proved themselves Comanche in every sense except blood.

With a wave of his arm, Crow Feather scared their horse away. Stone Flower grabbed the hand of her brother. Paints the Dead put his arm around her shoulder to comfort her. He spoke words that Crow Feather did not understand.

Crow Feather heard the sound of singing and shouting. He straightened on his horse and turned toward the parade coming to greet him. As leader of the raiding party, it was his place to ride in front to meet the people who came to welcome him.

The other warriors fanned out behind Crow Feather in the order of their coups and bravery on the journey. It angered Crow Feather to see Speaks Loudly turn his horse in front of Owl Eyes.

The young warrior, however, showed wisdom for his years and did not argue. Better warriors than Speaks Loudly would note Owl Eyes's accomplishments, and his reputation would soon exceed Speaks Loudly's.

When Crow Feather saw that all his braves, save Speaks Loudly, were in place, he tapped his horse with his knee and the pinto advanced. The warriors fanned out behind Crow Feather, the three captives walking behind him, the stolen horses, mules, and cattle trailing all.

As he rode, Crow Feather looked for Weasel and finally spotted her. She had never looked better. She waved at him, but he had to maintain his dignity. The distance between the returning warriors and the welcoming party narrowed.

Women, children, and old men greeted them, and the oldest woman of the band, Big Feet, carried high a scalp pole in front of the welcoming crowd. The women sang praises of the returning warriors and clapped their hands or beat sticks together.

When barely ten paces separated the warriors and the celebrants, Crow Feather halted his pinto and waited for Big Feet to approach.

The woman, whose face was wrinkled like old leather, gave a toothless grin. "You have returned victorious to the village."

Crow Feather dipped the lance that he carried until it touched the scalp pole. "We bring many horses and mules, we bring three children to join our families, and we bring many gifts for all."

The women shouted their approval, chanting his name.

"We took nine scalps. I shall give you the honor of removing the three from my lance and carrying them on your scalp pole."

The old woman smiled broadly, the folds of her wrinkled face parting upon a mouth empty of teeth.

Crow Feather lowered his lance, and she removed the scalps one at a time and hung them over her pole. A dozen young boys on horseback rode up from the creek and drove the stolen animals away to join the horse herd.

Once the horses were driven away, the other warriors approached Big Feet, who added their trophies to the scalp pole. When Big Feet had all the scalps, she spun about and led Crow Feather and his war party back to camp. The women and children of the village walked in parallel lines on either side of the warriors.

Those closest to the captives pitched rocks and sticks at them, a couple women darting past the warriors to strike the children with their palms or hit them with whips.

Stone Flower began to sob, while Willow Leaf mumbled and screamed at the attackers.

Crow Feather glanced over his shoulder and saw Paints the Dead walking steadfastly ahead, looking to neither side as he advanced, and ignoring the taunts of the women. "Stand proud, Paints the Dead," Crow Feather implored, "and one day you will head a great procession like this one."

Crow Feather knew that Paints the Dead could not understand his words, but one day he would. And perhaps one day Paints the Dead would be the son that Weasel had never been able to provide him.

The group followed the line of trees and rounded the bend, coming into view of the camp nestled on the opposite side of the creek in a wide grassy meadow. Those who had not joined the parade dropped their chores or emerged from their buffalo skin tipis to join the merriment. Big Feet drove the scalp pole into the ground where later they would hold their victory dance.

Crow Feather saw Weasel run to their lodge. He would join her shortly. Behind him, he heard the sound of Stone Flower's sobs as other little girls ran up behind her and tugged at her hair. Paints the Dead shoved back and protected her until the Comanche boys attacked him and beat him with their fists, laughing all the time.

They surrounded him, some throwing stones at him. One struck him in the face, bloodying his nose. He charged through the circle, taking their hits as he ran to protect Stone Flower. Comanche girls had surrounded her, taunting her. Willow Leaf lay beneath a pack of boys thrashing him and made no effort to help his terrified sister.

Paints the Dead flung a pair of Comanche girls from the circle, but other boys and girls rushed back in, like water after a stone hits the river. Seeing that he could never fight off all the attackers and protect Stone Flower, Paints the Dead pushed her to the ground, then fell upon her, shielding her with his own body while the others beat him with sticks and their fists.

Crow Feather had seen enough. Paints the Dead had passed his first challenge. His second and toughest would be at the victory dance. "It is enough!" he cried. "There will be time for more later. Leave the girl and boy."

"What about the other boy?" a Comanche youth asked.

Crow Feather pointed at Stone Flower's brother. "I call him Willow Leaf because he trembles. He has shown little courage even in protecting his sister. Do what you will with him, but do not kill him. We can trade him to the Comancheros."

With that, the Comanche children attacked Willow Leaf. His pitiful cries sickened Crow Feather. He would never be a warrior. Crow Feather watched Paints the Dead help Stone Flower to her feet. She leaned her head against his chest and he put his arm around her, then looked up at Crow Feather.

The captive seemed to understand that Crow Feather had stopped his punishment. Though his eyes watered, Paints the Dead did not cry. He stood small and defiant.

Crow Feather motioned for him to follow his horse, then turned toward his lodge, where Weasel awaited.

At the lodge, Crow Feather lifted his left leg over his horse, slid off and landed nimbly on the ground. He handed the reins to Weasel. It was her job to tend the horse, because the warrior must rest for the victory dance.

"I am glad you have returned," she said.

He took her hand. "Every night for three moons I have thought of you."

"I am proud to be the wife of Crow Feather, for your name is spoken of with great respect in camp when you are gone and when you return."

"Tonight we will celebrate."

"And even more so after the victory dance, when we are alone."

Crow Feather smiled, then pointed at the two captives. "The girl is called Stone Flower, and he is called Paints the Dead."

"The name is odd, Crow Feather. Are they brother and sister?"

"No, Stone Flower has a brother, but he has the heart of rabbit. He will not become a warrior. But Paints the Dead is a prideful boy. After we killed and scalped his father and brothers, he took a bucket of grease or paint and brushed it on their wounds, even though they were dead."

"It is a strange ritual."

"One I had never seen before, Weasel, but now I must rest. Tie Paints the Dead and Stone Flower to the stakes of our tipi. Give them food and drink to prepare them for the victory dance tonight."

"I shall do that, and then I shall bring you food and drink and news of the camp."

Crow Feather smiled. "And tonight, I shall bring you here for us to celebrate."

Crow Feather's woman brought Armando food and water, which he shared with Lupe. None was left by the time a pair of warriors dragged Esteban to the tipi and tied him to the stake. He was bruised and bloodied. Whimpering, he thrashed on the ground as if the others were still beating him.

Lupe reached over to comfort her brother. As she touched him, he swatted her hand away. She began to cry.

Armando patted her shoulder. "We'll be okay."

What was his fate to be? And Lupe's? He feared that the Comanches saw weakness in Esteban. Like animals in a pack, they ganged up on him. Armando knew he was no less scared than Esteban, but he hid his fear better. When he showed bravery, he realized the Comanches were easier on him. He listened, trying to figure out their words so that he might know what they were saying. If he could understand, then they would hold no secrets from him.

Lupe nuzzled against his chest while he tried to encourage Esteban to be brave.

"Esteban, you must be strong. Do not cry."

"Please, Esteban, do what Armando says," Lupe pleaded.

"They hurt me," he cried. "They are mean."

"Be brave, Esteban. Whatever they do, don't cry."

"But they hurt me."

"Just don't cry."

"I want water."

"We have none, Esteban," Lupe said.

Her brother began to sob. "I want water."

"When we get more, you can have mine."

Esteban turned away from them.

"I'm scared," Lupe said.

"Whatever happens, do not act scared, Lupe. Do not cry. They are meaner when you cry."

"I can't help but cry when they are mean to me."

"Please, Lupe, just try."

She nodded reluctantly. "I will try."

Lupe snuggled against him and finally went to sleep.

Though he was tired, Armando watched the activities of camp. Everyone seemed so excited, and he could not understand why. In the center of camp he watched men and women pile tufts of dried grass, then top it with wood until there was a mound as tall as him. All through camp ran dogs that were chasing or being chased by children, shouting and whooping as they ran.

As dusk neared, he saw the men plant in the ground the pole that the old woman had carried when the war party returned to camp. From the pole hung the scalps, including those of his father and brothers, that the warriors had taken on their raid. Their deaths, though, seemed a lifetime ago.

As he watched the sun disappear behind the canyon rim, the camp was enveloped in a great shadow. More and more men and women disappeared into their tipis, and emerged wearing their gaudiest attire. The Comanches wore trinkets and necklaces and paint upon their faces, the women favoring black and the men red, all in odd designs that meant little to Armando, other than they were sure to frighten Lupe when she awoke.

Then, as darkness finally drew a blanket across the sky, Armando's captor emerged from his lodge, the bottom half of his face painted red. His woman followed him and quickly untied Armando from the tent stake, leaving the leather thong tied around his ankle. The woman repeated the process with Lupe, who awoke with a start.

Armando saw Lupe's bottom lip quiver as she looked up into the painted face of the Comanche woman.

"Be brave," he reminded her.

She bit her lip and nodded.

Then the woman untied Esteban's tether and shook him.

He awoke, moaned, and pushed her hand away.

The Comanche bent down and yanked him up by the shoulder.

He squealed.

The Comanche said something that Armando could not understand.

Esteban let out a scream as he was pulled toward the center of camp.

Armando took Lupe's hand and trailed after Esteban. "Remember, Lupe," he said, "don't cry."

The woman led the three captives toward the pile of firewood. At the scalp pole, a warrior bent and tied Esteban's tether to it. When Armando and Lupe approached, he did the same and all three were secured.

Armando grabbed the pole and shook it, knowing that even a boy of his years could pull it down.

As soon as they were secured, the warrior backed to the circle of Comanches gathering around them. Then a warrior approached the woodpile with a torch. He touched the flame to the yellow grass, and fire swooshed up around the wood.

For a moment Armando feared that the Comanche planned to cook them. He felt the heat of the flames scalding his back and glanced behind him to see that he was a good ten feet from the fire. Equidistant in front of him, old men with war drums were sitting on the ground with their legs crossed. They began to beat the drums and chant. In the light of the fire, Armando saw that he was surrounded by the inhabitants of the village.

The beat of the drums and the chanting made a mournful noise. The men and women sat in a circle around the fire, the scalp pole, and the drummers. Children and dogs ran and played outside the circle.

The warrior who had captured him stood, and other men arose and began to chant with the drummers. Then they started circling inside the ring of spectators, first in one direction, then another.

"It's hot," Lupe said.

"I'm thirsty," Esteban whined.

"Don't cry," Armando answered.

The women began to chant and sing. Then one of the dancing warriors broke from the circle and charged at the scalp pole, screaming and waving a knife in the air.

Armando gritted his teeth, and heard Lupe gasp.

"Don't cry," he implored her. "Shut your eyes if he scares you."

Armando saw that she had obeyed, her eyes closed so tightly that her eyelids were disfigured.

Esteban screamed as the warrior ran straight for him.

"Don't look, Esteban."

The warrior grabbed Esteban's hair and yanked at it.

Esteban cried.

Then the warrior pretended to stab Esteban and take his scalp. Esteban's knees sagged, and when the warrior released his hair, he fell to the ground sobbing.

"Get up, Esteban, get up. They are taunting you! Do not let them scare you."

Esteban cried and tried to stand, but he tripped on his own feet and collapsed. When another warrior made a run at Esteban, he curled himself into a ball on the ground. Armando pitied Esteban, his body already bruised and battered. What little courage he had ever had was lost somewhere so deep within him that he might never find it.

The braves toyed with Armando a few times, and occasionally with Lupe, but mostly they tormented Esteban, the circle of women laughing at his cowardice and the warriors displaying their disgust at his performance.

Then the women got up and began to dance in a circle around the celebrating men. Sometimes the men faced the scalp pole and sometimes they faced the women. Occasionally both lines of men and women converged on the scalp pole.

Then the women danced through the line of men and circled the captives and the fire. The women flitted toward the captives, trying their best to frighten Lupe, but she held her eyes tightly closed and did not scream. Then some of the women produced willow switches which they had hidden in the folds of their dresses. They ran by the captives, swatting at Armando and Lupe especially, striking skin and drawing a wince and a yelp from them.

"They're trying to scare us, Lupe," he told her. He grabbed her, and the next time the women ran in with the willow switches, he shielded her with his own body.

Esteban stood up and was immediately attacked with a flurry of blows. The sudden pain on his already bruised body caused him to scream, then turn pale. Esteban fainted.

Some women retreated from the circle and returned with sticks which they stuck in the fire until the tips flamed. Joining the other dancers, they began to weave back and forth to the beat of the tom-toms, and jabbed at Armando and Lupe.

Armando protected Lupe from attack as best he could, though she winced and cried out when two burning sticks seared her skin.

One woman placed her burning stick upon Esteban's

shirt, producing a flame. Armando jumped to Esteban, knocked the woman's stick from her hand and slapped at the shirt until the flame disappeared.

While he was attending Esteban, the women attacked Lupe, touching her arms and legs with the burning sticks. She screamed, then knocked a couple of the sticks away and charged at her tormentors, but tripped when she reached the end of her rope. She fell with such force that she pulled the scalp pole down.

Armando saw the pole start its fall, and fearing it might strike Lupe, bounced to his feet and caught it before it hit the ground. He then shoved the end back into the soft dirt where it had been planted. When he looked at the twin circles of men and women, they all seemed to be staring at him. The warrior who had captured him stood with shoulders and head high. Armando thought it a prideful look.

The men and women backed away, the squaws throwing aside their willow branches and their burning sticks. Though the Comanches kept dancing and singing, they did not make another run at the captives.

Armando realized something had changed, but he did not understand exactly what. He stepped to Lupe and squatted beside her. She appeared stunned by her fall.

"It will be okay," he said. Lupe managed to stand up, though she was wobbly as a newborn colt. Once the dancers saw that she was on her feet, they ignored her and Armando. He did not understand why.

The beat of the drum quickened and the dancers increased their pace, now fully ignoring Armando, Lupe, and Esteban.

Tired from the trials of the long day, Armando backed to Esteban, helping Lupe move with him. They both sat down beside Esteban and leaned against one another. When the Comanches did not run at them or taunt them, Armando knew that he and Lupe would survive. They had met the challenge of the Comanche. He wondered if Esteban would.

Santa Fe, New Mexico Territory

With no word from Fort Laramie for almost three weeks, Jean Benoit grew even more anxious. Why had they not written? He had expected a letter from Inge or Jace Dobbs. When would they ever arrive?

His days fell into a pattern of reporting to the Ninth Military District headquarters, handling the paperwork and tasks assigned by Brigadier General Smedley, retiring at 11:45 for mess with the other officers, then returning to his office for more paperwork until six o'clock, when he returned to see what Consuela had prepared for the officers.

Some evenings after supper, he spent time looking for a house for his family, but he didn't find any place particularly suitable, nor particularly affordable on an Army officer's pay. He anticipated looking harder once he knew when his family would arrive in Santa Fe.

But most evenings when he was done with the final meal of the day, Benoit returned to his room, taking with him any newspapers he could borrow and reading about the political situation. Tensions were running high in the press, reflecting the mood of the country, he thought. Maybe it was best that he was on the frontier and away from the hotheads and sudden political passions that could turn the dispute into war.

The papers arriving in Santa Fe came mainly from St. Louis and Springfield, Missouri. The opinions were hard-edged, some pro-Union, some favoring secession.

On this evening as he read by candlelight, the issue of nullification dominated the St. Louis paper. Nullification had long been a contention of the South because they believed that the individual states should and could nullify the federal law if it went against the will of the state.

Benoit was especially amused to read that the state of Wisconsin had adopted a resolution the previous month that supported nullification. The resolution stemmed from a contentious case five years earlier when the editor of the *Wisconsin Free Democrat* had been arrested for violating the federal Fugitive Slave Law, which required citizens to return fugitive slaves.

Benoit shook his head. Nullification always seemed to be linked to a slave issue, whether it was in the North or the South.

The accused editor was released by a judge of the state supreme court on the grounds that the federal law was unconstitutional and void. The editor was tried, convicted in federal court, and sent to jail, stirring the passions of citizens until the state supreme court released him again. The U.S. Supreme Court then overruled the state court. The editor was rearrested and sent to jail, where he remained.

Benoit grinned at the irony of a northern state supporting the idea of nullification. He read the wording of the resolution aloud:

"We regard the action of the Supreme Court of the United States, in assuming jurisdiction in the case before mentioned, as an arbitrary act of power, unauthorized by the Constitution, and virtually superseding the benefit of the writ of habeas corpus, and prostrating the rights and liberties of the people at the foot of unlimited power.

"Resolved, that this assumption of jurisdiction by

the federal judiciary in the said case, and without process, is an act of undelegated power, and therefore without authority, voice, and of no force."

The paper indicated that the citizens of Wisconsin were up in arms, and talk abounded about secession. Benoit had often wondered what state, if the problems of national unity could not be resolved, would be the first to secede from the Union. He had thought it would be Virginia, South Carolina, Alabama, Mississippi, or even his home of Louisiana, but never would he have guessed Wisconsin.

The legislature in Wisconsin was arguing what the southern states had contended for years: that the federal government did not have the power to tell the states what to do. Benoit agreed that the federal government lacked such authority, save in matters related to the defense of the nation. After all, the seat of power in the District of Columbia was too far removed from New Orleans or Santa Fe, for instance, to provide effective and efficient government.

He wished that Jace Dobbs was around to argue this issue. Would he defend the right of Wisconsin to nullify the federal law in light of his insistence that the southern states didn't have that right? Or would he say Wisconsin was as wrong as the South? Benoit's thoughts were interrupted by a loud rap on the door.

"Captain Benoit, Captain Benoit," called a voice.

Benoit thought it was Sergeant Hamilton Phipps. What was he doing well after dark unless it was an emergency? He moved quickly to answer the door.

Phipps saluted hurriedly. "Sir, you have someone to see you."

Benoit just made out a bulky figure behind him that seemed to be a hulking man.

Phipps stepped aside and the figure advanced.

The form was difficult to make out in the dim light thrown off by the candle.

Then he saw her.

It was Inge!

His heart leaped to his throat.

"Inge?"

"Jean," she answered, her voice like music to him.

Her broad silhouette was a result of the bundle she carried in each arm.

His daughters. He stood speechless, not believing that the moment had finally arrived. He was so surprised, he merely stared.

Inge walked to him. "Aren't you going to kiss me?"

"Yes, yes, but let me see my girls first," Benoit said, feeling foolish. He looked around. Sergeant Phipps had disappeared. "Thank you, Sergeant Phipps," he called, then backed into the room, not letting his eyes leave Inge and the two babies she carried.

Inge moved toward him into the candlelight, and he caught the first glimpse of his two daughters.

"This is Colleen," Inge said, shaking her right arm. The baby giggled. Colleen was dark-haired, with blue eyes like his own.

"And this is Ellen." Inge shook her left arm. Ellen was light-haired, with the turquoise blue eyes and pink cheeks of her mother. She was cuddled in her mother's arms, sucking the two middle fingers on her right hand.

"Girls, meet your father, Jean Francois Xavier Benoit."

Benoit stood dumbfounded, not knowing what to do. Then he lunged to his wife and kissed her hard upon the lips.

Inge broke away from him and stepped back. "Jean, not in front of the girls," she chided him.

Then Benoit leaned over and gently kissed each girl.

Colleen giggled and Ellen just sucked her fingers harder.

Benoit took Colleen from her mother and laid her in the crook of his left arm. Then he slid his arm under Inge's and took Ellen in his right arm. He marched around the room, humming to the girls. He had a thousand questions.

"When did you arrive?"

"Just after dusk."

"I never got a letter you were coming. I wasn't expecting you."

"There were sudden orders at Fort Laramie for a troop of soldiers to report to Fort Union. We left sooner than we had planned, all packed in an ambulance."

Benoit danced around the room, almost giddy, until Ellen yanked her fingers from her mouth and began to squall.

Benoit never remembered feeling so helpless.

"What do I do?"

"Don't panic, Jean. You won't break them."

Inge took Ellen and quickly comforted her. Soon, Ellen was sucking her fingers again.

Benoit rocked Colleen in his arms, then stared at Inge.

She was more beautiful than he remembered. Her hair was the color of corn silk and tightly braided, her eyes the blue of turquoise and her cheeks pink. Her broad shoulders gave way to a bosom that seemed bigger than before. Her slim hips had broadened a bit, but she was still fully appealing.

"What about Erich?"

"He is with us, but is being taken care of for the night. He did not want to intrude upon our privacy, and

I think he is still embarrassed to be so helpless. Tomorrow will be time enough to talk about him and see him."

Benoit grinned.

Inge nodded her head. "Tonight I wanted it just to be us. You and me. Of course wherever I am now, that's where the girls are as well."

Benoit looked around the room. "Where will they sleep?"

"Sergeant Phipps promised to bring the wagon around and leave their cradles and bedding outside the door." Inge surveyed the cot that was her husband's bed. "As for us, we'll have to make do." She winked.

"There's so much I want to know," he said.

"And so much for me to tell you."

Benoit heard a wagon and then noises outside his door. He started in that direction to help Phipps, but Inge grabbed his arm.

"Stay with me. He said he didn't mind unloading things for you."

"How was the trip?"

"Long but safe. The weather was pleasant and we encountered no problems or Indians."

"And the girls, how did they travel?"

"They had their days."

"How is Jace?"

Inge smiled. "He sends his best and thinks you and he will be together before too long."

"I sure miss him."

"As much as you missed me?"

Benoit walked to Inge and kissed her on the forehead. "I missed all of my girls, but especially my big girl. Now tell me all about my daughters."

Inge and Benoit circled each other in the room, keeping the girls occupied while Inge spoke of their hard birth and the first few days, when Dobbs had been uncertain if they would live. She told how he had made sugar teats—a tablespoon of sugar tied in a permeable cloth that was then dipped in milk. The girls had sucked on them until they were strong enough to nurse.

Then she told him about Colleen's love of cuddling and Ellen's independence. She told how the babies had discovered their hands, fingers, and arms, then their legs and toes.

And how they laughed when they were tickled. Benoit tried to tickle Colleen, but she began to cry.

"They're tired," Inge said. "It's been a long day and a long trip. Maybe it's time for their feeding."

Inge sat down on the cot and began to unbutton her blouse. Shortly, she exposed her breast and put Colleen against it. The baby began to suckle.

"I'm envious," Benoit said.

Inge laughed. "From now on, Jean, you're third in line."

He smiled. "There's not two I'd rather be behind than these girls."

Outside, he heard the wagon drive away.

"Maybe I should get our things."

Inge nodded.

He stood there looking around the room, not knowing what to do with Ellen.

With her free hand, Inge patted the cot. "Put her here and I'll watch her so she doesn't fall off."

Benoit obeyed, then brought in the cradles and bedding that had been left outside his door. He set them beside one another as Inge switched babies. After Ellen was done, she put both babies in their cradles and set them to rocking. When the girls were asleep, she took the remaining bedding and made a pallet on the floor. She blew out the candles before she started removing her clothes.

"I have a surprise for you tomorrow," she said.

"I'm not thinking past tonight," he said as he fell into her arms.

5

Jean Benoit awoke tired. He dressed quietly so as not to wake the girls, who were light sleepers. Inge was still an exuberant lover, but the girls kept waking whenever Benoit wished they were sleeping the hardest. Inge had explained that the girls would eventually adapt to their new surroundings and sought his patience. Benoit admitted it would take time to accustom himself to his family.

"'Morning," Inge said, stirring on the makeshift mattress she had spread out on the floor with her quilts. She sat up and the sheet fell away from her shoulders so Benoit could admire her bosom.

"I can't believe you're here and I've finally seen my daughters," he said. "They're beautiful, like their mother."

"They missed their father, just like I did," she whispered.

"I'll go to headquarters, see if General Smedley can do without me today so I can find us a better place to stay."

"We'll need a place big enough for Erich as well."

Benoit had been so overjoyed to see Inge that he'd forgotten about Erich. "Where'd he stay?"

"The wagon."

"I should have invited him in."

"He wouldn't have come, not until you'd had a chance to see me and your daughters alone. Besides, he's got a surprise for you." Inge smiled.

Benoit clapped his hands. "He's walking again?"

Ellen's eyes flew open and she jerked her fingers out of her mouth to squall.

Benoit felt his face redden with embarrassment.

"You'll learn quickly," Inge said, crawling across the bedding and grabbing the bundle of covers that surrounded Ellen. She began to hum to the baby and soon had her asleep again.

"What's this surprise?" Benoit asked.

"If I told you, it wouldn't be a surprise," Inge answered coyly.

"Where'll I find Erich?"

"They said they'd park the wagon at the end of the street."

"They? Who's they?"

Inge slid softly back on the bedding and pulled the sheet over her. She yawned, then smiled. "I'm sleepy."

Benoit scratched his head. "Your mother and Jim Ashby didn't come, did they?"

Inge shook her head. "Mama has finally adjusted to Jim Ashby as a husband, though it hasn't been easy, not with his mountain man ways, but Jean, my darling, I want to rest. You should find Erich."

Benoit slipped to the bedding. Kneeling, he kissed Inge on the forehead. He retreated to the door, took his hat and stepped outside, where the light was still soft and the morning air cool.

He glanced first toward the plaza, then marched up the street to the wagon parked at the end. The horses were hobbled and the back end of the wagon was open, the tailgate dropped. Benoit saw Erich sitting in a chair in back of the wagon. A man in uniform at the side of the wagon stepped around the front and out of sight. Erich waved slightly.

Benoit smiled, but felt especially helpless now. His letter speaking of the miracles at Chimayo had brought Erich to Santa Fe. What if the miracles never happened? What if the trip had been futile for Erich? As those thoughts raced through his mind, he studied the shell of the young man he once knew. Erich sat somberly, watching him approach.

Benoit tried to hide the concern over his brother-in-law's deterioration. Not yet nineteen, Erich Schmidt had sported huge shoulders, a thick chest, and thighs the size of telegraph poles, but that Erich had withered away. As a result of the injury, this Erich was slight and sullen. Jason Dobbs had thought the injury was a compression of the spinal cord which might repair itself, though most likely not.

"Erich, it's good to see you," Benoit said. "Glad you came with Inge. I know it was a relief to her to have you in the wagon." Benoit shoved his hand at Erich.

Erich took it limply and shook it weakly. "The wagon's the only place I could be with these useless legs," he replied.

Benoit grimaced at the resignation and bitterness in his voice.

As Erich slid his hand from Benoit's, he slapped his own right leg, then ran his fingers through his shoulder-length hair, which was as fair as his skin. His blue eyes seemed as lifeless as his legs, and his spirit as withered as his shoulders.

"I'm grateful for the night alone with Inge and the

girls, but you're welcome to stay in my meek quarters from now on."

"I'll stay elsewhere until I can get to the miracle church."

"You're kin and you're welcome to stay."

"It'd be too painful a reminder." Erich looked away. "Every night when you went to bed with Inge, it would remind me that I'd never have a chance to sleep with a woman."

"Erich, you've got to have faith. The archbishop says faith can produce a miracle."

Erich twisted his head to stare at Benoit. "Faith? Every day since I was thrown from that horse, I believed I would awake and be able to get out of my bed and walk, even run. I've had faith. Now I want a miracle."

"The archbishop has promised to go with us to Chimayo and talk with the priest."

"Jean, did Inge tell you what this really means, being paralyzed below the waist?"

Benoit didn't care to hear, but could not stop Erich.

"I soil my britches like your daughters soil their diapers. I wet my pants without knowing it. A grown man doing that. I'd be better off dead than forced to live like this."

"Inge doesn't think so. I don't think so."

"But I think so, Jean, and I know so because I'm the one who has to live with this."

"The archbishop says nothing bad happens without a reason and there's a godly reason behind this."

Erich spat on the ground. "Do you believe that, Jean?"

Benoit doubted it, and his delay in responding gave Erich his answer.

"You don't believe it."

"I believe in you, Erich."

Erich turned away. "Just help get me out of this wagon."

Benoit nodded. "I'll go get someone to help."

Erich shook his head toward the side of the wagon. "There's a soldier around there."

Benoit moved from behind the wagon and saw the soldier, the man he'd spotted beside the wagon as he approached. The soldier's back was to him, and he was leaning against the wagon as though he'd been eavesdropping on them.

"You," Benoit called. "Give me a hand with this man."

The soldier turned around, his head drooping so far forward that the brim of his hat screened his face. Benoit saw by his uniform that he was an army lieutenant. "I expect proper military protocol, Lieutenant, as I am a captain."

"Yes, sir," the lieutenant replied, his voice vaguely familiar. "Of course we'd all be captains if we had a crooked senator getting us promotions like you."

"Lieutenant," Benoit cried out, "stand at attention."

The soldier snapped straight as a pole, save for his drooping head. He was at least six-foot-two and lean as a reed.

Benoit's anger was building. "Lift your head, Lieutenant, immediately."

The officer nodded and slowly raised his head, the brim of the hat rising until Benoit saw a chin, then a broad smile followed by a patrician nose and mischievous eyes.

Benoit gasped. "Jace Dobbs, what are you doing here?"

Dobbs laughed. "Mouthing off to my superiors."

Benoit lunged for Dobbs and trapped him in a bear hug. "I can't believe it. Why didn't you let me know?"

"I wanted it to be a surprise."

"You here at Fort Marcy now?"

Dobbs shook his head. "Wish it were so, but you know the Army."

Benoit broke his grip on Jace. "That's for saving my daughters."

"They're a pair of cuties, Jean."

"But tell me about the Army."

"I requested a transfer to Fort Marcy and got a transfer . . ."

"Great," Benoit shouted, slapping him on the shoulder with joy.

". . . to Fort Bliss."

"Fort Bliss?"

"In El Paso. At least it's closer than Fort Laramie."

"Damn."

"And I sure missed you, Jean. After you left, I didn't have anyone to argue with on everything."

"They weren't as smart as me, huh?"

"No, they weren't as wrong as you on everything."

Benoit shook his head. "You haven't changed. I guess that's why I've always enjoyed you."

"Well, we could talk all day, but we've some work to do." Dobbs pointed toward Erich Schmidt. "Sad situation," he whispered.

The two officers walked to wagon tailgate.

"I designed a chair for Erich," Dobbs said. "I put a pair of wheels on the back two legs of his chair. All you've got to do is tilt the chair back on the wheels and push."

"Like a wheelbarrow," Erich said.

Both men reached into the wagon, grabbing the

front legs and pulling the chair closer to the edge until they could grab the back legs and remove Erich. Benoit was surprised at how light he was.

They sat Erich gently on the ground, then Dobbs pushed him down the street. "I'll take him to your quarters."

"How do you know where my quarters are?" Benoit asked as he walked alongside.

"It was me that unloaded the bedding on your doorstep last night. I hope you made good use of it?"

Benoit grinned. "We did as good as we could with the girls in the room."

Dobbs laughed.

Benoit glanced from Dobbs to the two six-inch wheels that revolved around a iron rod axle running through holes in the rear legs. It was a crude and perhaps undignified way to transport a cripple, but it worked, and created less embarrassment than carrying a man around like a sack of potatoes.

When they reached Benoit's quarters, he slipped inside first to make sure Inge was properly dressed. She smiled when he entered.

"Quite a surprise," he said.

Inge smiled. "It was Jace's idea."

Benoit opened the door. "Okay," he whispered.

Dobbs wheeled the brooding Erich into the middle of the room, then turned to Benoit. "We've the wagon to unload and other chores to do, Captain."

Benoit nodded. "I had best check with headquarters first to see if the general can do without me."

The two men stepped outside and closed the door behind them, then marched toward headquarters.

"I've never seen Erich so morose," Dobbs said. "If

this miracle doesn't come through, I fear he'll be paralyzed for life."

"Do you think there's a chance he'll walk again?"

"Sure there's a chance. One chance out of a million."

"I talked to the archbishop, and he says it's a matter of faith. Without faith there are no miracles."

"Some things even faith can't cure, and for my money this is one of them. Backs are tricky, and I've never seen in any of the medical literature any indication that anyone's close to understanding the spine and how it works. Hard as it may sound, the war that everyone's talking about might help medicine, might help Erich."

"How's that?"

"There's a lot of savage injuries in battle, the type of thing doctors don't ordinarily see. While they're treating the wounds in such great numbers, they try things they wouldn't ordinarily do. It's desperation. In war, doctors with inquisitive minds can learn things to advance the cause of medicine."

"That's the first time I've ever heard that war could have a beneficial side."

Dobbs slapped Benoit on the back. "That's why you need me around—to keep educating you. Now educate me. I hear General Arnold Smedley's related to Jefferson Davis."

"He's a third cousin of Jefferson Davis, but as straight and loyal as they come. You'll not find a better man in an Army uniform out West."

They reached headquarters and went inside. Benoit started to introduce Dobbs to Sergeant Hamilton Phipps, but discovered they had met the night before. General Smedley overheard him and invited Benoit and Dobbs into his office.

After exchanging salutes, Smedley eyed Benoit. "You sure seem in better spirits than I can remember, Captain."

"My wife and girls arrived last night, General."

"Well, congratulations. I know you are relieved."

"Yes, sir. Lieutenant Dobbs accompanied them from Fort Laramie."

"Every mile of the trip, sir," Dobbs answered.

"Where you from, Lieutenant Dobbs? It's not from south of the Mason-Dixon line, I can tell from the sound of your voice."

"No, sir, New Hampshire, sir."

Smedley motioned for them to sit, then he plopped in the chair behind his desk. "I don't remember seeing any orders assigning you to the Ninth Military District," he said.

"No, sir. I requested a transfer to Fort Marcy, Jean being a decent man and a Southerner I can get along with, but the Army assigned me instead to Fort Bliss. I've got three weeks before I'm to report there."

"Good, you'll have a chance to spend some time with Captain Benoit, then. And you're in luck—in two weeks the paymaster will be coming through on his way to Fort Fillmore. You can accompany him there. Fort Bliss is just another thirty-five or so miles south of Fillmore."

"That would be fine, sir."

Smedley turned to Benoit. "And I suppose, Captain, that you would like some time to spend with your family and Lieutenant Dobbs."

"Yes, sir. I must find larger accommodations for my family. Then there's my brother-in-law, Erich Schmidt. He's a cripple."

"I will ask Sergeant Phipps to cover your responsibilities for the next ten days, Captain Benoit, until the paymaster arrives. Then I will expect you at your desk assisting. Until then, you can do what you want."

"Thank you, sir. And may I ask if we've heard anything more from Senator Couvillion?"

Smedley eyed Dobbs, considering how he should respond.

"Lieutenant Dobbs is trustworthy, sir, and knows the troubles I've had with Senator Couvillion. He's a man of honor, sir."

The general stroked his handlebar mustache, then nodded. "Your word's good enough for me, Captain. I have not heard anything else since we last wrote. We will respond whenever we do hear from him."

"Sir," Dobbs interrupted, "might I ask if it is true that you're a third cousin of Jefferson Davis?"

Smedley's eyebrows arched. "I do not advertise that fact, Lieutenant."

"I was just curious, sir, the type of man he is. I know the type that Senator Couvillion is. I was just curious about Senator Davis."

"There's no comparison between the two, if that's what you mean. Though we played together as kids and were fairly close growing up, he has not once asked or threatened me to provide him information on the Army and its activities. He is certainly one of the smartest men I know. I might even say brilliant. He stands for what he believes and does not back down. His beliefs are grounded in reason and he does not manipulate others as Senator Couvillion tries to do. Why do you ask, Lieutenant?"

"A natural curiosity, sir. These are difficult times and everyone is preparing for war. Should war come, I like to know the character of my enemy, for he will surely be an enemy of New England because it is an enemy of slavery."

"Jefferson Davis is an honorable man. Clement Couvillion is not. Men of honor and dishonor will fight on both sides."

Dobbs nodded. "The men of the South I know talk as if chivalry will win the day, if war comes."

"Numbers will win the day, Lieutenant, and the North has the numbers. Factories, railroads, men, munitions, those are the numbers that count. The South has cotton, sir, but cotton will not win the war, nor will right. Only might will triumph."

"You sound discouraged, sir, as a son of the South."

"I am realistic, Lieutenant. Slavery is doomed, and the issue of states' rights is so closely tied to slavery that it, too, is doomed. The South would be far wiser to abolish slavery gradually and to try to cling to the idea of local self-determination or states' rights. The argument of nullification can never be sustained if slavery remains the issue. I fear slavery is like Thomas Jefferson himself said, 'A fire bell in the night.'"

Dobbs lifted his hands and applauded. "You, sir, are wise."

Smedley shook his head. "No, sir, I am merely realistic."

Jean Benoit used his time wisely, finding a small three-room adobe he could lease on the edge of town. The adobe had a kitchen and two other rooms. Inge and Benoit used one for their bedroom and offered the other to Erich, but he insisted that the girls have it and that he sleep in the kitchen. Dobbs, meanwhile, stayed in Benoit's old quarters.

They unloaded the wagon of all Inge's belongings and furniture and furnished the house as best they could. Dobbs also brought his books and belongings, which he would send for once he was settled at Fort Bliss. They stored his items in the girls' room. When all that was done, they spent the days exploring Santa Fe together, Benoit introducing Dobbs to Father Machebeuf and Alejo Ortiz. And they planned a trip to take Erich to the miracle church in Chimayo.

When the first caravan of the season reached Santa Fe from Missouri, Benoit escorted Dobbs to the plaza to enjoy the spectacle. Dobbs could find virtually anything he wanted, though greatly overpriced. He spotted a silver pocket watch with an alarm, and picked it up while eyeing the merchant behind a table hastily covered with the goods brought from Missouri.

"Fifteen dollars," the merchant demanded, pounding the table for emphasis, realizing the watch had caught Dobbs's fancy.

"Too high."

The merchant, a Mexican, was lean, his clothes as dusty as the Santa Fe Trail. He was hard to read because his eyes seemed to be in a perpetual squint from always riding westward into the sun. "Good watch, loud alarm," the merchant explained, snatching the silver watch from Dobbs's hands. He set the alarm and then placed it on a clear spot on the table.

Dobbs reached for it, but the merchant grabbed his hand. "*Alto,*" he said. "You will see."

In a moment the alarm sprang to life so loudly that the watch bounced from the vibration. "Alarm move and rumble like thunder." The merchant picked up the watch, snapped off the alarm and handed the timepiece to Dobbs.

Dobbs offered it to Benoit, who held it in his hand. It was heavier than the pocket watch Inge had given him for their first anniversary. The watch was a fine timepiece, with a case that had an embossed eagle on the cover and a United States flag on the back.

"Keeps good time, accurate time," the merchant said. "Only fifteen dollars. Good price."

Benoit handed the watch back to Dobbs. "What do you need an alarm watch for?"

"To keep me from oversleeping at Fort Bliss. I want to make a better impression on the commander there."

"But fifteen dollars?"

Dobbs winked, then whispered, "I can get him to come down. Absolutely."

Benoit laughed when the merchant held his ground.

"Fifteen dollars. No more, no less, no watch."

"Army pay isn't that good," Dobbs pleaded.

"Dangerous to get watch to Santa Fe, must cover much ground between Missouri and Santa Fe. Many Indians. Comanches meanest of all. Risk scalp to bring fine merchandise to Santa Fe. Fine merchandise cost more. Fifteen dollars or I keep watch."

Dobbs shrugged and put the watch back on the table. "Can't afford it." He turned away from the table, winking at Benoit as if to say this ploy would convince the Mexican to reduce his price.

Dobbs took a couple steps.

"Adios, soldier," the merchant called after him.

Benoit laughed when Dobbs spun about and marched straight to the table, grabbing the watch.

The Mexican smiled. "You buy?"

"I'll buy it, if you provide me a watch chain."

"Watch chain expensive."

"Then throw in a cheap one for free."

Shrugging, the merchant nodded. "You pay fifteen dollars. Watch and chain, cheap not expensive, yours."

Dobbs grabbed his money roll from his pocket and counted out fifteen dollars.

"Soldier, *muy rico*."

"Not anymore," Dobbs answered as he handed over the money.

The merchant picked up the watch, opened a wooden box and picked out a chain. He offered both to Dobbs.

"Why don't you put the chain on the watch for me?"

"Cost fifty cents more," the merchant replied.

As Benoit laughed, Dobbs snatched the watch and chain from the merchant's hand, spun around and marched away from the plaza.

Benoit teased him. "Sure glad you didn't negotiate the treaty after the Mexican War. Everything west of the Mississippi would've become Mexico's if you had."

Dobbs grinned. "So much the better, if you think about it, because we wouldn't be out here fighting Indians, drought, scorpions, rattlesnakes, and everything else that bites, stings, or scalps."

"And we wouldn't've met," Benoit replied.

Dobbs laughed. "Another good reason."

Dobbs and Benoit had loaded the wagon with everything but the girls and Erich by the time Father Machebeuf arrived atop a donkey for the trip to Chimayo. After greeting him, Dobbs and Benoit removed the canvas from atop the wagon so Erich could see everywhere as they traveled, instead of just out the back of the wagon. When they were done, they retreated inside the adobe and wheeled Erich out as the priest dismounted.

The archbishop extended his hand. "I am Father Machebeuf."

Erich shook it without enthusiasm and said nothing.

Inge, standing nearby, grimaced. "Forgive him, Father, as he feels half a man since he cannot walk."

"I can speak for myself," Erich replied, looking at no one in particular.

"Then do it," Inge answered curtly. "Show the good manners that Mother taught you."

Erich looked up at Machebeuf. "I am sorry, Father."

"You are forgiven, my son, and what is past is forgotten." Machebeuf looked at the deep blue sky overhead and the mountains shining like towers of gold in the early morning sunshine. "Enjoy the day as another glorious moment that God shares with us."

"Do you really believe in God?" Erich asked.

Machebeuf seemed flustered for a moment. "How could I be a man of the cloth and not?"

"But do you really believe in Him? Have you no doubts?"

"I am a believer of many things, but in none do I believe more strongly than God."

"Does God create miracles?"

"He has that power."

"Does God cripple people like me?"

"He has that power, but it is the devil that causes the bad in this world."

"Then how can God allow that to happen?"

"My son, remember that it is not what God allows to happen that matters but what God does to make even the bad moments of our lives turn out for the best."

Benoit and Dobbs stepped between the man of God and the young man of doubt.

"Time to get you in the wagon, Erich," Benoit said.

"You'll have time to talk with Father Machebeuf on the way to Chimayo."

The two men grabbed his chair and lifted him into the back.

"Will I ever walk again, Father, so that men do not have to lift me into the back of wagons?"

"With faith you will, my son."

"But how do you get faith?"

"Start with things small, the beauty of a new day, the aroma of a field of flowers, the call of a songbird. Faith, like a cathedral, is built one stone at a time."

"Thank you, Father."

Machebeuf nodded. "I will pray not only for you, but also for your faith."

Inge scurried out carrying a cradle and put it in the back of the wagon by the seat. Then she hurried back inside and returned with a second cradle, placing it opposite the first. This done, she climbed in the wagon seat and grabbed the reins. The six mules picked up their heads.

"Do you want me to drive?" Benoit asked.

"I drove every mile of the way here from Fort Laramie," she said.

"That's a fact, Jean," Dobbs interjected. "I offered to drive, but she said no."

Benoit turned toward Father Machebeuf. "Since you know the way, Padre, you should lead."

The priest gathered his robes, then mounted the donkey. For a moment the donkey balked, but Machebeuf leaned over and bit its ear. When the priest realized the others had seen this, he smiled. "Sometimes, I give instructions with a bite."

Benoit and Dobbs laughed. Even Erich managed a grin as the priest rode by. Benoit and Dobbs mounted their horses and followed him to the front of the wagon. After they passed, Inge released the brake, shook the reins and started the mules to walking, the trace chains rattling and the dry wooden wagon frame creaking.

The morning was crisp and clear. They could see for miles as they rode toward Chimayo. Between the mountains to the east and west, the trail north climbed gradually as they advanced. Erich sat looking backward instead of forward, as if he could not forget the Crow attack that had crippled him.

The trail took them through badlands where wind and water, ice and time had carved sculptures across the landscape. The browns, tans, and yellows of the earth melded into a soft hue that was pleasing to the eye.

Dobbs took it all in as he rode, but mostly he conversed with Machebeuf because he loved to gab. Benoit looked at Dobbs once and saw by the surgeon's sly grin that Dobbs was warming up for a major discussion. Benoit figured the topic would be religion. Dobbs had an inquisitive mind and loved to argue for the pure sake of debate. Just as he had asked General Smedley what Jefferson Davis was like, Dobbs would certainly ask Machebeuf something sensitive.

Finally, Dobbs winked at Benoit and turned to Machebeuf. "Father, I have a question about the priesthood."

"What is it?"

"Celibacy. There are what I would call natural urges that a man must deal with. I've never understood why priests must be celibate."

"It's biblical."

Dobbs smiled. "I have another theory."

Machebeuf looked at Dobbs. "The Apostle Paul spoke of celibacy when he established the Church. In

First Corinthians, chapter seven, he says that 'he that is unmarried careth for the things that belong to the Lord, how he may please the Lord. But he that is married careth for the things that are of the world, how he may please his wife.'"

Dobbs grinned. "As we know, Father, the Bible can be used to defend anything good, such as marriage, or evil, such as slavery."

"I would never defend slavery because I do not believe in it."

Dobbs laughed. "Then how can you defend marriage if you yourself do not believe in it?"

"But I do believe in marriage. For man and woman, marriage to each other. For me, it is marriage to the Church."

Dobbs smiled. "I cannot say if that is possible, Father, though I have read the scriptures many times."

"Then you are a religious man?"

"No, Father, I am a man who does not believe in what the Bible or the Church says. And I believe celibacy is merely the Church's way of making certain that property and money given to the Church remain the Church's rather than being passed on to the offspring that would result if marriage was allowed."

Benoit feared Dobbs had offended the priest.

Father Machebeuf scratched his chin, then looked at Dobbs. "I can tell you are a thinking man, Lieutenant Dobbs. That is certainly a reason I had never thought about, an interesting theory, no doubt, but the cynicism reflects a lack of understanding."

Dobbs looked at Benoit and shook his head approvingly. "No offense, Jean, but Father Machebeuf is my intellectual equal, a challenge to debate, and you know how much I like challenges."

Benoit nodded. "As long as you don't offend him."

"I can't help it. I'm just being me."

"That's what I'm afraid of, Jace."

Machebeuf laughed. "It is good to have occasion to talk with an intellectual. It can be stimulating. A muscle grows weak unless it is used. It grows stronger when it is used. Your brain needs the challenge of hard questions and solid logic. A man such as Lieutenant Dobbs, no matter how wrong he may be, presents a challenge to me, and I to him. It is stimulating."

Dobbs laughed. "Wrong, am I? Well, by the time we get to Chimayo, I'll have you convinced you are wrong."

The two men grinned and began a debate on religion and science and the incompatibility of the two.

Benoit eventually grew tired of their discussions and slipped back to the wagon to visit with Inge and Erich, who said little. After they stopped for a brief lunch of jerked meat, Benoit tied his horse behind the wagon and climbed in the seat with Inge. Colleen and Ellen made odd noises as if they were singing. Their jabbering was music to Benoit's ears. When they got squawky, Inge breast-fed each in her turn. Then the children took their naps, and awoke feisty as they approached Chimayo.

They entered the town shortly before sundown. Men, women, and children acknowledged the priest as he passed. He blessed them in Spanish, and they smiled. Dobbs had fallen back to the wagon, letting Machebeuf bless his flock as he passed.

"I feared you might offend Father Machebeuf," Benoit said.

"Not at all," Dobbs answered. "He respects me more because I have the intellect to challenge his faith and his beliefs."

Before Benoit could answer, the noise of a loud ringing pierced the air. Both Ellen and Colleen stopped their cooing as Dobbs pulled his watch from his pocket and shut off the alarm.

"It's a game I play to see if I can set my watch to coincide with the exact moment the sun disappears behind the horizon. This is the closest I've been in the days since I bought the watch."

Benoit looked west.

"The mountains blocked my view so I cannot tell if I won."

"Do you do it in the morning, as well?" Benoit asked. "Because I will strangle you if you wake those girls from their sleep."

Dobbs grinned. "I won't tomorrow."

They rode through Chimayo, and on the outskirts of the village came to Sanctuario de Chimayo. The adobe church was modest, with twin bell towers, each supporting a wooden cross. The church was enclosed by a low adobe wall that ballooned into an arch with a wooden entry gate. The gate, though, was open, as if welcoming all.

Father Machebeuf drew up in front of the gate and dismounted. He dropped the reins and walked through the gate into the chapel.

Dobbs rode to the back of the wagon. "Here we are, Erich."

Erich rocked around on his chair until he faced the modest church. He studied the simple chapel, which seemed insignificant compared to the mountain directly behind it. "I will walk before I leave here," he said.

Dobbs sighed. "I hope you are right, Erich, I hope you are!"

In a moment, Father Machebeuf emerged from the

chapel escorted by another man in a priest's garments. The two clergymen strode through the gate side by side, heading straight for Erich.

Machebeuf introduced Father Candid Zavala.

Father Zavala smiled and shook Erich's hand. "Welcome to Sanctuario de Chimayo." He turned to face the others. "Welcome to all of you."

Machebeuf then introduced the remainder of the party.

Zavala turned back to Erich. "But I should like to have time with you alone to discuss your needs. Father Machebeuf has told me of your infirmity, and I have agreed to let you stay in the church with me, if you like."

"Father, this is my last chance. If I leave here without walking, I shall never hope or dream again."

Dobbs dismounted and walked to the back of the wagon. He dropped the tailgate and pulled the chair. "Care to help, Father?"

Zavala stepped to the back and helped lift Erich from the wagon. Gently, they placed the chair on the ground, then Dobbs yanked it back and began to push it toward the fence and through the gate.

Benoit helped Inge from her seat, then handed her Ellen before he took Colleen. Machebeuf led them into the church, where he pointed out the two dozen sets of crutches supposedly left by the cured. The chapel was cool and dark, the candles burning around the altar the only light.

"Behind the altar to your left, Erich, is a room," Zavala said. "In it you will find a hole in the middle of the dirt floor. Scoop out dirt from the hole and rub it into your legs."

Dobbs started to wheel Erich in that direction, but Erich lifted his hand. "No," he said, "I must do this myself." With those words, he slid out of the chair onto the floor and began to worm his way toward the back room, pulling himself with his arms and shoulders.

Benoit grimaced at the exertion it took for Erich to inch toward the room. He wanted to help, as did everyone else who watched, but he sensed this was something Erich must begin to do for himself if he was ever to overcome his lameness or restore his pride.

"Can this cure him?" Inge asked Father Zavala.

The local priest looked from Inge to Machebeuf. "The archbishop and I disagree on many things, but miracles do happen with faith. Upon that we can agree."

Machebeuf nodded.

"Will he ever walk again?"

"Perhaps," Machebeuf said, "but we must leave him on his own to determine it. We should leave first thing in the morning."

Dobbs laughed. "See, Jean, I can use the alarm on my watch in the morning, after all."

6

Comanche Camp, Llano Estacado

Excitement ran through the camp like a prairie wildfire. The buffalo herd had been spotted. Soon the shriveled bellies of the women and children would be full with sweet buffalo meat.

The hunt would occupy everyone in camp. The men would do the stalking and killing, then the skinning. The women would assist with the butchering, cutting the meat into strips for drying and tanning the hides, making use of practically every part of the buffalo. Only the rump, spine, and sometimes the skull had no use among the Comanches. Everything else—blood, bones, flesh, skin, horns, kidneys, liver, paunch, and hair—was consumed.

Crow Feather would lead the hunt, for he had found the buffalo a mere hour's ride from the village. The women began to break camp, quickly gathering their belongings in bundles and leather bags. They lowered the skins that sheathed their tipis and used the poles to make travois on which they carried their belongings.

As he rode toward his tipi, Crow Feather watched

Paints the Dead help Weasel gather their belongings and bedding. Paints the Dead had a good heart and had learned to speak rudimentary Comanche. Crow Feather was proud of him and even Stone Flower. She was durable, unlike her brother, who Crow Feather had traded to Speaks Loudly for two horses.

When Crow Feather drew up his dappled gray by the skeleton of his tipi, Paints the Dead greeted him. "It is good, the buffalo?"

"Yes, for the buffalo is a sacred animal put upon this earth to provide us food, clothing, shelter, and everything else. One day, you will be man enough to hunt with me. It is an honor to ride on a buffalo hunt."

Paints the Dead smiled. "Will I have a horse of my own?"

"When the day is right, you will have a horse."

Crow Feather nudged his horse forward, passing Weasel.

She smiled without stopping her packing. "He is a fine captive," she said, "and the girl is good, too. Her brother was not worth two horses."

When she began to lower the lodge poles, Crow Feather rode off to the horse herd, returning quickly with the four packhorses that would carry and drag their belongings to the buffalo herd. Weasel began to hitch the travois to the animals, then pile bundles and buffalo robes atop them. Stone Flower and Paints the Dead worked diligently. When the animals were loaded, Paints the Dead took the halter lines and led the animals away from camp.

Crow Feather was proud his brood was the first to be packed. Gradually, other women and children drove their loaded animals in behind Weasel, Paints the Dead, and Stone Flower. Crow Feather glanced at the camp of

Speaks Loudly and saw that his woman was whipping Willow Leaf. He smiled and reined his horse, about to join the procession, but Speaks Loudly rode out to intersect his path.

"I will return Willow Leaf for one horse," Speaks Loudly said.

"No!" Crow Feather replied.

"You would still have one horse, and Willow Leaf for a slave."

"I don't want him back."

Speaks Loudly grumbled. "Then I shall trade him when the Comancheros come. They will take him."

Crow Feather shrugged. "He is yours. We must kill the buffalo. The herd is small, maybe a hundred buffalo. I want twenty of our best hunters, no more. The buffalo are just beneath a rise near Creek that Runs Crooked. You gather the men."

As Speaks Loudly galloped off, Crow Feather, stricken by a sudden whim, turned his horse toward the horse herd. At the herd, he cut out a pony, then drove it to the head of the caravan.

Paints the Dead looked up at him with wide eyes.

"This pony's for you, Paints the Dead. You shall ride with me."

Paints the Dead smiled nervously.

Crow Feather instructed Paints the Dead to pull another halter from one of the parfleches, but the boy did not understand the word. Crow Feather rode over to the bundle atop one of the packhorses and yanked a halter free. He repeated the word so that Paints the Dead would understand.

The boy nodded. "*Sabe.*" He grabbed the halter and pulled it over the pony's head.

As he did, Crow Feather produced a length of buffalo hair rope. "Tie that around your pony's chest. When you ride, slip your legs beneath the rope. You will not fall when you are galloping."

Paints the Dead did as he was instructed, tying the rope beneath the pony's belly, then said, "I need a weapon? A knife?"

Crow Feather shook his head. "Watch how we hunt."

The boy quickly boosted himself atop the animal. "I'm ready."

Crow Feather smiled as Paints the Dead fell in beside him.

The hunters gathered in advance of the procession of women, children, and pack animals. The men carried their bows and arrows and lances. A few carried rifles, but most still preferred to hunt buffalo as their fathers and grandfathers had, galloping beside the animal and loosing an arrow for the soft spot between the buffalo's protruding hip bone and his last rib. An arrow accurately placed would traverse the animal's entrails and pierce a lung, knocking the animal to its knees and its death. There was nothing more exciting than killing buffalo from atop a galloping pony, nor many things more dangerous.

"When we join the others," Crow Feather said, "say nothing. As a boy, you are merely to listen and observe. Do not whine or complain like Willow Leaf or the hunters will think less of you."

"I'll do what you say."

Crow Feather joined the men and issued instructions on the location of the buffalo and how to attack them.

~

Armando smiled as his pony moved into the lead with Crow Feather. He had never seen a buffalo before, though he'd seen evidence of the animal nearly every moment he had been with the Comanches. He drank water from the paunch of a buffalo and ate meals cooked over dried buffalo chips when wood was not available. The cups and spoons of his Comanche family were fashioned from buffalo bones, hoofs, and horns. Sinews from the spine of the buffalo became bowstrings and thread. Ropes were twisted from buffalo hair. The covering of the tipi where he slept was buffalo hide. The hide provided the clothes the Comanche wore as well as the parfleches they used to carry their belongings. The buffalo was everywhere in camp.

Though he was glad to ride with the braves, Armando wished Crow Feather had given him a knife. He wanted the knife so he could kill Speaks Loudly in revenge for how he had killed his father. When that deed was done, he would be satisfied with his lot. The Comanche life could be fun for a boy who did not whine all the time like Esteban.

Armando rode proudly with Crow Feather, glancing over his shoulder occasionally to see if any braves were watching him. They rode with solemn, inscrutable faces, looking beyond Armando to the horizon. After an hour, the riders approached a rise where Crow Feather lifted his hand and quickly dismounted. He tossed his reins to Armando, who held them.

Crow Feather dropped to his knees, crawled to the top of the rise, and fell flat on his stomach, studying what lay before him. He grabbed a handful of grass and tossed it in the air. The gentle breeze carried the grass in the direction from which they had ridden. Then Crow

Feather crawled back to the others. Reaching his horse, he stood up. "They are there."

Quickly the other warriors jumped off their horses and started removing their leggings and their tops, stripping down to their breechcloths. The men left their clothes on the ground by their horses, then took their bows, stretching the bowstring and flexing their shoulders.

One by one the men remounted their horses and notched arrows on their bowstrings.

Crow Feather jumped on his horse and turned to Armando. "Stay on your horse. After we top the crest, you can ride up and watch. Should the buffalo break and charge this way, turn and run, angling away from the stampede."

Armando nodded.

Without instruction, the braves fanned out behind the rise. Upon Crow Feather's signal, they topped the slight incline and started down toward the buffalo.

Armando waited until the last warrior slipped from view, then he eased his horse atop the rise and beheld his first buffalo herd. He gasped at the size of the beasts grazing a hundred yards away. The hunting party advanced slowly at first. When the first buffalo sighted them, the riders charged ahead, shouting and screaming.

The buffalo came to life, turning at once to run away from the warriors. The hunters narrowed the gap between themselves and the rumbling herd, which headed toward the creek.

With Crow Feather in the lead, the line of warriors rushed to cut off the herd before it reached the water. Crow Feather and the lead bull appeared headed for a collision, but at the last moment the buffalo twisted away and the herd began to circle, kicking up dust and clumps of spring grass.

As the herd revolved in on itself, the cows and calves worked to the center while the massive bulls with their huge humps and their black horns charged about the perimeter.

The rumble was thunder without lightning, the black heaving hulks like roiling clouds. An animal on the perimeter fell, tumbling head over hooves, brushing against a warrior's horse.

Then other animals began to fall, some dropping dead in their tracks as arrows found their marks, others slowing, then finally stopping and collapsing in front of other stampeding animals. Armando thrilled at the spectacle, while struggling to keep his nervous pony from bolting. Through the dust he spotted Crow Feather and watched him attack a buffalo bull. Guiding his horse by the mere touch of his knees, Crow Feather eased behind the great lumbering animal, snot flinging from its nose as it ran. The bull tossed its head, and the gray shied away.

Crow Feather eased the gray closer to the bull, then leaned over the side of his mount until he was almost vertical. His strong arms pulled back the taut bowstring and virtually touched the bow to the soft flesh behind the great animal's last rib.

Crow Feather released the arrow.

The bull flinched.

Crow Feather pulled himself back atop his horse.

The bull turned suddenly and tossed his head, missing Crow Feather by inches with the wicked curve of his horn. Crow Feather yanked the reins and pulled his gray away.

The bull butted the rump of the dappled gray, and the pony stumbled briefly, then bolted ahead as Crow Feather charged for the next animal.

Their numbers thinning, the herd moved in a

ragged circle, animals breaking away alone and in pairs and darting for the water. They plowed into the creek, splashing water and flinging mud as they clamored up the opposite bank.

A few terrified cows and calves darted back and forth among the bodies of the fallen. A couple calves, orphaned by the attack, bawled by the carcasses of their mothers.

One by one the Indians killed the calves, until the grounds were silent save for the heaving and blowing of the horses. As the veil of dust began to thin, Armando counted fifty-seven carcasses scattered upon the ground.

All the hunters and their mounts survived with nothing but bruises. Crow Feather lifted his hand over his head and motioned for Armando to join him. Armando galloped down the rise, his path intersecting with Crow Feather's at the body of a great bull.

Crow Feather said, "There will be meat for the village and we shall have a great celebration tonight. One day, when you have learned the ways of the Comanche, you will ride and kill with us."

Crow Feather dismounted, pulled his knife from his belt and cut into the belly of a buffalo calf. He spilled the entrails until he came to the purple clump that was the liver. He cut it free, lifted it to his mouth, and took a bite. He smiled and extended his bloody hand toward Armando.

Armando swallowed hard, then slid off his horse and stepped to Crow Feather. Reluctantly, he took the warm, slippery liver and held it to his face, inhaling its pungent aroma. He closed his eyes and took a bite of the warm meat. He swallowed it quickly, without chewing.

Crow Feather examined him with a stern gaze, and Armando knew that he had not pleased the warrior with his modest bite. Taking a deep breath, he lifted the warm liver to his mouth and bit off a chunk that he chewed slowly, forcing himself to smile.

Then Crow Feather grinned, his lips smudged with blood, and took the liver from him. He congratulated Armando before consuming the remainder of the liver.

Armando turned so that Crow Feather might not see the grimace from the bitter taste of raw liver. He watched other warriors climbing over their kills, beginning the butchering. The warriors worked quickly on the carcasses, slicing across the neck, then drawing their sharp knives along the spine and pulling the hide away. The hides crackled as they parted from the pink and purple flesh.

After the hides were loosened, the hunters began to carve up the buffalo carcasses, severing the fore and hind quarters, then cutting the flank and brisket and peeling the meat away, rolling it into bundles that they deposited on the fleshy side of the hide. Then the butchers removed the entrails and began to separate the ribs from the spine or pull sinew from the spinal column.

Armando turned to help Crow Feather work the great bull onto its belly and spread its spindly legs out. The animal's legs were wedged beneath its great weight, and Crow Feather struggled to free them.

Armando dove to the ground beside Crow Feather, grabbed a hoof and tugged with the warrior. Gradually, they worked the limb free.

Crow Feather nodded his approval as he began to skin the great bull. While he worked, the procession of women and children reached the site. They shouted and sang when they saw the dead buffalo. The women ran down the hill to help their men, and the young children swarmed through the buffalo, climbing on the unskinned carcasses or drawing back imaginary bows and arrows as if they were responsible for the kills.

The women celebrated with the men. Packhorses were cut from the herd and driven among the scene of the slaughter, to be loaded with bundles of meat and driven downstream where camp would be set up. The work of the men was almost over, but the work of the women was just beginning. The meat was to be salted and dried. The hides had to be scraped and treated so they would be supple and useful as clothing, parfleches, and blankets.

Weasel arrived with Stone Flower and began to bundle the meat in fresh hides. "How many buffalo did you kill?" Weasel asked.

"Two bulls, a cow, and a calf," Crow Feather replied.

"Is that more than any other hunter?"

Crow Feather tossed a slab of meat on the hide. "I think so."

"I am glad that you are my husband. I wish that I could provide you with a child."

Crow Feather shook his head, then pointed to the two captives helping them out. "We have a son and daughter ready born."

Armando thought he understood what Crow Feather said and he was proud that his captor spoke so of him.

"Now that we will have plenty of food for us all, it is time that I lead another raid."

"Not to Mexico. The way is far and you are gone too long."

"I do not know. Only my medicine can tell me which way to go."

— —

Chimayo

Father Candid Zavala lived modestly in a back room of the chapel, and Erich Schmidt stayed in an adjacent room, barely bigger than a closet. But why should he need a bigger room? Erich asked himself. After all, he was paralyzed. The room was barely wide enough for the narrow bed and the chair that Dobbs had made. Erich had not used the chair since arriving at Chimayo, and he vowed never to use it again.

Whenever he left his tiny quarters, he dragged himself on the floor, his useless legs following him everywhere and taking him nowhere. Four times a day he would crawl to the miracle room and slip his hand into the hole in the floor. He would extract a handful of moist earth and rub it on his useless legs. Then he pulled himself back to his room. His forearms and elbows were callused.

Every day Father Zavala was patient and understanding. Every day Zavala would clean and wash the britches Erich had soiled. Every day Zavala would talk with him, encourage him and pray for him. Every day Zavala would prepare his breakfast and dinner without complaint. Zavala was patient and kind. Erich admired him.

The Hispanos admired the priest as well. They came to him daily with their problems and concerns. The women approached him modestly, their dark shawls demurely covering their heads. The men sought his counsel humbly, with heads bowed and hats in their hands. They were a faithful people, and devout.

And on the eighth day of his stay, Erich had emerged from his room and pulled himself toward the miracle room, stopping short when he heard the voice of Father Zavala praying at the altar not for his flock of

Hispanos, but for him. The priest beseeched God to heal Erich's crippled legs and show Erich the comfort and peace of mind that had eluded him since his injury.

After Father Zavala said amen, he arose and marched out the front of the chapel, not seeing Erich on the floor. And then Erich did something he had not done since the fall from his horse.

He cried.

All the rage, all the frustration, all the anger and doubt that had welled in him in the months since he was paralyzed burst from him in great wails and sobs. He felt embarrassed and ashamed, but he also sensed relief that what was past was indeed past, and that whatever the future held, he would be prepared to meet it. Then he crawled the rest of the way to the miracle room with no less physical effort than before, but certainly with less mental anguish.

He scooped handfuls of dirt from out of the hole. He untied his pants and pushed them down, then rubbed the dirt into his shriveled legs until they were red with the abrasion. Still he felt nothing.

He cried again, and while his cheeks were still moist with tears, he did something else he had not done since the accident. He prayed.

Erich asked not for a cure, but for strength, compassion, and understanding. He asked that his life not be wasted.

"If I cannot walk, oh God, please let me stand. And if I cannot stand, then please let me crawl. And if I cannot crawl, then please let me continue to pull myself on the ground."

He extracted more earth from the floor and rubbed it into his legs. And more soil yet he pulled from the hole, until the soil was mounded up around his legs, and yet the hole never seemed to be any deeper. And when he was done, he pushed the soil back into the hole and the hole seemed to have no more or no less dirt in it than when he began or ended.

He did not understand how it could be unless it was a miracle, the type of miracle he had hoped for. He pulled up his pants and dragged himself from the room, back past the altar, pausing in the chapel's central aisle to look at the crutches propped against the back well, and then pulling himself to his room.

Reaching his bed, he pulled himself onto the corn-husk mattress and wormed himself fully onto the bed. And then he prayed the entire afternoon, not for himself, but for Father Zavala, Inge, Jean, his two nieces, and Dobbs.

When Father Zavala came to check on him in late afternoon, Erich knew he had soiled his britches. For the previous eight days, Erich had refused to ride in the chair, and the priest had carried him out the back of the chapel to the spring that fed a gentle stream with waters pure and cold.

"You must be cleaned," Zavala said.

Erich nodded.

Zavala leaned over the bed to pull Erich up and carry him to the stream. "What has come over you?"

"A change."

"Are you more contented, as you seem?"

"I heard you praying for me today."

"I pray for you every day."

Erich sat up in his bed and the priest lifted him awkwardly until he had a solid grip. Zavala eased him through the narrow door.

"But why do you pray for me every day?" Erich asked.

"It is my duty as a priest."

"But why? You didn't know me, not like you know the Hispanos around here, and you minister to them every day."

Zavala moved down the hall, then turned out the back door, the exertion delaying his response.

"Their hearts are not as callused as yours. You are a challenge." He turned toward the stream.

"You think I will ever walk again?"

"Only God can answer that."

"But you are a man of God."

"And so are you, Erich, if you will just listen to what he has to say." The priest sat Erich on a pile of rocks at the stream. "I must fetch your clean britches." He retreated to the chapel.

Unlike other days, where Erich merely let the priest remove his britches and clean him, he untied the rope that served as a belt, slid the britches down his legs and slipped into the cold water. Chills ran up his spine as he washed himself, then began to launder his dirtied britches. He felt better just having done what he could instead of relying entirely on Father Zavala.

The priest soon returned with clean britches. Erich spotted the glint of surprise in his eyes.

"Something has changed about you," Father Zavala said. "I don't know what it is, but your spirit is stronger."

"Why do you say that, just because I cleaned my own pants?"

"It is more than that. There is a determination I have not seen before."

"I cannot explain it," Erich answered, "other than watching you with the Hispanos, your patient manner and soothing voice."

Father Zavala drooped his head and his shoulders seemed to sag.

"What is it?" Erich asked. "Should I not have been watching you with them?"

The priest shook his head. "Oh, no, it is not that, but I fear that I have not been totally honest with you."

Erich pulled himself from the stream onto the rock and let the air dry the water on his legs. "How can that be?"

"There is a selfishness on my part, Erich, that I must explain or I cannot in God's grace face you."

"But what?"

"There have been miracles here at Sanctuario de Chimayo, but none of them have been confirmed by the Church."

"Why does that matter, if the miracles changed the lives of the sick and crippled?" Erich asked.

"Because I am a vain priest. I want the other clergy to know that I have presided over miracles. Father Machebeuf believes in miracles, but not in ones that occur here."

"But why should he doubt them?"

"He is from France, where he was educated. I am merely from here. My education is modest."

"The people love you and respect you here more than Father Machebeuf, for all of his education."

Zavala smiled. "They are my people and I love and respect them, that is sure."

"Then what more can you want?"

"To be recognized for what I—with God's direction and assistance—have done."

Erich took his clean britches from Zavala and worked them up his limp legs. "Who determines miracles, Father?"

"God and the Church."

"What about the individual whose life is changed? Can't he accept a miracle, even if the Church disagrees?"

"I suppose."

"You told me just minutes ago that something had changed in me. Was that a miracle?"

"I would say so, but the Church would never agree with me."

"I think it was a true miracle."

Zavala's face lit up. "Then perhaps a miracle of the spirit is greater than a miracle of the body."

Erich looked at him and smiled. "What I'm saying is that there's already been one miracle performed on me, and if the Church won't recognize that miracle of the spirit, we'll just have to see that they do recognize a second miracle, a miracle of the body."

Santa Fe

When the paymaster arrived in Santa Fe, Jean Benoit had mixed emotions. He needed his Army money to help pay for the place for his family, but once the paymaster left, he would take Jason Dobbs with him to Fort Bliss. The Army being what it was, they might never see each other again.

On the evening before Dobbs was scheduled to depart, Benoit invited him to their adobe, where Inge had promised to fix him a fine going-away dinner. Benoit had even convinced Father Machebeuf to donate a bottle of brandy from his cabinet. Benoit had been hoarding some coffee beans sent by his sister Marion from New Orleans, and planned to make Dobbs a pot of his special coffee. Inge was fixing sauerkraut and spiced potatoes along with apple strudel for his dinner. Then, when the girls were put to bed, Benoit planned to take him to La Estrella for a few rounds of something stiffer than coffee or brandy.

By the time Dobbs arrived for dinner, Inge was totally frustrated. Unlike Fort Laramie, where she had a stove to cook with, all she had in the adobe was a corner fireplace. It required a different style of cooking, and more squatting and bending than she was accustomed to. She managed, though not without a few strong words of German.

Benoit greeted Dobbs at the doorway a half hour before sundown.

Dobbs carried two small bundles wrapped in burlap as he came inside. He placed the bundles on the rough-hewn table where they would dine. "Evening, Inge, supper smells delicious." He walked to her and kissed her on the cheek.

Blushing, she straightened her apron. "I hope it tastes good."

"You all packed?" Benoit asked.

"All that I can carry on horseback." He stepped to the door leading to the girls' room and looked at his belongings: stacked crates of books, his telescope, and other curiosities.

"I will miss my books, but you are free to pick out any of them to read, Jean, until I can send for them."

Benoit laughed. "I don't read as much as you do, Jace."

"And that is why you never win any arguments with me."

"Is that a fact?"

"Indeed."

"Then what about the state of Wisconsin, a good northern state, solidly opposed to slavery, threatening to secede from the Union? Wisconsin's solidly with the South on nullification. The legislature passed a resolution as such."

Benoit motioned for Dobbs to join him on a bench by the table. "This nation cannot survive if every state is free to come and go as it wants," he said.

"This nation won't survive with the government telling every state how to conduct its affairs," Benoit replied. "That's why nullification is important, it allows the states to disregard the laws and unfair burdens placed upon it by the national government."

"But where does nullification stop, Jean? Is it over slavery in Louisiana, over a court case in Wisconsin, over tariffs in Massachusetts? There's no end to it once every state is allowed to pick and chose what laws it obeys."

"You're wrong, Jace. Nullification will keep the national government in check."

Dobbs shook his head slowly. "You're a soldier, are you not?"

Benoit nodded.

"When you give an order, Captain, do you think the soldiers under your command should have the option of obeying or not?"

"Absolutely not," Benoit answered. "It's not the same thing."

"Sure it is. There has to be an ultimate decision, and that decision has to reside with the national government. Otherwise, we will be squabbling from now on, all the states. Wisconsin's wrong and so are the southern states." Dobbs grinned like he knew he had won the debate.

Benoit shook his head. "Why should all the laws be the same among the states? This is a big country with great differences between the states, their climates, their culture, their economies. Why shouldn't Louisiana have slaves if that's what it wants, and New Hampshire not have them if that's what New Hampshire wants?"

"Because slavery is morally wrong. It is a sin upon mankind. A government cannot sustain immoral institutions and hope to survive."

"But, Jace, the South can't survive without slavery."

"It can't survive with it, Jean. Nor can this country."

For a moment an odd silence hung between them, then Inge dropped a pot on the table. "Politics, politics, no more discussion of politics before I throw you both out of this house."

Benoit grinned sheepishly.

"See, Jean," Dobbs laughed, "someone's got to make the final decision, and in this house it's apparent that someone is Inge."

"I'm just glad she's here to call the shots, Jace, and that you were with her in Laramie to save the girls. I thought it was a mistake to leave her up there, but it was the right decision."

"Too often, doctoring's associated with pain, death, and sadness, but bringing a baby into the world is a source of joy for everyone."

For an instant there was a profound silence between them, but it died with a sudden and jarring ringing in Dobbs's pocket.

Benoit jumped and the babies started fussing.

Dobbs shoved his hand in his pocket and pulled out his watch, quickly shutting off the alarm. "It's sundown."

"You still playing that stupid game?"

"Sure am."

Inge went into the next room and returned with a fussy girl under each arm. She stepped to Jean and gave him Ellen, then handed off Colleen to Dobbs.

"Now, you can keep them occupied until I can finish supper." Inge spun around and went back to the fireplace to bring food to the table. By the time she finished setting the food on the table and removing the lids from the pots and pans, the two girls had calmed down. The room filled with the pleasant aroma of supper.

"I can't wait," Dobbs said.

Inge took Colleen from Dobbs and sat down at the table.

Soon they were scooping out sauerkraut, potatoes, and slices of roast onto their plates. They ate in silence, except for the cooing of the babies. Jean mashed up some potatoes and placed a tiny bit on the tip of his spoon. He offered it to Ellen. She ate the potatoes quickly, and Jean fed her some more.

"Delicious, as always, Inge," Dobbs said. "I shall not only miss you and the girls, but I shall also miss the occasional taste of your cooking."

When they finished eating, Inge excused herself and went into the back room, where she breast-fed the two babies, who seemed to be tiring for bed. While she was tending the babies, Benoit pulled a sack of coffee beans from a tin can.

Dobbs's face lit up when he saw them. "I tried to boil some good coffee after you left Fort Laramie, Jean, but I never could do it. My brew was always bitter, never sweet like yours."

Dobbs watched Benoit scoop out some beans and place them in a mortar that had been passed through the family for years. With its companion pestle, he ground the beans and then measured out the amount to be placed in the receptacle of his long-necked coffeepot.

Next, Benoit retrieved an iron skillet and poured a

half inch of water into it, then sat the skillet in the fireplace until the water boiled. Then he spooned water into the coffeepot. Patiently, a spoonful at a time, he dripped water over the grounds until the coffeepot was half full. Finally, he poured the coffee in a pair of tin cups, then topped each off with a couple more spoons of water.

Dobbs lifted the cup to his nose, sniffed at the sweet aroma, then took a sip. He savored the flavor, and cut loose with an expletive. "Damn! I've watched you make this coffee a hundred times and I've tried to do it just the same, and mine never tastes this sweet. What's the secret, Jean?"

"Many things we southerners do better than you northerners."

Inge returned. She prepared them each a dish of apple strudel while Benoit retrieved the bottle of Machebeuf's brandy. He filled three more tin cups with the brandy and sat them on the table at his, Dobbs's, and Inge's places.

When they finished the strudel, Benoit lifted his cup of brandy. "A toast to Jason Dobbs: soldier, surgeon, intellectual, and the friend who saved my wife and daughters."

The three clinked cups. Then Dobbs said, "To the Benoits four, may your futures be filled with the happiness you deserve."

The three drank again, and Inge began to cry.

"I'm sorry," she said, "but I can't tell you what you've meant to me, and I just hope we see each other again someday." She sobbed and burst away from the table and into the adjacent room to cry.

"We owe you a lot, Jace, and there's no way we can

ever repay you, but you'll forever be in our graces for what you did."

"I am a doctor, just doing my job as best I could."

"Thank you."

Dobbs seemed genuinely embarrassed.

"So we can talk without disturbing the babies, Jace, you care to go to La Estrella for something a little stronger than brandy?"

Dobbs nodded and arose.

Benoit stepped back to tell Inge they were leaving. She reemerged from the back, her eyes red with tears. She hugged Dobbs.

"Good luck," she said, then broke down again.

He kissed her on the forehead, then joined Benoit by the door. The two men stepped outside into the night, where the air was cool and pleasant. They walked beyond the plaza and down the side street that led to the saloon and gambling den.

Opening the door to the building, they stepped into a noisy, dimly lit, smoke-filled room and moved through the crowd to the bar. There, they ordered a couple glasses of whiskey. Then Benoit and Dobbs visited and watched the men thronging around the gambling tables, most especially that of Doña Rosalia, the proprietor.

"That's not poker, is it?" Dobbs wanted to know.

"Monte."

"How's it played?"

"I don't know. Alejo Ortiz explained it once to me, but I didn't pay him any mind, not figuring I'd ever play."

"Well, Jean, I don't think that I'll be able to leave Santa Fe without playing monte."

"Even if you don't know how to play?"

"It's gambling, Jean. Look at all the people who know how to play and still lose."

Benoit laughed as he followed Dobbs to the table. Except for Doña Rosalia, the only person he recognized around the table was Eduardo Crespin, the shady Comanchero.

Dobbs observed a couple hands while Benoit tried to remember how the game was played. It had something to do with the card order and which suit would come up next, but before he could recall, Dobbs pulled out five dollars in paper money and placed a bet.

Doña Rosalia looked at him and smiled, while Crespin called him a name in Spanish. She turned another card and her smile faded into a frown. She passed him silver reals the equal of his bet.

Dobbs tipped his hat to her, then gathered his money.

"The luck of a bastard," Crespin mumbled.

Dobbs turned to the Comanchero, staring into his hard face. "And good luck to you, fellow."

Crespin growled something in Spanish, seemingly irritated by Dobbs's response.

Benoit grabbed Dobbs's arm, pulling him away from the table and toward the door, not wanting to risk any trouble. They were out in the street in a moment.

Dobbs laughed. "Friendly group, wouldn't you say?"

"That was Eduardo Crespin. He's a Comanchero, trades with the Comanche."

"No wonder he's so sour."

"Some think he's evil."

"I figure he's just a bad loser."

"Not the kind you want to get tangled up with your last night in Santa Fe."

Dobbs shook his fist with his money in it. "Maybe my luck's taken a turn for the better."

"What's luck to you, Jace, you're not a gambler?"

"Everybody who lives in the West is a gambler, Jean," Dobbs replied. "Everybody!"

7

Llano Estacado

A half day's walk beyond the Comanche camp, Crow Feather had thrown his buffalo robe and waited. Without food, without water except that in Crooked Creek, and without weapons, he waited for a vision. He wore a breechcloth and moccasins. By his left side lay his bone pipe, tobacco, flint, and steel. By his right side lay his medicine bag, a leather pouch the size of his foot. Inside were the amulets that had given him power since he had first sought medicine as a youth. The crow feather that he had found on his buffalo robe the first time he sought medicine was in the bag. A crow foot, the hair ball from the stomach of the first bull buffalo he had killed, the gristle of a bear snout, a bear claw, and the tail of a mountain lion stayed in the medicine bag with the four additional crow feathers he had found at momentous occasions in his life.

For two days he had fasted and waited. Relief from his overpowering thirst was but a dozen steps away, yet he did not drink. It tested his manhood and his medicine to resist. His medicine would grow stronger if he did not surrender to his hunger and his thirst.

At daybreak he arose and faced the sun as it climbed the sky over his head. There was power in the sun and he soaked it up. He waited as the sun traveled from east to west. As the day became night, he smoked his pipe and prayed for power that might carry him and his band to great triumphs. Sometimes he chanted, but mostly he awaited his vision.

The third day he arose weak and weary, his hunger and thirst gnawing at his mind. His tongue was swollen and his lips parched. He craved water so much that he wanted to surrender his body to his cravings. Drowsiness set in and he reclined on his buffalo robe. Then it came to him, his vision.

He saw a fury that he could not fathom, and men emerging from it, white men in pursuit of a mule. The men were naked and helpless, and then arrows appeared in them from the magic bows of Comanche warriors. And then a great Comanche warrior stormed from the tumult of battle. The warrior reminded Crow Feather of Paints the Dead as the captive would surely look in fifteen years. The great warrior looked over the dead, then disappeared as in thin air.

Crow Feather knew the terrain in his vision was unlike any he had ever seen. As he looked for landmarks that might identify the place, his vision vanished. He awoke with a start, dazed for an instant. Then he heard the caw of a solitary crow. The crow was bringing him a message. He looked skyward, his eyes focusing only reluctantly. He glimpsed a black bird flying away from him toward the setting sun. The crow was directing him to the west. West was where his vision would be fulfilled.

His vision complete, his thirst intense, he arose feebly and stumbled toward the creek, throwing himself in it, relishing the cold shock of the water against his dried

his parched face. The water was as cleans-
ision.

cupped his hands and lifted water to his lips four ti then stopped. He must not satisfy such a deep thirst in such a short time. Pulling himself from the creek, he retreated to his buffalo robe, where he spent the night. Sleep came suddenly and ended as quickly when the sun cleared the horizon on the fourth day. He went to the creek and cupped his hands to lift water to his lips. Gradually he eased his thirst.

Returning to his buffalo robe to gather his belongings and start back to camp, his heart beat faster when he found a crow feather upon his robe. He sang and clapped, then put the feather in his medicine pouch. The feather was a sign that his medicine was strong. He walked to camp with feeble legs but strong spirit. At the village, he went straight to his lodge, where Weasel had boiled a pot of buffalo meat.

"You are back," greeted Paints the Dead.

Crow Feather nodded, then walked past him wordlessly, as he was drawn to the aroma of food. Weasel squealed her delight that he had come home and handed him a spoon made from a buffalo horn. Crow Feather ate from the pot, then drank water that Weasel brought him fresh from the creek.

When he finished, he fell upon his bed and slept until late afternoon, oblivious to Weasel's cooking. Awaking, Crow Feather arose, put on his leggings and his shirt, and marched through the camp inviting warriors to his lodge to eat. The warriors knew this ritual as the first step of a war party, and those who believed their medicine was right accepted his invitation.

Before sundown the warriors crowded into his lodge, seventeen men in all, sitting in the circle around the fire and partaking of the buffalo Weasel had stewed. Then Crow Feather filled his pipe with tobacco and lit it from an ember. He drew on the pipe and exhaled a ribbon of smoke.

"I have just returned from a quest for medicine, and I have had a powerful vision," he said.

The solemn-faced warriors nodded.

"I saw a crow fly toward the sun, and to the west we will find a great fury, like a swirling fog, and from it will emerge white men who we will kill and scalp with many coups."

Wordlessly, the warriors watched Crow Feather's every move, for each had to decide if his medicine was strong enough at this time to accompany Crow Feather on this war party.

"And from this swirling fog will emerge a great Comanche warrior, and it is not me, but another, younger warrior." Crow Feather looked around the circle, knowing that his last words had captivated the imagination of the young braves who had not won reputations for themselves as daring warriors.

Then Crow Feather lifted the pipe to his lips and inhaled. He passed the pipe to the next warrior. For each, it was the moment of decision. If he inhaled of Crow Feather's tobacco, he had committed to join the war party under Crow Feather's command. If he passed the pipe, then he passed this opportunity to raid.

When the pipe returned to Crow Feather, thirteen braves had agreed to accompany him on his war party, including Owl Eyes, Speaks Loudly, Big Wolf, and Gives Gifts. The men nodded to each other and one by one arose and departed. As soon as the last man left, Paints the Dead entered. He took the pipe, inhaled, then coughed and spit.

"You are young now, but one day you will smoke the pipe and lead other warriors against our enemies," Crow Feather announced.

Paints the Dead handed the pipe to Crow Feather. "How can I be a warrior when I have no weapon?"

"Patience. You must have patience. When I return, I shall give you a bow and arrow so that you may learn."

"Can I have a knife? It will help with my chores."

Crow Feather nodded. "In the morning I will ask Weasel to give you a knife."

Paints the Dead smiled.

"Now," Crow Feather said, "I must sleep, and sleep well so I am rested for tomorrow."

Armando was pleased with the promise of a knife. Though he would surely like to kill Speaks Loudly for his cruelty, he had come to admire Crow Feather, perhaps because he had no one else to turn to. But Speaks Loudly he hated, not only for killing his father, but also for his meanness to Esteban. Esteban was weak, but he could grow strong if Speaks Loudly did not pester him.

Armando slept restlessly that night and awoke early. Weasel shooed him out of the tipi while Crow Feather and Lupe still slept. It was well after high sun before Crow Feather arose, and Armando spent his time talking with Esteban, who Speaks Loudly had tied to a stake in back of the tipi. Esteban was still forced to sleep on the ground outside, unlike Armando and Lupe, who slept on soft buffalo robes inside the tipi.

"Crow Feather is leaving to make war," Armando said.

"Is the one that treats me mean leaving too?"

Armando nodded. "I think so."

"Maybe we can escape when they leave?"

"Escape to where? We are hundreds of miles from home. I cannot find my home and we cannot travel so far without weapons and horses."

Esteban began to cry. "Then we will never get home?"

"Do not cry or you will anger Speaks Loudly."

"He is always angry. Nothing I do will change that."

"Do not cry in front of him. The people admire bravery."

"But when I try to be brave, I fail."

Armando saw Lupe pass, carrying a paunch to retrieve water from the creek. "I must go to help your sister carry water."

"Send her to visit me."

Armando ran away and joined Lupe. He took the paunch from her hand. "Your brother is sad. You must visit him."

"I will when Speaks Loudly leaves, but he is mean."

At the creek they quickly filled the container, then returned to Crow Feather's lodge. Weasel gave them chores to do. Lupe was to scrape from the buffalo hide they were still conditioning, and Armando was to gather firewood.

When he finally returned to the tipi with his fifth armload, Weasel spoke. "That is enough." She motioned for him to enter the tipi. "Crow Feather must see you."

Armando stepped inside. Crow Feather sat with legs crossed opposite the entrance. He wore his war paint and his war regalia. His weapons were at his side: bow and arrows, lance, shield, two knives, tomahawk, and rifle. Between his legs was a war drum.

"I am here, Crow Feather."

"And your knife is here, Paints the Dead." Crow

Feather picked up one of the sheathed knives beside him and handed it to Armando. "I give you this knife. By your actions you must prove that you deserve it."

"I will."

"You must."

Armando nodded.

"Now you must leave until I have gone. When I return, I will teach you how to hunt and fight and you shall become one of us."

Armando looked at the knife and pulled it from its sheath. It was shiny and sharp.

"I have had a vision that one day you will be a great warrior. Do not disappoint me, Paints the Dead."

"I will not," he answered.

Crow Feather nodded. "You speak enough Comanche now that you must play with the other boys. They may tease and taunt you for being a captive, but do not strike them back or ever pull this knife. They will know that I trust you by the gift of it. Now, be gone until I leave this tipi."

Armando had barely gotten outside before Crow Feather had begun striking the war drum and chanting war songs. Shortly he was joined in his tipi by other warriors in paint and regalia.

The ritual continued until sundown, when Crow Feather and the warriors emerged from their tipis and went to prepare their horses for the departure.

Armando, like the other children, followed them, dancing through the village. As he passed Speaks Loudly's tipi, Armando saw that Esteban was still tied to the tent stake. Armando's hand went to the knife at his side and he thought about cutting Esteban loose, but feared that would be breaking the trust Crow Feather had placed in him. So Armando pretended he did not see

Esteban and kept on dancing through the village.

After the warriors rigged their horses, they rode back through the camp, gathering in the center for a war dance. Only those men who were going on the raid could participate. Armando watched the ritual. The warriors danced intermittently until midnight, when they slipped away, mounted their horses and left.

When the war dance ended, Armando watched Weasel carry the sleeping Lupe back to the lodge, then he scampered to see Esteban.

He found him asleep, still tied to the tent stake.

"Esteban, Esteban," he said, shaking him awake, "did you not see the war dance?"

His friend awoke, rubbing his eyes, then pushing Armando's hand from his shoulder.

"Did you see the war dance?"

"No. Last dance, they tortured me. I feared they would do it again. How do you know it was a war dance?"

"I am beginning to understand more of their language."

"I don't want to understand their language. I just want to get back to Mexico."

Armando pulled his knife and waved it in front of Esteban. "See what I have now."

Esteban turned away. "You are becoming a Comanche, Armando, a stinking Comanche."

Lieutenant Jason Dobbs had never ridden with a more sullen, inarticulate bunch of soldiers than those he accompanied from Santa Fe. The paymaster, a narrow-waisted, narrow-shouldered, and narrow-minded captain, may have been good at keeping books, but certainly not at keeping a conversation going. Captain Farragut introduced himself, then said nothing more.

The paymaster's party included ten other soldiers sent to guard the money in the satchels carried on the pack mule, and, Dobbs figured, to make certain no unnecessary words escaped from the captain's mouth. Dobbs expected he could carry on a more intelligent conversation with the pack mule than with any of the soldiers.

Dobbs believed silence was meant to be filled. He enjoyed talking or arguing about nearly anything. For the sake of conversation, he would even argue a position opposite his beliefs, just to have something to talk about. Captain Farragut must have believed silence was golden, he thought.

After leaving Santa Fe the previous afternoon, the only pleasure Dobbs had had on the trail was the jangling of his watch alarm around sundown. The alarm startled the captain, who'd given Dobbs a hard stare that left no doubt he was annoyed.

With no one to talk to, Dobbs studied the landscape along the trail that roughly paralleled the Rio Grande River. The land was dry, and even the cactus seemed to wilt in the afternoon sun. Sweaty though he was, Dobbs was grateful this wasn't the full heat of summer. He had never been to hell, but was sure he was in the right neighborhood.

The dry soil beneath the horses' hooves arose after each footfall, floating up and sticking to their faces. Whenever he swiped at the sweat on his brow or wiped away the salty sting of perspiration from the corner of his eyes, the grit rubbed like sandpaper against his skin. The landscape looked like it hadn't seen rain since Noah.

The soldiers made poor time because of the heat upon their heads and the dust that settled in their lungs with each breath. Toward mid-morning of the second day, Dobbs glanced west and saw a brown cloud unlike anything he had ever seen before. The cloud tumbled over the ground toward them, blotting out the horizon. Farragut, who rarely looked anywhere but straight ahead, failed to notice it.

Dobbs stared and realized that it was a great wind that was blowing out of the west and kicking up the sand as it went. He remembered the great winds of Wyoming Territory, where gales howled off the slopes of Laramie Peak and swooped east across Fort Laramie and the plains of Nebraska, but never had he seen a wind carry such sand.

"Captain, we've a blow coming."

"What, Lieutenant?"

"To the west, sir."

The captain looked halfheartedly to the west. "God almighty," he exclaimed.

Dobbs realized he had just heard the most profound statement the captain had made since Santa Fe, and possibly in his entire life. Dobbs took his army kerchief, folded it corner to corner and tied it over his face, so the top came to his eyes and the remainder covered his nose. He tugged his hat down tighter.

Captain Farragut twisted in his saddle. "Close up, men, and bunch together."

Dobbs looked around for cover, but there was nowhere to go. A rush of wind blew over them in advance of the cloud. Then the sand began to pick up, softly at first, then harder and harder, until the full force of the wind slapped against them. The rush of wind spooked their horses. The men fought their mounts and cursed the wind and the sand, which stung them like a million vengeful insects.

The wind yanked Dobbs's hat off and flung it into the roiling sand. The hat disappeared while he struggled to control his horse and to keep the mask over his mouth and nose.

The air was thick with sand. Dobbs could barely make out the captain two arm lengths away. The wind slapped Dobbs, and the roar drowned out most of the cries of the men. The sand hid the sun, replacing the light with a red haze that reminded him of the odd light at dusk. But it was not dusk, it was not even noon. The light was eerie, the wind maddening.

At first Dobbs had thought the gale might die down after the first strike, but instead it seemed to grow stronger. It was a dry, hot wind, as if the very gates of hell had been opened and the heat had rushed to escape.

The horses stumbled and fought the wind and their riders, tossing their heads, stamping their feet as the gusts hit them broadside. They battled against the reins. The flying grit stung their eyes and terrified them as much as a fire. It was useless to fight his mount, Dobbs decided. He let the animal turn away from the stinging sand. His horse calmed for a moment, then butted into the neck of Captain Farragut's animal.

"Damn you, Lieutenant, keep your horse headed south."

"It's no use, Captain. We'll exhaust them trying to keep them on track."

"Do as I command!" Farragut yelled.

Dobbs yanked the bridle of his horse as the wind whipped into his face. The horse resisted, then gave in at the pain of the bit in its mouth. Before Dobbs got his horse moving again, the captain's decision was overruled by the mule.

"Captain, Captain!" one of the men cried from behind. "The mule got away."

"What?" The captain halted.

All the soldiers clumped around the captain. "Who lost him?"

Nobody admitted the mistake.

"It'll be a court-martial for somebody. There was upward of five thousand dollars in greenbacks on that mule, plus the ledger for all the men we've already paid. There'll be hell to pay for this."

"If you want the mule back, Captain," Dobbs yelled, "you best understand he did what my horse was trying to do: turn his head away from the wind. He won't be standing still waiting for us either. He'll trot with the wind. The mule's probably halfway to Texas by now."

"There's nothing to stop him until he gets to the Pecos River," a soldier said.

Farragut cursed. "Spread out men, but not too far. Number off and line up in that order. Then distance yourselves just far enough that you can still see the man on your side."

"One," Farragut yelled.

"Two," Dobbs called.

The other soldiers numbered off until they reached twelve. Then the soldiers separated.

"Count off every few minutes to make sure we don't get separated," Farragut commanded.

Soon the men were heading east, their mounts trotting with the wind. Intermittently, Farragut cried out, "One."

Then Dobbs yelled, "Two," and the other men counted off. The wind howled so loudly that Dobbs could not hear soldiers nine through twelve. He assumed that the word would pass back down the line if they weren't in their place.

The wind roared like a fire without flame, and the heat seemed to intensify. The sand bit into the back of

Dobbs's ears until he thought they were bleeding. He had endured heat and cold, snow and sleet, and wind and hail, but never had the elements dispensed such misery.

For once, Dobbs wasn't interested in talking. Just breathing was an effort. His chest was tight. His nostrils, even with the kerchief to filter out sand, were clogged. His sense of smell was overpowered by the odor of dry, silty earth, until it seemed like a stench that almost turned his stomach.

The noise of the wind was so loud that he could no longer tell if it was the wind itself or the ringing in his ears that he was hearing. He stared ahead through squinting eyes, watching the ears on his horse and glancing occasionally to either side where the riders were struggling as hard as he was.

"Damn," he cried.

"Three," the solider beside him called out, mistaking his curse for another call to count off.

"Four," the next in line yelled.

The horses kept trotting east. The men kept numbering off. The sand kept stinging every spot of exposed flesh on man and animal.

The storm seemed without end. Past high noon, the wind continued to blow. Past mid-afternoon, the torture continued. Only after the sun set and after his alarm watch went off did the winds begin to die down. Finally, after full darkness set in, the storm began to lose its bluster. But even when darkness arrived, the men did not dare to dismount, for fear their horses might stampede without them.

When the wind died away altogether, the air was filled with a fine sandy silt that settled slowly upon the land like the dried tears of a vengeful god. Dobbs was surprised when the men counted off and all twelve remained together. Then the captain called for the men to halt, and Dobbs wrapped his reins tightly around his right hand and jumped off his still skittish mount.

Quickly, he hobbled the animal, then took his canteen and sipped slowly at the hot water within. Hungry though he was, Dobbs was even more tired, so he pitched his bedroll and fell asleep while the captain and his men discussed their plans for finding the mule the next day.

Dobbs awoke around sunup, guessed at the time and set his watch accordingly, then fixed the alarm to go off as close to sunset as he could estimate it. The day broke still and gently, the men arising and brushing off what dirt they could before a breakfast of jerky.

"We're probably twenty miles from the Pecos," Farragut announced. "We'll hope the mule is there."

Riding on tired horses, the men didn't reach the Pecos until almost noon. The thirsty horses caught the smell of water and trotted to the river, drinking until they were bloated and sluggish.

Then the men rode twelve miles up the Pecos, backtracked and rode another twenty miles down the river in search of the mule. The Pecos was a muddy stream without a stretch of clear running water. It ate into the banks and cut out dozens of places where the mule—or Indians—could be hiding. The longer they rode, the more frustrated Captain Farragut got. By late afternoon they were all discouraged, and as dusk approached they had lost all hope.

Then one of the men shouted, "Look," and pointed downriver.

Dobbs grinned when he saw the mule drinking from the Pecos. Most miraculous of all, he still wore his pack. One of the soldiers started for the mule, but Farragut slowed him. "Take it easy, soldier. I don't want to spook him."

"Yes, sir."

"If it looks like he might run, shoot him. I don't want to chase him anymore. We're already far enough behind schedule."

The men fanned out, a couple riding up the embankment, wide of the mule, returning to the river downstream from him, then converged on the mule. The animal was docile, as if the wind and the sand had blown all the fight out of him. The soldiers surrounded him, but the mule never budged from grazing on the spring grass along the riverbank. One of the soldiers threw a rope around his neck, and another dismounted and hobbled him.

Farragut glanced to the west. "Almost sundown. We'll make camp here and head out at sunrise for Fort Fillmore."

Dobbs rode his horse to the river's edge and let the animal drink its fill, then retreated to a patch of grass away from the other soldiers. He quickly hobbled and staked his gelding, then unsaddled the animal.

Dobbs searched through his bundled belongings to find his spare uniform. Though he knew it would be filthy by the time he got to Fort Fillmore, he could not stand the stiff, gritty feel of the pants and blouse that he wore. He carried his clean uniform and union suit to the river and found a spot of grass near some rocks where he could slip into the river. He deposited the clean union suit, pants, blouse, and socks on the grass, then removed his boots, unbuckled his holster and pistol and placed them on the ground. He pulled his pocket watch from his trousers and placed it atop his clean uniform.

Then he waded into the Pecos River. Muddy though

it was, the water felt good around him. The river barely ran waist deep, so he sat in the mud and ducked his head under the water, washing and brushing dirt from his hair before he came up for air.

Dobbs unbuttoned his blouse, removed it and dunked it in the water, knowing he could never clean it without hot water and soap, but hoping he could at least wash away a few pounds of sand from it and his pants. When he was done, he flung the blouse to the rocks. He repeated the process with his pants, union suit, and socks, until he was naked. Then he washed himself as best he could without soap.

Finally finished, he stood up and walked back to the shore. The soldiers were so dull—or tired—they didn't hoot and hurrah him for his nakedness. He shook like a dog trying to dry off, dressed, and checked the time on his watch before slipping it in his pocket. Last of all, he buckled on his gun belt, then returned to his horse.

Captain Farragut had pointedly ordered the men to set up camp about fifty yards from Dobbs. That was okay with him. Dobbs tossed his bedroll and removed a St. Louis paper he had rolled up inside it. Thinking he'd read every story in the paper, he started back through it so he could get in a little reading before dark. A man's mind grew weak around weak minds like Farragut's.

As he read he heard the men begin to shout and holler. He glanced up from his paper and saw them undressing and diving into the Pecos clean off. Even Farragut stripped and jumped into the water.

As the long shadow of day fading fast fell across the river, the men grew friskier in the cool water.

Dobbs realized his hobbled horse was fidgeting and shaking his head. "Easy boy," he called. "They're just playing. Nothing to get nervous about."

The horse danced away from Dobbs. When the horse moved, Dobbs caught a glimpse of the opposite embankment. Terror raced through his body. Twenty or more Indians were lined up on the bank, their arrows and carbines readied.

Dobbs flung his paper aside and jumped to his feet.

"Indians!" he yelled. "Indians, goddammit!"

He yanked his carbine from its scabbard on the ground beside his bed, aimed his rifle at the nearest Indian, cocked the hammer and pulled the trigger. The hammer clicked without discharging a shot. He thumbed back the hammer again and pulled the trigger, but the gun answered with silence. The sand must have fouled the firing mechanism. He cursed, then flung open the flap on his holster and yanked his pistol free. Before he could fire, the Indians attacked.

Crow Feather had never seen men with skin so pale. They flailed naked in the water, bathing, playing. They were so inattentive that they would die clean. He nodded and his men notched arrows on their bows and cocked the hammers on their carbines.

The warriors on either side of him were ready, but he hesitated just because it was laughable that the soldiers were oblivious to their own danger. Naked and dozens of paces from their weapons, they would die quickly.

Then from across the bank came the shout of another soldier, the only one dressed. He was sounding the warning, but it was too late to save his allies.

Crow Feather yelled and his band of warriors charged down the embankment toward the water.

The soldiers screamed and ran for the shore and their weapons.

Crow Feather guided his horse with his knees as it hit the water and splashed ahead after the terrified soldiers. He pulled back his bowstring and loosed an arrow that sailed true into the back of one. The coward fell into the river thrashing with his hands, half trying to walk, half trying to swim.

Crow Feather barely had time to notch another arrow before it was over.

All the naked soldiers were dead and dying.

Only the one upriver was unscathed, and he was firing his pistol. Once, twice, three times the gun fired.

Crow Feather leaned low over his horse and guided the animal toward the only soldier still standing. He shouted as his gray bolted out of the water.

The enemy pistol exploded a fourth and fifth time at others, then the soldier aimed it at him.

Crow Feather gritted his teeth and nudged his mount with alternating knees so the horse followed a crooked path toward the soldier.

Bang!

Crow Feather smiled. The sixth shot had missed. Now he would count coup upon the soldier. Feats of bravery were many among the Comanche, but not even killing and scalping an enemy warrior could compare with touching a live enemy.

Crow Feather charged the soldier. He was a brave man, for he did not run. Seeing he could not reload his pistol, the soldier flung it down, grabbed his carbine from the ground and held it by the barrel. He lifted it over his shoulder like a club.

Crow Feather was upon him before he could swing the rifle, the gray passing within inches of him. Reaching out, Crow Feather touched the man's head, yanking at his hair.

The soldier tried to swing the carbine.

The horse passed so quickly that the carbine barely glanced the animal's rump. Crow Feather turned the gray in a tight circle, then yanked the reins and stopped not twenty feet from the soldier. Lifting his bow, he drew back the bowstring until the bois d'arc wood bent from the pull of his muscular arms.

The soldier never flinched, even though he was almost a dead man. Behind the bluecoat, Crow Feather saw the warriors of his band watching. Crow Feather saw no fear in his enemy's eyes. He saw only courage. He must surely be smarter than the other soldiers for he had not been caught weaponless. He had stood and fought with bravery.

Crow Feather relaxed his arms and the bowstring went straight. He lowered the bow.

The enemy lowered his rifle.

The two men stared at each other.

Then Crow Feather screamed.

Instantly the warriors who weren't taking scalps converged on the brave soldier. Five warriors jumped from their horses and swarmed him, tossing his carbine away and grabbing his arms and legs.

"What shall we do with him?" Gives Gifts asked.

"Stake him to the ground," Crow Feather said. "Later we shall torture him."

The warriors shouted with anticipation.

They quickly bound his wrists and ankles and yanked him down, beating stakes into the ground with their hatchets.

"Be quick with their animals and their weapons. Get what you want and bring wood for a fire."

The warriors plundered the dead men's belongings, taking their weapons and ammunition and their horses.

Soon they had a fire going behind the captive's head. It was close enough that his head beaded with perspiration. Darkness had set in and the flickering fire cast dancing shadows upon the ground.

Crow Feather knew this man was brave. They would soon find out how brave. He picked up a burning stick and held the red-hot end over the captive's left eye. In an instant there would be no more defiance in the soldier's eyes because he would have none.

Crow Feather drew back the stick.

The man gritted his teeth.

Crow Feather slowly inched the burning stick toward his left eye until he was but a thumb's length from it.

Suddenly, there came a loud ringing from the man.

Crow Feather jumped back.

The circled warriors flinched and looked at each other. They had never heard anything like it.

The ringing seemed to be coming from the man's hip.

Crow Feather threw the stick back in the fire. The other warriors looked from him to the captive.

Then the noise faded away.

"Crow Feather?" Speaks Loudly said. "Are you afraid?"

Crow Feather answered icily. "You can poke out his eyes, if you are so brave."

Speaks Loudly said nothing more.

"What are we to do with him?" Owl Eyes asked.

"I do not know. He must be a man of great medicine."

"If we kill him," Big Wolf said, "we may offend a great spirit."

"I did not see this in my vision," Crow Feather said,

"only that a great warrior would emerge from this raid."

Gives Gifts pointed at the captive. "Maybe he is that warrior, Crow Feather. Was the warrior you saw Comanche, or was he of some other people?"

Crow Feather hesitated. He thought he had seen Paints the Dead as a great warrior. Paints the Dead was not a Comanche. Neither was this man. Could he have misread his vision? He shook his head. "He was not a Comanche."

The men gasped.

"Then maybe this is the great warrior, and maybe he will become one of us, a Comanche." Big Wolf stated.

Crow Feather shrugged. "I do not know that, but we should not kill him. We should take him to our village and decide his fate."

8

War Camp, Pecos River

Before sunup the Comanches cut the thongs that bound Jason Dobbs to the ground. A pair of strong braves lifted him to his wobbly feet and tied his hands together. Dobbs's back and muscles were stiff. His feet were numb. The two braves pulled him toward a horse. He stumbled with each step. His feet tingled at first, then ached with the prick of a thousand needles.

The two warriors boosted him atop the horse, then one tied his feet beneath the animal's belly. He knew the Indians thought his watch some kind of magic. He patted his pocket to make sure it was still there. It was!

The horse stepped forward as one Indian led him away by the reins. In the darkness Dobbs could just make out the powerful shape of the warrior jumping gracefully atop his horse. Without a saddle, Dobbs wobbled on horseback and clamped his knees against the horse's rib cage, fighting his dizziness.

He heard the sound of other horses and warriors around him as his horse moved down the bank. As the animal splashed into the river, Dobbs tried to lift his feet from the river, but the rawhide thong at his ankles lacked slack to clear the water. Dobbs cursed. The rawhide had gotten soaked. The day's hot sun would dry it and it would shrink. If not removed, the rawhide would squeeze the circulation from his feet and might cut into his flesh and possibly sever his Achilles tendon.

He would worry about that later. The thing that kept running through his mind was his watch. The alarm that had saved him the night before had run down the watch. He knew he had to wind the watch without the Comanches observing so they would think him magical.

But even if he did that, when should he set the alarm to go off with maximum effect? Would they expect it every day at sundown? Would they start to torture him again, then kill him if the alarm did not ring? The possibilities seemed endless, the probability of him guessing right small. Once the sun rose, the Indians could better observe him. In the darkness he could get his watch without being observed, but he could not see the watch face and thus know what time the alarm was set for.

He decided to risk the uncertainty of setting the alarm in the dark rather than being seen with the watch in the daylight. He twisted his stiff arms around and tried to slide his hand in the pocket. He could not reach the watch for it had worked its way to the bottom. He cursed silently, then patiently began to push the lump on the side of his thigh up in the pocket. Finally he managed to slide his hand partially into his pocket and pull the watch free. Though he couldn't see the hands, he twisted the knob to move them forward, then quickly wound the watch and pulled the alarm button. Carefully, he slid the watch back in his pocket. Now all he could do was wait. And pray. Dobbs noted the irony, having never believed in any god, much less a God, and now he had nowhere else to turn. He mouthed a silent prayer.

Dawn exposed the Indians around him. They rode single file with Dobbs in the middle of the procession. Some men led Army horses that had been ridden by Captain Farragut and his men. One Indian even led the pack mule, still loaded with the bags of money and the Army records.

The warriors spoke little, intent upon reaching their destination. As he rode amidst them and their silence, Dobbs wondered if he would live out the day.

Chimayo

Erich Schmidt awoke thirty minutes before dawn. He had a strange sensation around his waist. At first he touched his hips and then his groin. Something was different! He tried to move his legs but his withered limbs were as useless as they had been for months. This sensation was strange, yet familiar. Then he realized he had to pee!

It had been months since he'd felt that sensation. He needed to pee and he needed something to pee in. Lacking a chamber pot, Erich sat up and pushed his legs off his bed.

"Father, Father," he cried, "I need a pail. I need a pail."

Erich heard a stirring next door, then saw a flickering light outside.

"Father, come quick."

Padre Candid Zavala entered the room in his nightshirt. He carried a candle which created a ball of light that engulfed his head like a halo.

"What is it, my son? What is it?"

"A pail, Father, a pail or a chamber pot. I need to pee."

Zavala stood speechless for a moment, his mouth dropping.

"Hurry, Father, hurry."

"Yes," Zavala cried, "yes, yes!" The priest ran from the room. "Hallelujah!" he cried. "Hallelujah!"

Erich slid his loose britches down past his knees and scooted forward on the bed until he sat on the edge, where he could urinate into the pail. "Hurry, hurry," he cried. "I can't wait."

He heard a clattering in the hall, then Zavala bolted into the room. He slid the pail beneath him.

Then Erich relaxed. He heard the sound of himself draining into the pail and laughed until tears began to stream down his face.

Zavala too was laughing, so hard that he accidentally blew the candle out.

"Is it a miracle, Father?"

Zavala relit the candle, then scratched his head. "It is a miracle, yes, but not one we can share or even speak about. Imagine trying to explain this to Father Machebeuf."

"Maybe I should show him instead."

Both men laughed again.

Erich's laughter died suddenly. "Thank you, Father, thank you for all your prayers."

"Perhaps it was your faith! Build upon this miracle so that you can one day walk out of here a new man, a man who has life again."

Erich nodded humbly. He felt suddenly ashamed of his nakedness before this man of God. He struggled to pull up his britches. "I'm gonna walk again, Father, I am. I hoped, wished it, dreamed it, but never fully believed it until now."

Zavala smiled. "Don't underestimate your faith, my son, or God's faith in you. Perhaps you are marked for a destiny you do not know."

"But how will I ever learn what it is?"

"God will reveal it to you when the time is right."

"Thank you, Father." Erich slid off the bed, his numb legs scraping the floor. He rolled over on his stomach and found himself at the priest's bare feet.

Zavala retreated a step.

Erich reached out and grabbed Zavala's foot, then wormed his way to him. Reverently, he kissed both feet. "Thank you, Father."

Zavala squatted and ran his fingers through Erich's hair. "What is meant to be will be. God will see to that."

"I believe you, Father, and I believe God. I am going to pray at the altar and visit the room of miracles."

The priest smiled. "God will be pleased." He retreated to his room, leaving his candle holder on the floor in the hallway.

By the flickering light, Erich pulled himself into the hall then dragged himself to the chapel, where he lay before the altar, dimly lit by six candles.

As he prayed he thought he felt a tingling sensation below his waist, a sensation unlike any he had felt since he'd been injured. Maybe he was only imagining things, he thought, but he hoped and prayed not. He wanted to walk again, but the reason for that wish seemed more complex than it had a day before. He did not understand what had come over him, but felt more at peace with himself than at any time in his life, crippled or not. He prayed until sunrise, then crawled into the room of miracles. "I will walk again," he said. "Amen."

The warriors sat around the campfire, discussing what to do with the captive soldier. They had staked him to the ground again and argued about his fate.

Crow Feather was still troubled by the ringing they had heard when he had prepared to blind the soldier with the burning stick.

"If he is a great warrior," Speaks Loudly said, "then why does he not free himself and escape?"

"Perhaps he wants to find our camp and kill our women and children too," Big Wolf said.

"One man cannot kill our camp. No warrior is that great."

Crow Feather listened and considered.

"We all have our medicine pouches, but nothing in our pouches makes noises when we are attacked," Owl Eyes said.

"What do you say, Crow Feather?"

Crow Feather hesitated as he considered suggesting that they kill the soldier and take his medicine, whatever it was.

Before he could respond, however, the bell rang again.

All the warriors looked at the captive, then back at Crow Feather.

Crow Feather did not want to show it, but he was scared. Even thinking about killing the captive produced his medicine.

"We shall take him to camp and learn his medicine. Then we will be stronger warriors."

The ringing died away after Crow Feather finished speaking.

The warriors nodded to one another that Crow Feather was wise.

Come morning the Comanche band rode out again after feeding themselves and the captive on dried buffalo meat. They rode three more days and rejoined the camp near the site of the buffalo kill.

They rode into camp victorious again, the women and children coming out to escort them. At first the villagers taunted and threw rocks at the captive, but Crow Feather lifted his arm.

"Do not attack this man for he has great medicine. When we threatened to kill him, his medicine spoke like a bell. I started to kill him but his medicine told me no. His medicine is powerful. Do not trifle with him. Tonight we will celebrate our victory and eleven scalps. Tomorrow we will discuss his medicine."

The throng chanted and the warriors rode to their lodges to prepare for the scalp dance. Weasel awaited him.

"Where is the boy I call my son?"

"He gathers firewood."

"And Stone Flower?"

"She is helping. They are good workers, not like the one you traded for two horses to Speaks Loudly."

"They shall be our children."

Crow Feather placed his weapons by the buffalo skin he used for sleep. Weasel offered him a bowl of stew.

"I must see that our captive is bound so that he might not escape." Crow Feather retreated from the tipi and went to the center of the circled lodges. There he watched Owl Eyes, Big Wolf, and Gives Gifts tie the captive.

As the captive struggled against them, something fell from his pocket. Seeing this, Crow Feather walked over and picked up the amulet. It was round and shiny and attached to a tiny chain.

"What is it?" Owl Eyes asked.

"Maybe it is his medicine." He examined the eagle engraved on one side, then lifted it to his mouth and licked it. It was flavorless. He held it to his ear, then jerked it away.

"What is it?" Big Wolf asked.

"It has a heart like an animal."

"It cannot be," Owl Eyes said. "No rock has a heart."

Crow Feather offered the captive's medicine to Owl Eyes.

Skeptically, Owl Eyes held it to his ear. He shook the metal, then listened again.

"Crow Feather is right. This iron eagle has a heart that beats." Owl Eyes passed it to Big Wolf.

Big Wolf nodded. "Its heart ticks, but who can make it sing like before?" He looked at the captive staked to the ground. "This warrior is weak without his medicine."

"We all are," Crow Feather answered, taking the metal from Big Wolf.

"We should keep his medicine," Speaks Loudly stated.

"Does my medicine protect you or make you strong," Crow Feather countered.

The warriors shook their heads.

"Then we should not keep it," Crow Feather said, "for it might bring us great harm."

Speaks Loudly looked at the captive. "He is weak. We should kill him."

"We do not know that he is weak," Crow Feather responded.

"Then what should we do? If he escapes, he could come back to do us great harm," Speaks Loudly said.

"He will not escape," Crow Feather answered, pulling his knife from his sheath, "I will see to that." Crow Feather strode to the captive. He squatted between the captive's feet, then slid the blade of the knife under the soldier's right heel and sliced at the tendon.

The soldier gasped and fought the bindings but he did not scream. He was brave, but henceforth he would be lame. Crow Feather dropped the watch on his chest and then moved away.

The feeling had returned enough that he could control his bowel movements as well as his bladder. Erich cried with relief. No more humiliating experiences while the priest or anyone else cleaned his soiled clothes and redressed him. The feeling seemed to be returning to his legs though he could not be certain. Sometimes he wondered if his mind was playing games on him. He looked at his legs and they still seemed shriveled and useless from atrophy.

Erich no longer prayed for his healing, but that God's will would be done with his life. He prayed unselfishly, spending more time in prayer than even the priest. He spent as much time at the altar as he did in the room of miracles, dragging himself between the two and even dragging himself out into the small flower garden that Zavala tended for his own peace of mind.

As Erich lay on the ground, he watched hummingbirds and bumblebees kiss the flowers for their nectar. When he had been a scout, he watched wildlife for signs of danger. Now he observed solely for the beauty. He listened to the chirping of the birds in the trees, no longer for what they might tell him, but for the melody of their songs. He had known so much of the world in the mountains of Wyoming but had learned so little of its beauty.

Father Zavala emerged from the chapel and was surprised to find Erich outside. "I did not realize you had come out here," he said.

"I'm watching."

"Spring is a delightful time. The flowers are magnificent, the birds are feisty, and winter is too far away to worry about."

"When you crawl, you see the world like the animals do. It is more beautiful than I ever realized," Erich said.

"People, too, are more beautiful than you ever realize until you watch them. People can bloom just like the flowers," the priest said.

"How do you mean?"

"I once knew a young man who came to this place embittered by the unfairness of life, but that young man grew and believed. Then he began to blossom spiritually."

Erich nodded. "That young man was me, wasn't he?"

Zavala smiled softly. "It was."

"I have learned much from you, Father."

"And I from you."

"How can that be?" Erich asked.

"My faith was being tested. I have seen miracles here but the archbishop did not believe me. I wanted so for you to walk again."

"But that is good."

"No," Zavala replied. "I wanted those miracles for the wrong reasons, so I would have proof that God did amazing miracles in this out-of-the-way place in New

Mexico Territory. I wanted to show the bishop and archbishop that I was a powerful man of God. My vanity wanted to show them I am a better priest than they are. It was wrong. And now God has shown true miracles in you, but they are not miracles of which I can speak in decent company. That is God's way of teaching me humility."

"But you were humble, Father."

"Perhaps of body, but my heart was vain, and I have learned from God's miracles in you. God works in mysterious ways, my son, and we can only be the chosen implements of his earthly works."

"My legs don't work but my spirit seems freer than ever."

"That may be the biggest miracle of all," the priest said.

Erich thought about that for a moment and nodded. "I think it is time for me to return to the altar to pray."

Zavala smiled. "Prayer frees the spirit."

"Yes, Father," he replied, then turned himself on the path and retreated to the chapel, trying to make his legs move by his sheer willpower. They did not respond, but he reached the chapel, pushed open the door, and wormed his way inside the dark and cool building.

He inched past his room and for an instant thought he might have felt some stirring in his legs, but the moment was so fleeting that he realized he might be dreaming it.

Erich reached ahead with his right arm, then his left. His legs seemed different. They were not moving, but they were not necessarily static either. It was strange, the tingling that pricked his thighs. He wondered if he was imagining things, then he actually felt his thigh move and thought he felt his kneecap against the hard-packed floor. He pulled himself to the altar, thinking he felt life in his legs. He wanted to walk more than ever. Not just for himself, but for Father Zavala as well.

At the altar, he prayed that he could be the miracle that Father Zavala had so earnestly desired. Then he pulled himself into the room of miracles. He scooped a handful of soil from the hole and rubbed it not on his legs, but on his chest, over his heart.

Jason Dobbs cried during the night. He knew the Indians had cut his Achilles tendon. He knew he would never run again and that for the rest of his life he would walk with a pronounced limp.

Dobbs wished for his medicine bag so he could put some salve on his wound, but he did not know if the Indians had even picked it up after the raid.

When the morning light was finally good, the Indian who had captured him and later cut his tendon freed him. Dobbs grabbed the watch on his chest and quickly wound it. He slipped the watch in his pocket, then rubbed his legs to work out the stiffness. As he rubbed his right leg, he felt the severed end of the tendon knotted behind his calf.

He touched the gash on his heel. It was tender and clotted over. Dobbs pointed at the knife in the warrior's hand. "Give it to me."

The Indian eyed him suspiciously and hesitated.

"Now."

The warrior did nothing.

Dobbs yanked the watch from his pocket and held it up at the warrior, who stepped back.

Though his muscles were cramped, Dobbs stood up gingerly and held the watch before the warrior's face. Dobbs lifted his right leg and it went unnaturally high before falling back to the ground. He stepped with the left, then limped with the right. He shook the watch.

The warrior froze.

Dobbs stepped to him and yanked the knife from his hand. The warrior did not resist. Dobbs hobbled toward the embers of the previous night's fire. He slid the blade into the embers until it was red hot, then pulled the blade from the fire, bent down and touched it to the gash across his heel. He cried out as the blade seared his flesh. Painful though the procedure was, it would cauterize the wound and prevent gangrene from setting in. When he was done, he stepped awkwardly toward the Indian, who stared with wide eyes and an amazed countenance.

He handed the knife back to the warrior.

The warrior looked around to see if anyone else was watching, then spoke words Dobbs could not understand before turning away.

Suddenly, Dobbs found himself alone in the middle of the Comanche camp. Though men and women walked by, they ignored him. Desperate as he was to run away, he could not, not on a lame foot. If he took a horse, they would only catch him. He knew he must wait for another time, when his chances for success were greater.

He also knew he had to convey to the village that he was not a threat. So he limped through the village, dodging the staked buffalo hides which had been taken on a recent hunt, and moved down toward the creek. He could feel the eyes of many watching him, but they made no effort to stop him.

At the creek, Dobbs gathered pieces of brush and what tree limbs he could find and carried them back to the camp, stacking them by the embers of the previous night's fire. Several Comanches watched him but made no effort to halt or help him. Then he wandered awkwardly around camp, his limp drawing more stares. It hurt to walk and his severed tendon felt like a huge cancer beneath the skin of his calf. The Achilles tendon was the tendon critical for bending the leg or walking. Though he could still lift his leg, he could no longer pull it down with a muscle. That meant that his heel and foot dragged. To walk, he lifted his right leg up as high as he could, then let his foot and leg fall. He walked around camp, taking in the activity of the day. In the distance he saw the horse herd.

As he came to one tipi, he saw a young boy staked behind it.

The boy looked frightened and beaten. Though he was dark-skinned, he appeared more Mexican than Indian. Dobbs knew enough Spanish to get by, so he asked the boy his name.

"Esteban," the boy said. "Comanche, *muy male.*"

So these were the dreaded Comanche. Dobbs tried to speak more with the boy, but he seemed scared of being spotted with him, so Dobbs went on. At the edge of camp he found where the packs from the paymaster's mule had been discarded. In addition to the money, there was paper, a pen, and ink inside.

He opened one of the bundles, pulled out an empty ledger, and retrieved a bottle of ink and a pen. He carried them to the middle of camp and sat down on a log where he had seen the wise men of the tribe gather. Then he began to write of his experiences with the Comanche, his captivity and his fears. He recorded his observations of their lives and work, knowing it might be months before he could escape or be rescued. In the interim he knew he must make the best of his predicament. He vowed not to let them defeat him.

Crow Feather had been frightened when the soldier with the magic talisman had taken his knife. Then, when he saw the soldier burn himself with the knife, he knew the man had great powers, but was surprised when he started to gather wood. This man was a brave, yes, but strange. He had great medicine, but he wasted it on woman's work. Crow Feather trailed the captive around the camp, observing him talking to Willow Leaf and fearing he might talk to Paints the Dead and convince him to escape the Comanche.

Then he saw the man move to the worthless belongings they had dumped from the Army mule. He watched the captive pull out a book and some other materials, move to the center of camp, and draw on the papers like Comanche men drew in the sand.

Crow Feather returned to his lodge, where Paints the Dead and Stone Flower were eating. Paints the Dead had learned the Comanche language quickly and Stone Flower was doing well for her age. Crow Feather sat beside Paints the Dead. "Today I shall teach you about the bow and arrow. You must practice so you can become a warrior."

"I will," he said.

"Do you like your new tribe?" Crow Feather asked.

Paints the Dead looked up from his bowl of stew. "All but Speaks Loudly. I don't like him. He is cruel to Willow Leaf."

"Would you ever run away from your new tribe?"

"Where would I go? I cannot find my home!"

"It is just as well, but you must stay away from the new warrior captive. He is a man with desires to return to his home. Do not listen to him or let him convince you that you should leave."

"I would not do that."

Crow Feather patted Paints the Dead on his shoulder. "I am proud that you are my son."

Paints the Dead did not seem to understand the import of his words, but Crow Feather knew that one day he would.

When Paints the Dead finished eating, he placed his bowl on the buffalo skin and looked at Crow Feather.

"Can we practice with the bow and arrow tomorrow, too?"

"No, for tomorrow we start for Quitaque Canyon. It is there where we trade goods with the Comancheros. We have many horses to trade."

Jason Dobbs spent the day observing the camp and writing down descriptions of Comanche dress and life. No one bothered him, though everyone seemed to watch him warily. Dobbs knew that they would tolerate his activities during the day, but wondered what fate awaited him at night. Would they stake him out again?

By the afternoon he observed the women unstaking the buffalo skins that had been worked around the camp and gathering blankets and other belongings. Dobbs surmised that they would break camp tomorrow and likely take him deeper into Comanche country.

At dusk the warrior who had captured him approached and pointed for him to go to a lodge. Dobbs nodded and limped in that direction. As they neared it, the warrior pointed to a buffalo robe beside the tipi. A bowl of meat sat upon the robe. The warrior motioned toward the food, then grunted. Dobbs sat down and picked up the bowl. Once he began eating, the warrior squatted beside him and tied his good leg to a tent stake with a leather thong.

It was more a gesture that Dobbs was to stay there for the night, because the warrior left his hands free so he could feed himself. When Dobbs finished eating, he sat the bowl on the ground, then reclined and pulled the buffalo robe over him. It was a nuisance sleeping with a tethered leg, but certainly better than being staked out on the ground. For the first time since his capture, he slept soundly and awoke before dawn. Soon the camp was abuzz with people taking the village down.

After his captor came out, Dobbs pointed to the thong attached to his foot and began to untie it himself, trying to make the point that he could have done that at any time during the night had he wanted to, and possibly escaped. The warrior nodded at him as if he understood, then strode to another tipi.

When Dobbs realized no one was going to load the paymaster's mule with the pack and five thousand dollars, he gathered his book, pen, and inkwell and hobbled over. The money meant nothing to the Comanches, but it might mean something to the Comancheros or others who might trade for captives.

Since he could not speak their language, Dobbs merely waited by the packsaddle and pack until someone observed him. While he waited, he used the pen and ink to write his observations of the Comanche breaking camp. They scurried about like ants cleaning a rodent carcass. Horses were driven in and tipis taken down. Belongings were stacked on travois and the village was dismantled a layer at a time. By midday the camp was virtually packed. Then his captor strolled out to find him.

The warrior, accompanied by a young boy who

looked to be Mexican, motioned for him to come on, but Dobbs pointed at the packsaddle. The warrior grimaced and the boy drew back his play bow and arrow and aimed it at Dobbs.

Dobbs got down on his hands and knees, held his hands up to his ears like a mule and then put one of the small bundles on his back. Then he shook his good leg. The warrior seemed to understand, but the boy laughed, apparently thinking he was playing an animal for hunting. The boy released the arrow and it sailed over Dobbs's shoulder.

The warrior chastised the boy and sent him running toward the horse herd. Shortly, two Comanche youths, trailed by the young Mexican boy, led the Army mule to Dobbs. The warrior pointed toward Dobbs and the two youths handed him the mule's rope.

Dobbs hoisted the packsaddle atop the mule's back, then strapped it down snugly. One by one he began to place the money pack and other items on the animal's back, securing them quickly. Taking the rope, he led the animal back toward the procession of Comanches forming at the campsite.

The warrior, who had disappeared while Dobbs loaded the mule, reappeared shortly, riding a dappled gray and leading an Army mount without a saddle. Riding beside him on a pony was the Mexican boy.

When the warrior reached Dobbs, he tossed the reins to him and took the line from the mule while Dobbs mounted.

Without a saddle Dobbs struggled to mount the gelding because of his injured leg, but finally he pulled himself aboard. The warrior pointed to Dobbs's place in the procession. Dobbs nodded and angled to the northeast.

For the first time since the Indian attack, Dobbs

believed he might actually live long enough to escape and ultimately get back to civilization. Though he desperately wanted to escape, he knew he must be patient. If haste resulted in failure, he would surely die.

Everywhere Crow Feather went on the trail north, Paints the Dead rode beside him, proud of his own pony. Paints the Dead still had much to learn about horses, their quirks and their capabilities. The horse was more important to the Comanche than even the buffalo, for without the horse the people might never catch the buffalo.

"Have you had a horse before?" Crow Feather asked.

His Comanche still shaky, Paints the Dead asked him to repeat the question.

"Did you have a horse in your previous life?"

"I had ridden a horse, but even my father did not have a horse."

"Among the Comanche a horse is a sign of prosperity. To own many horses, you must be a good warrior, and to be a good warrior you must be a good rider. On your trip from Mexico you showed promise as a rider, but you have much to learn. You should be able to ride without using the reins, guiding the horse with the touch of your knees. You cannot shoot a bow and arrow if you cling to the reins. You must be able to hang from your horse's side on raids to protect yourself from enemy bullets. You must learn to scoop up a wounded warrior in your arms to save him from the enemy. You must learn many things."

Crow Feather gave riding instructions to Paints the Dead all day. Often Crow Feather glanced over his shoulder to check on Draws Something, as he had decided to call the captive, but the man remained in line and accepting of his fate.

Noticing the knife in Paints the Dead's belt, Crow Feather pointed at it. "Show me your knife."

Paints the Dead pulled it proudly from his scabbard. Crow Feather took it from him. He ran his finger along the blade, then shook his head. "You have used it many times?"

"Yes, to cut sticks and rawhide. I made a doll for Stone Flower."

"That is good, Paints the Dead, but you must learn when you use your knife, you must sharpen it on a sharpening stone. A knife is only half a knife when it is not sharp. When it is dull, you must work twice as hard."

Paints the Dead said nothing, and Crow Feather saw a frown of disappointment on his face.

"You have much to learn, Paints the Dead, but do not be discouraged, because I will teach you. Be patient. You are young, with many moons for learning."

"Okay."

"Now go ride with the other boys on ponies. Challenge them to a race."

Paints the Dead galloped away and Crow Feather turned his horse toward Weasel.

Astride her horse with Stone Flower riding in front of her, Weasel smiled. Stone Flower held up a crude doll made of sticks with rawhide template in the shape of a Comanche dress.

Weasel pointed to the doll. "See what Paints the Dead made for Stone Flower."

Stone Flower giggled. "My baby." She clasped the rough doll to her breast.

"Where is Paints the Dead?" Weasel asked.

"He is riding and learning with the other boys with ponies."

"He is a good boy."

"He will be a great warrior."

"And a great son," Weasel said.

"Now we have a son and daughter, ready born."

"They both have many lessons to learn, Crow Feather."

"And they will. I have told no one this, Weasel, but in my vision I saw Paints the Dead as a great warrior. It is meant to be."

Weasel seemed suddenly saddened.

"What is it, Weasel?"

She hesitated.

"What is it?"

"I have a great fear."

"What?"

"That someday Stone Flower and Paints the Dead might run away to their homes."

9

Santa Fe

Jean Benoit could not remember a happier time. With Inge at his side and his girls at his feet, he relished life. The girls seemed to understand his importance to their existence, and their faces brightened each time he returned home. Inge had adjusted to cooking in the small corner fireplace and was serving delicious meals, so much so that Benoit felt his uniforms growing tighter. Ellen and Colleen talked gibberish and giggled and cried, and Benoit enjoyed every moment of it. Inge was at his side to love, and the separation had made him value her even more.

While he treasured his time with his family, he did miss Jason Dobbs. Benoit enjoyed their intellectual debates and their political discussions, and he could use his friend's advice now. Benoit had received another letter from Senator Couvillion, who wanted more information on the Colorado gold find. He had passed it on to General Smedley, who drafted a puerile response. As before, Benoit put the letter in his own handwriting and sent it on. Couvillion had made threats to his brother, which disturbed Benoit. Theophile was scheduled for a final round of ship maneuvers before graduating from Annapolis, and, according to the letter, the senator had plans for him. Benoit hoped his brother could get out of the senator's grip.

The only black cloud in New Mexico was Erich. Benoit thought about him daily, wishing that he would regain the use of his legs but knowing the chances were remote. Inge's spirits had lifted once she left Erich at Chimayo, and that made Benoit feel so much better himself. He did not look forward to Erich's return. It was wearing enough having to look after the girls without having to take on a full-grown man.

All in all, things had never seemed to be going better until the morning two weeks after the paymaster left for Fort Fillmore with Jason Dobbs. When Benoit arrived at the headquarters, he found General Smedley earlier than usual, a somber look upon his face.

"I have had a message from Fort Fillmore," Smedley announced.

Benoit's first fear was that murder charges that had been leveled against him during a stay at Fillmore the previous fall had been reopened.

"It's the paymaster," Smedley said, shaking his head. "He never arrived at Fort Fillmore and hasn't been seen since."

"Sacre bleu!" Benoit replied, then caught his breath. "What about Jason Dobbs?"

Smedley shook his head. "Nobody with the paymaster has been found."

Benoit's shoulders drooped. "What can we do?"

"Nothing," Smedley said. "I've sent men out to search for the missing. I just hope we find some alive."

Benoit nodded. Especially Jason Dobbs, he thought.

It was a miracle!

Erich Schmidt could explain it no other way.

First, he had regained control of his bodily functions. He no longer required Father Candid Zavala to clean him like a baby.

Then the sensation gradually returned to his legs, beginning with a slight tingle, and then full sensation. His arms, strong from pulling himself on the floor about the chapel, finally received a boost from his legs. He moved and then pushed his legs like a baby learning to crawl. Then he began to crawl, though not far because the muscles had shriveled. When he used his legs, they tired quickly.

Finally, one morning, he had slid his feet off his cot and gingerly pushed himself up, bracing his hand against the adobe wall. He stood but a moment, precariously balanced on legs as spindly and wobbly as a newborn colt's. He sat back down, desiring to surprise the priest. This miracle would be a gift to Zavala.

He slid down on the floor, then half crawled, half wormed his way to the altar, where he said a prayer of thanksgiving and praise for the wonder of God. As he had done dozens of times before, he pulled himself into the room of miracles and rubbed the holy earth upon his legs. Then he retreated to the back of the chapel where the crutches of the healed leaned against the wall. He found a pair that looked the right height, eased them to the floor and, with one in each hand, began to crawl back to his room, hoping that Father Zavala would not discover him.

The crutches made a clunking sound as he crawled on the floor. When Erich reached his room undetected, he dragged himself inside and shoved the crutches beneath his bed so the padre would not see them. When he was certain Zavala was in prayer or meditating out in his garden, he would retrieve the crutches and practice standing, then walking.

For eleven days he practiced, first in his room, then in the hallway outside when Father Zavala was out of the building. Finally, he could use the crutches to walk the hallway to the chapel, up and down the aisle, then back to his room. The exercise was tiring and left him exhausted, but with each day, he could feel his legs beginning to steady. Though he knew he would never have the strength he once had, as long as he could walk by himself, he did not care.

On the morning when the day was right for his surprise, he waited until he heard the shuffle of Father Zavala's sandals in the hallway as the priest went to pray at the altar, as was his habit.

Erich took the crutches from beneath his cot and carefully stood up. He slipped out his door toward the chapel, where the flickering candlelight barely illuminated the sanctuary. He moved as quietly as he could until he could reach out and touch Father Zavala with one of his crutches. The priest knelt reverently before the crucifix, his eyes shut, his palms pressed against each other under his chin. In the soft light, Zavala seemed as innocent as a child.

The priest mouthed the word "Amen" and gently arose. He turned toward Erich, seemingly oblivious to his presence in the dimly lit room, then startled when he realized he was not alone.

"I'm sorry," he said, "I did not realize someone had entered."

Erich answered. "It is me."

The priest's mouth fell open. "Erich? I cannot believe it!"

Erich let the crutches drop to the floor. Then he walked tentatively forward, stepping past the priest and to the front pew. "I cannot walk very far on my own." He sat down.

Zavala stood shocked. His lips moved but no words came out.

"I'll get stronger and walk farther so that you will have your miracle and can prove it to Father Machebeuf."

Zavala shook his head, then clasped the crucifix that hung from his neck. His eyes watered and a tear rolled down his cheek. He brushed it away.

"How can I thank you, Father?"

The priest waggled his finger. He pursed his lips as he fought his emotions. The single tear was followed by others. "Thank God."

Erich nodded. "I have done that, but I want to thank you. God spoke to me through you."

"If He did, I am but a humble instrument in His glorious hands."

"It was you, Father, not just God, because you gave me the faith to believe in Him. You did not have to show me the kindness and the patience you did. I needed you."

"I needed you as much as you needed me, my son."

"It was more, Father, and I have learned from it."

"How to walk, yes."

"No, not just that, I have learned about the power of God, the ability to touch people and change lives. I came here because as much as my mother and my sister loved me, they couldn't cure me. Nor could they touch me as you and God have over the last weeks."

"That is the power of God."

"But it was more than my legs."

"What do you mean, my son?"

"My legs were crippled, Father, that you know, but my heart was also crippled."

"You had reason, the bitterness of not being able to walk and the fear of such a life like that, but that is past. Now we should let your sister and Father Machebeuf know quickly."

Erich lifted his hand and responded emphatically. "No."

Zavala was shocked. "I do not understand. We should share the good news."

"No, I do not want them to know until I am stronger. Then I want to walk before them in Santa Fe, so that the power of the miracle is not diminished."

"You are wise, for how can Father Machebeuf disbelieve what he sees with his own eyes?"

"And I want you to escort me to Santa Fe."

"I shall be honored."

"And, Father, there is one other thing."

"Yes?"

"I have thought greatly about how God has changed my life and brought me peace, even when I couldn't walk. I have watched your kindness to all people, me especially, and I have seen the good that you do. I think there is but one course for me to follow from this day forward."

"And what is that?"

Erich sighed, then smiled. Nothing he had ever done in his life felt as right as his next words. "I want to become a priest, like you."

Zavala began to sob. He stepped up to Erich and hugged him. "This is not a celebration of a single miracle, but of two miracles."

Quitaque Creek, Texas Panhandle

Eduardo Crespin licked his lips, then stroked his black untrimmed mustache. In all his years as a Comanchero, he had traded for horses and buffalo robes and captives, but when Crow Feather's band arrived at the creek to trade, he saw an Army mule carrying what had to be the money of an Army paymaster, the paymaster who had disappeared after leaving Santa Fe.

The mule was led by a captive soldier who looked vaguely familiar. Where had he seen him? In La Estrella? Crespin thought so, but he did not understand why the Comanches hadn't killed him. Perhaps the soldier had convinced the Comanche of the value of the mule and its cargo, but that was unlikely, as the Comanche would put little stock in a few sheets of colored paper. How could such paper have the value of horses?

Crespin realized that, for once, he might actually trade with the Comanches for money.

The Comanchero camp was a beehive of activity as the Comanches moved among the goods Crespin's seventeen men had brought to the Texas Panhandle in ten caritas and on twenty-four mules. There were wool blankets and bolts of cloth, trade rifles and gunpowder, steel arrow points and lead, copper kettles and trade beads, knives and hatchets, copper pots and kettles, whiskey and trade bread that the women of Crespin's men had baked in rounded ovens. The bread was baked until it was dark and crisp. Though burnt to the Hispanos' tastes, the rounded loaves were considered delicacies by the Comanche. There was also coffee and sugar, tobacco and dried pumpkins, onions and spices.

As the mule with the Army payroll passed, Crespin surveyed his kingdom, preferring this trading location among all others because of the creek nearby and the boxed canyon with springwater where the horses traded by the Comanche could be penned. He had used the canyon for so many years that he had given it and the nearby creek their names: "Quitaque," which was Comanche for horse dung.

Crespin followed the Comanches of Crow Feather's band to the clearing, where they erected their tipis. They moved quickly, working excitedly, knowing that when they were done they could trade.

Crespin watched to see where the mule was staked, then retreated to his men. He would not tell them what he had observed, hoping that he could trade for the mule and cargo without them knowing. Then he would have all the money to himself.

He walked among the blankets his men had thrown on the ground to display their varied wares and instructed each trader to send Crow Feather to him, for he alone would deal with that particular brave. Then in twos and threes the Comanches returned from their hurriedly arranged camp. Crespin knew they held their horse herd out of sight, not wanting to give away their numbers because it would diminish their bargaining power. He understood that tactic, and had stationed a man with a telescope atop the canyon rim, and so he already knew that there were close to 350 animals in the Comanche herd.

Crespin, watching for Crow Feather, moved among the Comanches as they bartered with his men. Crow Feather, ever cagey, was slow to approach the Comanchero camp, as he did not care to appear too anxious.

Crespin patiently awaited him, meanwhile greeting the others he knew, including Speaks Loudly, who yanked a young boy about.

"It is good to see you, Speaks Loudly. I have heard many reports of your bravery in battle," Crespin lied.

Speaks Loudly straightened his shoulders and nodded as if it were all true. "And I have many captives, more than I can handle."

Crespin nodded, though doubtful, because he had not noticed an abundance of captives around Speaks Loudly's lodge. Instead, he guessed Speaks Loudly wanted to trade away a lazy captive.

"I'll offer the boy for a rifle and powder," Speaks Loudly said.

"You know, Speaks Loudly, that I do not trade for captives until I head back for Santa Fe. They are too much trouble to watch while we are still trading."

"He's a good captive, hard worker," Speaks Loudly said. "He is called Willow Leaf."

Crespin studied the boy and could tell by the bruises on his arms and face that he was not a favored captive. "Captives have no value to me," he said.

"Captives always have value," Speaks Loudly argued.

"Once, perhaps, but since the Americanos have taken over Santa Fe, any captive I take in trade, they free."

"Trade him to another tribe."

Crespin sneered. "That is the way to make enemies, not friends." Crespin saw Crow Feather and turned away from Speaks Loudly, lifting his hat and waving it at the leader of the band.

Crow Feather moved toward Crespin, who greeted him warmly.

"Many are the stories of your bravery in Mexico. It is told you took many scalps and many captives."

Crow Feather nodded, but not being as vain as Speaks Loudly, he said nothing.

"I have many good things to trade for you this season. Rifles and powder, knives and axes, and many blankets."

"I have few horses this season."

Crespin knew Crow Feather was bluffing, but he saw it as an occasion to bring up the mule. "I can use mules, not just horses." He pointed toward Crow Feather's lodge. "There is a mule there with packs and bags that I should like to trade for. I will give you three rifles, a keg of powder, and six blankets for the mule, its pack, and its load."

Crow Feather scratched his chin. "It is the mule of a captive. His medicine is strong. To trade will bring bad luck to the tribe."

The Comanches were a superstitious people, Crespin thought. If the soldier had such good medicine, he wouldn't be limping around a Comanche camp. Crespin scratched his head. "Three rifles, a keg of powder, and six blankets is a lot for one mule and his packs, more than you will get from anyone else."

Crow Feather shook his head. "All the guns and all the powder you have cannot fight off bad medicine."

"I'll throw in five bottles of whiskey."

Crow Feather walked away.

Crespin knew not to follow him. "I'll trick you, you suspicious fool," he said softly to himself. He walked among his men, watching them bargain and barter with the Indians.

He ignored the Comanche who called out to him, pondering how he could convince Crow Feather to give him the mule and the packs that held the Army payroll. Then it came to him as simple as Crow Feather's name. The crow was central to Crow Feather's personal superstitions.

He called one of his men, the best among them with a rifle, but the man was busy bargaining with a brave over a mirror for his squaw. "Let him have it," Crespin commanded.

"For nothing?"

Crespin nodded. "I have something more important for you to do." He grabbed the hunter by the arm and pulled him away from his blanket of trade goods to a spot where no Comanche might overhear him. Leading him to the creek, Crespin stopped and looked around to see that no one was within hearing range. Only then did he speak. "Take your fowling piece and a horse and ride far enough from here that a gunshot cannot be heard by the Comanches."

The man nodded.

"Shoot some crows and bring me the tail feathers, but let no one see you."

His lackey scratched his head.

"Be quick," Crespin said, and shooed him away. He laughed as the man departed. "Stupid Comanche."

Jason Dobbs limped among the Comanches and traders, trying to find a Comanchero who might take pity upon him and bargain for him. Then he spotted the Comanchero who looked like he was in charge. He recognized Eduardo Crespin by the untrimmed mustache and the red serape that he wore everywhere.

Dobbs eyed the Comanchero as he talked to the Comanche warrior who had captured him. He saw the warrior walk away from Crespin, who retreated with one of his men to the creek.

When the Comanchero disappeared, Dobbs slipped back to his captor's lodge, where he had staked the payroll mule. He pulled a handful of paper bills from the packsaddle and slipped them in his pocket. Then he ambled back to the camp, watching for Crespin to return from the creek. When the Comanchero neared, he started toward him, trying to walk as fast as he could, but his lame leg seemed to convulse on its own accord.

The Comanchero observed him, then stopped, seemingly amused by his awkward gait.

Dobbs planted his lame foot in front of the Comanchero and nodded. "I need your help."

The Comanchero sneered. "The Comanche stay my friends because I don't help their enemies."

"I am a captive. Buy me, trade for me, help me escape them. I will repay you tenfold what it costs."

The Comanchero laughed. "You have nothing to bargain with."

"For God's sake, don't abandon me. If you can't buy me or take me with you to Santa Fe, at least tell the Army where I am."

"Bad for business."

As Dobbs jerked the wad of bills from his pocket, he accidentally pulled out his watch as well and it fell to the ground. Before he could pick it up, the Comanchero bent and snatched the watch.

Dobbs extended his hand.

The Comanchero shook his head.

Dobbs reached for the watch.

The Comanchero lifted his foot and kicked Dobbs's left leg from under him. Dobbs right leg collapsed beneath him and he tumbled to the ground. Instantly the

Comanchero was atop him, pulling the money from his wrist.

"Stop, you bastard."

The Comanchero laughed as he counted the money. "Four hundred dollars."

Dobbs got to his hands and knees.

The Comanchero kicked him in the ribs.

Pain shot through Dobbs like he had been struck by lightning. He gasped, then slumped to the ground.

"I'll have all the money before I leave here, and you'll die a captive's death." The Comanchero strode away, laughing while Dobbs gasped for his breath.

Dobbs was bewildered. The Comanchero knew there was more money. Worst of all, the Comanchero had taken his watch, the sole source of his magic before the Comanche.

Without the watch, Dobbs feared he might be killed.

Eduardo Crespin had watched Crow Feather for two days. He knew the warrior kept returning to a carbine that had a stock studded with brass tacks. It was a gaudy weapon, the kind that often attracted an Indian's attention.

Crespin passed the word among his men that only he could sell the carbine. He knew Crow Feather wanted it so bad he could almost taste it. The warrior would be cagey, but Crespin now had the tail feather of a crow hidden beneath his red serape. He waited until Crow Feather neared, then he lifted his arm and looked skyward, letting the crow feather fall from his serape over the carbine.

"What is it?" Crow Feather asked as Crespin watched the sky.

"A bird lost a feather as it flew overhead." Crespin looked at Crow Feather, then at the blanket where his rifles were displayed.

Crow Feather glanced from the sky to the blanket.

Crespin smiled when he saw that the tail feather had landed across the stock of the carbine. It was a good charade and Crow Feather was bound to fall for it. Crespin squatted. "Well, look at that, would you?" He reached to pick up the tail feather, but Crow Feather grabbed his wrist.

"It is from a crow and good medicine for me. I will trade you a horse for this rifle." The warrior released Crespin's hand.

The Comanchero shook his head. "Can't do it."

"Two horses."

"Not for any number of horses. You can have any other weapon for a horse, but not this one."

"Ten horses."

Crespin shook his head and took the rifle. "I'll keep it."

"This carbine has great powers for me. The feather is a sign. What will you bargain for?"

Crespin crossed his arms, then spoke. "The mule and all its packsaddles and their goods."

Crow Feather realized the sign was unmistakable. The carbine had special medicine for him. The crow feather proved it, but at what cost? The mule and the goods had been the captive's. He feared challenging Draws Something's medicine, but the tail feather had signaled the power of the carbine to kill many enemies. He knew he must have the carbine, but would his medicine stand up to the captive's?

"I will trade you the mule for the carbine," Crow

Feather answered in spite of the knot of fear in his stomach.

"The mule, the pack, and all the papers they hold?"

Crow Feather nodded. He bent to pick up the carbine and the feather for his medicine bag, then departed for his lodge. He called for Paints the Dead and gave him the carbine to put with his other weapons as he slipped the feather in his medicine pouch. When Paints the Dead returned, Crow Feather smiled. "Come with me."

Together they ran to the mule and quickly loaded it the way the captive did, then led the mule to Eduardo Crespin.

Crow Feather offered Crespin the rope to the mule. "This is what you wanted."

Crespin hesitated to take the rope. "I have had many thoughts while you were away, Crow Feather. Since the falling feather was a powerful sign of your strong medicine, I fear to keep the mule might bring me bad medicine."

"It is possible," Crow Feather answered.

Crespin nodded. "Then keep the mule and I will keep the cargo that it carried on its back."

Crow Feather smiled broadly. So did Crespin.

Toward the west, the sun was setting. Campfires blazed as the Comanches and the Comancheros finished their bargaining.

Paints the Dead wished he had something to trade for a gift for Stone Flower. He walked among the merchants, taking in the excitement of the last minute trading. He grimaced when he saw Speaks Loudly leading Willow Leaf by a rope.

Willow Leaf looked tired and scared.

Speaks Loudly had been acting oddly, and when he passed nearby, Paints the Dead smelled the aroma of liquor on his breath.

As Speaks Loudly passed, Paints the Dead fell in beside the other boy. "Are you okay, Willow Leaf?"

His companion frowned. "My name is Esteban and yours is Armando. I will not become a Comanche, no matter what you call me."

"We have nothing else to call you by."

Willow Leaf shook his head. "Then don't call me anything. Just leave me alone," he answered, and lurched forward as Speaks Loudly yanked the rope.

Speaks Loudly turned around, and Paints the Dead felt a sudden fear as the warrior eyed him.

"Scat," Speaks Loudly said.

Paints the Dead moved a few steps away and made a stubborn stand, not planning to move again, but Speaks Loudly yanked the rope around Willow Leaf's neck and moved on. Paints the Dead watched Speaks Loudly stop to talk to the Comanchero who had traded the mule for the carbine and then released the mule. He inched closer to listen.

Speaks Loudly shoved Willow Leaf to the ground. "I have come to trade the captive," he said.

The Comanchero shook his head. "I do not want him."

"I'll trade him for one horse, a broken-down horse."

"He is worthless to me."

Willow Leaf pushed himself to his feet and slowly stood, tears welling in his eyes.

Crespin waved for Speaks Loudly to leave. "We must finish our trading and pack our goods so we can leave with the sunrise."

Speaks Loudly protested. "A mule. I'll take a mule for him."

Willow Leaf began to cry.

"He is no good," the Comanchero said. "He is worse than a girl who whines. At least you can sleep with a girl."

"He is worthless, then," Speaks Loudly shouted.

Willow Leaf cried louder.

Paints the Dead feared for him. "Be quiet, Esteban," he pleaded.

Suddenly, Speaks Loudly yanked his knife from the scabbard at his belt.

"Get away, Esteban," Paints the Dead called. "Run away."

Willow Leaf looked at Paints the Dead.

Then Speaks Loudly slashed the knife across Willow Leaf's neck. The wound spurted blood.

Willow Leaf grabbed his neck and wailed, his hands covered with blood instantly. Comanches and traders looked up from their bargaining. Paints the Dead started toward Willow Leaf, then backed away when he saw the flash of Speaks Loudly's knife.

Willow Leaf collapsed on the trader's blanket, the blood staining the cloth and the ground. Willow Leaf kicked and moaned, then his life drained from him like his blood.

Paints the Dead felt as though he might throw up. He turned away, hating Speaks Loudly even more than before. Willow Leaf had not deserved to die.

Speaks Loudly turned to the Comanchero. "He's yours now."

The trader hurriedly gathered his goods from the blanket and yanked the cloth from beneath the body. Examining the large stain on the blanket, the Comanchero cursed in Spanish, which Paints the Dead could still understand. Then he flung the blanket atop Willow Leaf's still body.

"I will not trade with you, Speaks Loudly, ever again," the Comanchero said.

"Your goods are worthless," Speaks Loudly answered back.

"You owe me for ruining my blanket," the trader shot back, then spat at Speaks Loudly's feet.

Speaks Loudly laughed and turned around, striding away with the eyes of the other Comanches upon him.

Paints the Dead wanted to cry, but it was not the Comanche way. He tried not to, but he felt tears running down his face. He was scared for himself, but most of all fearful that Stone Flower might see her brother's body. He did not want her touched by another tragedy.

The Comanches and Comancheros returned to their bargaining as if Willow Leaf's body was no more than a piece of firewood. Paints the Dead stepped softly to the corpse. Squatting, he grabbed the blanket and laid it out on the ground. Next he pulled Willow Leaf onto the edge and rolled the body up inside.

He looked around to make sure Stone Flower was nowhere about, then tried to pick up the bundle, but Willow Leaf was too heavy to carry. When no one came to help him, he grabbed the end of the blanket and began to drag it toward the creek. There, where the ground would be softer, he would dig out a grave with the knife that Crow Feather had given him.

Once he was clear of the camp, he began to cry aloud.

When Crow Feather returned to his lodge, he picked up his new carbine and held it.

Weasel smiled as she braided Stone Flower's hair. The young girl sat smugly on the ground in front of Weasel and grinned.

Crow Feather nodded his approval. "You will be a beautiful girl when Weasel is through fixing your hair in the way of the Comanche."

She nodded, but Crow Feather was uncertain if she understood. She had not picked up the language as quickly as Paints the Dead. He was about to question her when he heard his name called.

"Crow Feather, Crow Feather, are you in your lodge?"

He recognized the voice as that of Owl Eyes. There was tension in his voice.

Crow Feather stood up and moved quickly to the tipi flap, flung it aside and stepped out, carbine in hand.

Owl Eyes peeked into the tipi, then grabbed Crow Feather's arm and pulled him away.

"We must move from this place," Owl Eyes said, "so I can tell you something that Stone Flower must not hear."

The two warriors walked behind another lodge.

"It is Willow Leaf," Owl Eyes said. "Speaks Loudly has killed him."

Crow Feather felt a knot in his stomach. He had never cared for Willow Leaf, as he had for Paints the Dead and Stone Flower, but still he did not wish the boy dead. He might have one day become a warrior, though never a great one.

"Paints the Dead is dragging the body to the creek."

"Did Paints the Dead see him die?"

Owl Eyes nodded.

Crow Feather clenched his fists and shook his head as the anger welled in him. "I must go to the creek," he said. "Bring me clay and vermilion and rawhide thongs, then let me be alone with my son."

Owl Eyes ran off as Crow Feather raced for the creek.

He found the boy easily. Paints the Dead barely looked up when Crow Feather reached him. The boy was out of breath, and Crow Feather could see the tracks of tears down his cheeks. He placed his hand on Paints the Dead's shoulder, and the boy dropped the end of the blanket, spun around and hugged him.

"He didn't deserve to die. He was scared, that's all. What will I tell Stone Flower?"

Crow Feather ran his fingers through Paints the Dead's hair, trying to come up with an answer.

Paints the Dead pushed himself away. "Is that what will happen to me? I wasn't scared, but now I am. Are you going to kill me the way Speaks Loudly killed Willow Leaf?"

Crow Feather squatted and looked at him. "I will never treat you so. You have become my son." He handed Paints the Dead his carbine.

Paints the Dead hesitated to take the weapon.

"Here," Crow Feather insisted, "hold it."

The boy took the carbine and held it awkwardly.

"If you think I will harm you, then point the carbine at my heart and shoot me. I would not hurt you because you have become my son and Stone Flower my daughter."

Paints the Dead offered the gun back to Crow Feather.

"You carry the weapon," Crow Feather said. "I have come to help you bury Willow Leaf in the way of the Comanche."

Crow Feather moved to the blanket-shrouded body,

slipped his hands gently beneath the bundle and lifted Willow Leaf's remains. He started up the creek with Willow Leaf.

By the time he reached the creek, Owl Eyes had caught up with him. The warrior carried a dish of vermilion, a dish of red clay, and a handful of leather thongs. Owl Eyes said nothing, just fell in behind Crow Feather and Paints the Dead.

Crow Feather walked upstream, looking for a crevice where the body could be placed, then covered with rocks. It was much easier than the white man's custom of digging holes in the ground.

When he finally found a rocky crevice in the bank of the creek bed, he gently placed the body upon a grassy spot by the edge of the creek. Then Owl Eyes placed the vermilion, clay, and leather thongs on the grass beside the body.

Wordlessly, Owl Eyes retreated to camp.

Paints the Dead placed the carbine on the grass beside the body as Crow Feather unfolded the blanket. He saw Paints the Dead flinch when Willow Leaf's bloodied face appeared.

"We first will wash him," Crow Feather explained. "Then we will paint his face with vermilion and seal his eyes with the clay that Owl Eyes brought. We shall dress him in his clothes again because he has no finer, then wrap him in the blanket and put him in the crevice and cover his body with stones so the animals will not get him."

Crow Feather stripped Willow Leaf, then scooped water from the creek to wash off the blood. He took the boy's shirt and washed it in the water, the blood trailing away downstream. When he was done, he wrung the water out and placed the shirt back on the body. The pants were not bloody, so Crow Feather did not wash them. When Willow Leaf was dressed again, Paints the Dead placed the body on the blanket.

Next he took clay and used it to seal Willow Leaf's eyes, which were half open. Then he dipped his hand in the vermilion and painted the face. When he finished, he washed his hands in the stream, the vermilion joining the blood that he had washed from the body. Next Crow Feather bent Willow Leaf's knees and folded them back to his chest. With one of the leather thongs, he tied the legs in position, then bent Willow Leaf's head forward until his cheeks touched his knees. With that, he wrapped the body in the blanket and tied it forever with more leather laces.

"It is time that we bury your friend."

Paints the Dead nodded.

Crow Feather lifted the bundle and moved to the crevice in the bank. He forced the body into the hole where the earth had split, then turned to Paints the Dead. "We must cover him with rocks to keep the animals from uncovering him and disturbing his bones."

Without another word of instruction, Paints the Dead moved along the river gathering rocks and then tossing them atop the body.

Crow Feather took big rocks and dumped them on top of Willow Leaf. They spent close to an hour covering the body.

When they were done, Crow Feather grabbed his new carbine and then took the bowl of vermilion.

Paints the Dead took the bowl of red clay and the remaining leather thongs. Father and son started back to camp together.

"I hate Speaks Loudly. He is mean," Paints the Dead said. "Why did he kill Willow Leaf?"

"I do not know. Willow Leaf could one day have become a warrior, not a great one, but a warrior still."

"One day, I will be a warrior."

"And you will be a great one, Paints the Dead."

Paints the Dead pulled his own knife from his scabbard. "And when I am, I will kill Speaks Loudly."

"You should kill your enemies, not your Comanche brothers."

"He is not my Comanche brother," Paints the Dead said. "The others may be, but not him."

"You will learn," Crow Feather answered.

"I have already learned much." He waved the knife over his head. "I will keep my knife sharp, like you taught me, for the day that I shall kill Speaks Loudly."

10

"Let me take a troop of cavalry and search for the paymaster," Jean Benoit pleaded with General Arnold Smedley.

Smedley paced back and forth behind his desk. "It has been three weeks since we learned of the disappearance, Jean. What can you do that others haven't?"

"Find Jason Dobbs, that's what I can do. If the scout Tim McManus is around, he'll help. He's got the nose of a bloodhound."

"This is not just about Jason Dobbs. It's about eleven other men and five thousand dollars in cash to pay the soldiers at the forts in New Mexico Territory."

"If I find Jace, I find the others."

"Where do you start? They could be anywhere, if not dead. We need something more to go on than your good intentions. They were hit by that damned sandstorm, and it could've blown them to Texas. Could've buried them." Smedley pinched the bridge of his nose and shook his head. "Maybe they deserted and stole the money."

"Jace wouldn't do that!"

"Then Dobbs may be dead."

"But I owe him, General. He saved my wife and daughters."

Smedley lifted his gaze toward the ceiling and shook his head. "What you owe him and what the Army owes him are different."

"Damn!" Benoit replied, "I feel helpless."

"That's how we all feel, but troops from Fort Fillmore didn't find anything, searching twenty miles on either side of the Rio Grande. No bodies, no animals, no nothing. Bad part about it is the War Department's more interested in the money than they are the men."

"That's the Army, sir, and why we've got to do something!"

"What, Captain? I'm as frustrated about this as anybody." Smedley moved around his desk and clasped Benoit by the shoulder. "Take the rest of the afternoon off, go play with those daughters of yours, try to forget about this for a while."

Benoit shrugged. "Don't know that I can. Can you?"

"Likely not."

Benoit left out of the general's office, informed Sergeant Hamilton Phipps that he wouldn't be in the rest of the afternoon and left. It was too early for Inge and the girls to be up from their afternoon naps, so he walked to the plaza, lost in his own thoughts.

As he circled the square, he heard his name and turned to see Alejo Ortiz striding toward him, his disfigured face half hidden by the broad brim of his hat.

"Good afternoon," Ortiz said with a smile.

Benoit hesitated.

Ortiz cocked his head and stared at Benoit. "Your face is longer than the Rio Grande itself."

Benoit nodded. "My friend Jason Dobbs has disappeared with the paymaster's troops."

Ortiz shook Benoit's hand warmly. "I heard about the paymaster but did not realize your friend accompanied him. My sympathy, Jean, but let me ask a question. This money that the paymaster carried, was it coin or paper?"

"Paper, we were paid in paper."

"American greenbacks was it?"

"Yes! Why do you ask?"

"Just curiosity, my friend. Would you care to join me for a drink and a game of chance or two at La Estrella?"

Benoit shook his head. "I don't have the money to gamble, nor to spend on drink, now that my wife and girls are here."

Ortiz grabbed Benoit's arm and pulled him toward the saloon and gambling den. "No, come along. I insist."

Benoit shrugged, deciding it was easier to go along with Ortiz than to challenge him. Ortiz led him through the narrow streets of Santa Fe and between the squat adobe buildings that abutted one another except where streets intersected.

"You will enjoy your visit this time, I promise," Ortiz said as he stopped outside the nondescript adobe building that was the biggest saloon and gambling den in Santa Fe. Ortiz pushed open the door, yanked off his hat and bowed for Benoit to enter. "Welcome to La Estrella, where many secrets are hidden for those who seek them."

Benoit entered, confused by Ortiz's remarks and his intentions. Was his friend just trying to boost his spirits? Ortiz stepped inside and closed the door behind them before tugging his hat down low.

"I will buy you a drink," Ortiz said, then steered Benoit toward the bar, where he ordered a whiskey for both.

As Benoit looked around the room, he saw the Comanchero Eduardo Crespin at Doña Rosalia's monte table, gambling with her. Benoit knew his stay would be short in La Estrella because Ortiz hated Crespin.

But to Benoit's surprise, the moment Ortiz finished his drink, he grabbed Benoit's arm and steered him to Rosalia's table.

Rosalia was at least sixty years old, perhaps older, short and ugly. Her black eyes were alert and her tiny hands flitted over the cards with hummingbird swiftness. She sucked on a cheap cigar and dolled herself up with a spot of rouge on each cheek and a smear of red on her lips. She wore enough gold chains to weigh down a mule. Though she understood English, she refused to speak it in her saloon, making certain everyone knew she resented the invasion of Americanos.

When Ortiz approached her table, she smiled and motioned for him to sit. When he sat down beside Crespin, she greeted him in Spanish.

The Comanchero grumbled something that Benoit took to be an insult. Ortiz turned to Benoit. "Watch so you can learn how the game is played."

Benoit had seen the game before, but didn't pretend to fully understand its nuances. The object basically was for the gambler to bet on which suit would come up before another suit. If the gambler called it right, he won. If the other suit appeared first, then Doña Rosalia won.

Besides Crespin and Ortiz, two other Hispanos sat around the table. They each placed a bet with a real, a Mexican silver coin worth an eighth of a dollar.

Crespin tossed a pair of crisp bills on the table. The moment he did, Ortiz glanced over his shoulder. With a twitch of his head, he motioned toward Crespin's bet.

Benoit shrugged, and Ortiz turned back to the table

to place his own bet. Ortiz picked clubs to appear before hearts. Rosalia dealt three cards before a club appeared. Ortiz laughed and slapped the table. Then he nudged Crespin. *"Bueno,"* he said.

Crespin growled.

Again they placed bets. Crespin throwing more paper money on the table. Ortiz nodded, and Benoit realized his friend was trying to signal him about something, but he wasn't quite sure. Ortiz even pointed at Crespin's bills on the table. "Paper money," he announced.

Crespin looked at him and growled, speaking his Spanish slow enough that Benoit understood he had called Ortiz a disfigured bastard.

Ortiz yanked off his hat and grinned at Crespin. *"Gracias,"* he said with a mocking tone.

Crespin slapped the table and began to gather the paper money in front of himself. He folded the money and then pulled a silver watch from his pocket.

Benoit observed him open the cover, which was embossed with an eagle in front of an American flag. He realized then that he had seen the watch before. It was Dobbs's watch.

Benoit's jaw dropped. How had Crespin acquired it?

Crespin snapped the cover shut and stood up, nodding at Rosalia, then grumbling to her in Spanish.

Benoit understood him to say that he would return later, when the disfigured bastard was gone. With that, he shoved himself away from the table, bumped into Benoit, then headed for the door.

Ortiz placed another bet, which he lost. *"Muy mal,"* he said and threw up his hands. *"No mas."* He stood up, stretched his arms and looked at Benoit.

"Did you see what I saw?" Benoit asked.

"Outside, Jean."

Benoit nodded and the two men walked toward the door, neither saying a word until they were out on the street. They ambled toward the plaza.

"For the last several days Crespin has been flashing around a lot of paper money," Ortiz said. "You don't get paper money trading with the Comanches and other savages."

Benoit nodded. "That's not all, the watch—it watch belonged to Jace. But how do we get him to admit where he got it?"

"That's easy," Ortiz replied. "We threaten to kill him."

After supper and the babies had been put to bed, Benoit told Inge that he was going out and would not be back until well after midnight or later. Midnight, Ortiz, had said, was the time that Crespin normally left the saloon each night. They would accost him and find out where he got the greenbacks.

Ortiz was waiting outside when he left his house. "Crespin is at La Estrella," he said. "He's been spending a lot of paper money at the gambling table." They both guessed he might be involved in the disappearance of the paymaster.

"Bastard," Benoit said.

"I owe him a lot for what he did to me. I've had to be patient, but now the moment has arrived."

"We can't kill him. We need him to answer our questions, maybe even lead us to where we can find the troops and at least bury them."

At La Estrella, Ortiz left Benoit outside while he went in. Moments later he returned. "The bastard's still in there. We'll get him when he comes out."

The two men leaned up against the adobe wall of the building on the opposite side of the street. An hour later, as midnight approached, Ortiz slipped across the street and positioned himself just down from the door. Benoit watched carefully as each man exited. Shortly after midnight the door opened and Benoit recognized the profile of Eduardo Crespin in his red serape.

Crespin stepped out to the street, and Ortiz moved out in front of him. The Comanchero must have recognized Ortiz for he spun around and dashed down the street in Benoit's direction. Benoit ran too, blocking Crespin's escape, then lunged for his legs and knocked him to the ground.

The Comanchero thrashed at Benoit and yelled for help until Ortiz fell upon him. Benoit saw Ortiz loop a leather thong around Crespin's neck and begin to twist it. As it tightened, the Comanchero's cries for help became gurgles.

Benoit bounced up, then searched Crespin for weapons, taking a knife and pistol from his belt. Then he yanked Crespin to his feet. The two men escorted the captive down the street.

Ortiz finally loosened the garrote enough for Crespin to catch his breath. "Scream again, and you'll choke you to death."

Crespin gasped and nodded his head rapidly to make sure that Ortiz knew he understood.

"We will go to my adobe," Ortiz said, working the garrote like a bridle to steer Crespin down the streets.

Finally, Ortiz turned him toward a solitary adobe home that was bigger than the typical Santa Fe house. Ortiz pushed open the door and shoved Crespin inside. Benoit stepped in and quickly shut the door behind him. Though the room was lit only by the embers in the corner fireplace and by two candles on a table beneath a crucifix hanging in the corner, it was light enough to see the terror in Crespin's eyes.

"Throw some wood on the fire, Jean. I expect we may need a good fire before we're done tonight."

Ortiz tightened the leather thong around Crespin's neck. "Now when I release this, you better start talking."

Benoit added the wood to the fire and soon it blazed up, casting sinister shadows on the walls. When Benoit moved back to the captive, he slipped his hand under Crespin's serape and extracted Dobbs's watch.

"Where'd you get this?"

Crespin shrugged.

Ortiz twisted the strap and the Comanchero's knees buckled. Ortiz loosened the strangle strap.

Crespin gasped for breath. "I found it! I found it!"

"Liar," Ortiz said, and squeezed tighter.

Crespin tried to cry out, but a twist of Ortiz's wrist strangled his words.

"Where'd you get the paper money?" Benoit demanded.

Ortiz loosened the garrote.

Crespin coughed and sputtered, taking short, hurried breaths.

"We'll be here all night and all day and all week if that's what it takes to get answers, Crespin," Ortiz said.

The Comanchero nodded. "I found the money," he said.

Ortiz tightened the noose, then turned to Benoit. "Hold this."

Benoit was enraged that this man had taken Jace's watch and perhaps even his life. He gave the leather strand an extra twist. The Comanchero fell to his knees, his eyes bulging as if they were trying to draw a breath. Benoit watched Ortiz stick a metal poker in the fire. Benoit loosened the garrote so Crespin could breathe.

The Comanchero's hands flew to his neck as he tried to slip his fingers beneath the leather thongs. Benoit twisted the leather until Crespin dropped his hands, then loosened the noose again. Ortiz returned holding a poker. He brandished the red-hot tip of it not six inches from Crespin's nose.

"The money," Ortiz demanded.

"I found it."

"The watch," Ortiz growled.

"I found it."

Ortiz nodded, then touched the poker to Crespin's nose.

The Comanchero screamed and threw himself on the floor, yanking the choke strap from Benoit's hands as he thrashed in pain.

Ortiz stepped over him on his way back to the fireplace. "Next I'll get an eye. If I don't get the answer, then I'll get your other eye and you'll be blind as a bat."

Benoit bent to grab the garrote, just so Crespin wouldn't forget about it. Ortiz stabbed the poker into the fire until its tip was glowing again. He stepped back to Crespin, who still lay moaning on the floor. Ortiz lowered the tip until the glowing metal was but an inch from his left eye. "Where'd you get the money?"

Crespin didn't answer.

Ortiz touched the tip to his eye.

Crespin screamed, then rolled away. "From the Comanches."

"And the watch?" Ortiz demanded.

"From a soldier captured by the Comanches."

"How many soldiers were there?"

"Just the one, just the one," Crespin gasped, squinting through one eye now.

Benoit yanked the loop over the Comanchero's head. "What happened to the other soldiers?" he demanded.

"I don't know."

"Where are these Comanches?"

"I trade with them in Quitaque Creek, but they stay much of the year in the canyon of the Palo Duro."

Ortiz tossed the metal poker on the floor by the fireplace. "Bind him," he said to Benoit.

"Now we can take him to the general and get a troop of cavalry to save Jace."

"If he lives through the night," Ortiz said.

"No, Alejo, he's the only chance I've got to save Jace."

"Then let's take him now. He's already lost one eye, and I'd hate for something else to happen to him before he got a chance to talk to the general."

Ortiz looped the garrote back over Crespin's neck and pulled him up to a standing position. Together, Benoit and Ortiz steered him out onto the street and down to the plaza, then turned toward the headquarters and General Smedley's quarters.

He rapped on the door. "General Smedley, General Smedley."

"Who is it?" came Smedley's muffled reply.

"It's Jean Benoit. I've got some news about the paymaster."

The door opened. "Come in," Smedley said, then saw Crespin and Ortiz. "What's this?"

"Alejo Ortiz, a local merchant, and Eduardo Crespin, a vile Comanchero."

"What's this got to do with the paymaster, Captain?"

"Crespin's been gambling with a lot of paper money," Ortiz said.

Smedley's eyes broadened.

"And I found this on him," Benoit said, holding up the watch. "It's Dobbs's timepiece."

"The one with that infernal alarm?"

Benoit nodded. "He says that Jason Dobbs survived and is a captive of the Comanches in Palo Duro Canyon. I'm requesting permission, sir, to lead troops to find him."

Smedley hesitated.

"Please," Benoit begged.

Ortiz pushed Crespin forward. The Comanchero had one eye shut tight, and was squinting through the other one. "Eduardo has promised to lead us to their camp."

"I'll get Tim McManus to scout for us," Benoit said.

The general pinched the bridge of his nose.

"We'll search Crespin place for any of the missing money," Benoit begged.

Smedley nodded. "Go ahead then, and let me know if you find any more money. I will proceed to write out the orders for this expedition. We cannot spare men from Fort Marcy so I will send a messenger to Fort Union tonight with word for them to be ready to ride day after tomorrow. It will be your duty to get to Fort Union tomorrow and leave with them."

"Yes, sir!" Benoit saluted.

After only a couple hours sleep and a hard day's ride, Benoit reached Fort Union, accompanied by Alejo Ortiz and the scout Tim McManus, both of whom had come voluntarily, and by the Comanchero Crespin, who had not. They had found more than four thousand dollars in Crespin's adobe and turned it over to Sergeant Hamilton Phipps.

Benoit had found McManus drunk in La Estrella, but somehow managed to get him to understand the Army needed him. He was an excellent scout when sober, and a good one even when drunk.

At Fort Union they were met by Second Lieutenant Sean O'Hara, from Dayton, Ohio. O'Hara was thin as a toothpick and didn't look like he'd put on an ounce of weight since Benoit had met him when he first passed through Fort Union a year earlier. His hair was reddish-blond and his face was covered with freckles. They were joined by Lieutenant Gerald Hapworth, who made a habit out of quoting Shakespeare.

Benoit explained his odd company and that the Comanchero was being brought along to find the camp where Jason Dobbs was being held. The soldiers agreed to manacle Eduardo Crespin each night. The Comanchero was surly, but his bravado lessened when they put the chains on him and when Alejo Ortiz threatened to put out his other eye if he tried to escape.

O'Hara reported that he and Lieutenant Hapworth would have a hundred men to accompany them into the Comanche country of Texas. The soldiers had been issued rations and ammunition and would be ready to ride out at dawn the next day.

Based upon the rudimentary maps of the Comanche country, O'Hara estimated they were as far as 250 miles from the canyon of the Palo Duro. It would take five days, maybe more.

The men retired early and awoke even earlier. Benoit ordered McManus and Ortiz to get Crespin fed and mounted, while he checked with O'Hara and

Hapworth, two solid junior officers who had the respect of their men. Benoit was pleased to be in command of fine soldiers like these junior officers and the men under them.

When the sun cracked the eastern horizon, the cavalrymen were ready to ride. Benoit gave the command and word was passed down the line; chills went up his spine. He could not remember ever feeling prouder than that moment when he led the soldiers away from Fort Union and toward Texas. It wasn't just the thought of leading good men, but the knowledge that he was leading an expedition to rescue his friend. He just hoped he wasn't too late.

Benoit led the way with McManus at his side. Then came Hapworth and O'Hara, followed by Ortiz and Crespin, and then the rest of the men, two abreast, all heading east by southeast toward Texas.

"Ever been to Texas, Cap'n?" McManus asked.

Benoit shook his head. "Funny thing, being from Louisiana, but I've never set foot in Texas."

"I been there many a time, and it's a fine state long as ya ain't visitin' any 'manches. They're mean ones."

"They meaner than Apaches?"

"Don't know I'd say that, but they're better warriors, especially on horseback. Ya won't find any better riders anywhere than them. Once we reach Texas, we'll be wary."

The soldiers came to the Texas border the evening of the third day. Benoit examined the maps with McManus, O'Hara, and Hapworth while Ortiz kept watch over Crespin. Benoit planned to approach the canyon at its head and work southward in hopes of finding the camp.

In two days they reached the head of the canyon and then started down, moving cautiously through the land. At first it was a gentle depression like an elongated earthen bowl that followed a small creek, but as they moved farther along the creek, the walls grew steep until the canyon spread out before them like a cathedral without a roof. The layered walls were a palate of reds, yellows, browns, grays, and oranges like opaque stained-glass windows.

The canyon eventually broadened far from the creek. It was dotted with buttes and miniature mesas that could provide cover for an Indian camp, but also screened the troop's movements. The landscape also provided vantage points from which the enemy could observe the approaching soldiers.

McManus ranged far ahead of the troops, looking for signs that would indicate the village. He saw signs of past camps, but nothing current. For two days he saw little, but on the morning of the third day in the canyon, he rode back to Benoit with a smile on his face.

"Cap'n, I foun' 'em." He grinned. "There's sixty lodges, maybe three hundred 'manches, countin' women and children. They're about a mile down the canyon and they don't seem worried, no guards other than those around the herd, which is downstream from the camp."

"Did you see Jace?"

"Can't say as I did for certain, though there was one man that had a funny gait about him."

Benoit frowned. Had Dobbs been hurt?

"Ya think we ought to parley with 'em or just attack, Cap'n?"

Benoit was uncertain. He motioned for the column to halt, then signaled for Hapworth and O'Hara to join him.

"McManus has found the Indian camp," he told them. "My plan is to attack. I know of no reason to bargain with them. I fear they attacked the paymaster and his men and killed most of them. Any objections?"

Hapworth shrugged. "I joined the army to fight Indians, not debate them."

Benoit saw Ortiz ride up, leading Crespin's horse by the reins. "You found the Comanche?"

Benoit nodded. "A mile down the canyon."

"What are we gonna do with Crespin?"

"You keep him here. We can't risk taking him any closer. He might alert the Comanches."

Ortiz smiled broadly. "I was hoping you'd say that."

Crespin shook his head. "No, no."

"You had the Comanches attack me, didn't you?" Ortiz ripped off his hat. "You're the one that caused me to look like this."

O'Hara and Hapworth looked away, having never before seen Ortiz full in the face.

"No, no!" Crespin cried.

"Keep him quiet," Benoit commanded.

Ortiz drew his pistol and whacked Crespin across the head. "Damn you, you one-eyed bastard."

Benoit turned to his two lieutenants. "Gentlemen, tell your men to draw their arms and check their loads. We're gonna raid the Comanche camp and see if we find any of our soldiers."

"Yes, sir," both answered in unison.

"We'll spread out in a broad line and sweep down upon them. Kill any warriors you can, and if you see any captives—not only soldiers, but also stolen children—grab them and let's take them with us. Once we get the captives, we'll retreat, then make a defensive stand if they counterattack."

The two junior officers rode back along the line issuing their orders softly. A chorus of metallic clicks told Benoit that his men had pulled their guns. Benoit lifted the flap on his holster and pulled his revolver, checking the cap and ball loads. Looking back behind him, he saw the men fanning out amidst the scattered brush.

"Don't fire until I fire or they fire upon us," he called. "Pass it on."

He heard the order being repeated down the line. Then he waved his gun toward the village and the long line of a hundred cavalrymen advanced down the canyon.

They moved slowly, and Benoit thought the village would never appear. Finally, he spotted wisps of smoke from their fires and the tops of their tipis through the brush.

The camp seemed oblivious to their approach.

Then, behind him Benoit heard a distant shout, followed by a scream.

It was Crespin. He must have tried to warn the Comanches.

The scream was followed by one, two, three, four shots that seemed to echo off the canyon walls. Benoit knew then the guard had shot Crespin.

Benoit instantly heard cries from the village. "Charge!" he yelled, and bolted forward as the thunder of calvary horses roared through the brush and toward the village.

Jason Dobbs was gathering firewood by the creek when he heard the distant shout, then shots, and then the rumble of charging horses. He threw down the wood he had gathered and started limping as quickly as he could toward the northern end of the camp.

Was it cavalry or was it a warring tribe?

Dobbs stumbled ahead, hoping his prayers had been answered. He caught sight of the first horseman approaching the village. He wore a blue uniform, and Dobbs shouted with glee. It was the cavalry. He was saved, if only they didn't shoot him.

He moved as fast as he could, but he could not run, not with his Achilles tendon cut. As he saw blurs of blue soldiers dashing through the camp, he raised his hands above his head and started waving at them.

"First Lieutenant Jason Dobbs!" he cried. "United States Army!"

A soldier rode almost out of nowhere, his pistol leveled at him.

"Don't shoot, don't shoot!" he cried. "I'm cavalry!"

The soldier yanked up his pistol and reined in his steed. "Hop on behind me and let's get out of here."

Dobbs grabbed the saddle as the soldier clenched his arm. He jumped, and the soldier pulled him atop his mount's rump.

"Jason Dobbs is my name!" he cried.

The soldier nodded. "You're the one we came for. I'll get you back to our defensive position."

The soldier reined the horse around and galloped back to the spot where the charge had begun. He halted beside a mounted civilian holding the reins to a second horse, at the foot of which was a dead man wearing a red serape.

Dobbs eased off the horse and looked at the body, then up at Alejo Ortiz. "It's the damned Comanchero that stole my watch."

"You owe him your life," Ortiz said. "Jean Benoit recognized your watch and convinced the general to send troops."

Dobbs laughed. "I should've known Jean wouldn't let me down, that glorious Louisiana son of a bitch." Dobbs limped to Crespin's horse and pulled himself up on it. "Can one of you spare a gun? I want to kill some of those Indians if I get a chance."

Crow Feather heard the distant shots and then the rumble of the charging horses. He grabbed his new carbine with the strong medicine and bolted from the tipi, knocking Paints the Dead down as he emerged. At the northern edge of the camp he saw a line of soldiers charging in. Glancing over his shoulder, he saw Paints the Dead and Stone Flower outside the tipi.

"Stay with your mother," he cried, then ran to meet the charging soldiers. He fired, as other Comanches were firing, but they were unprepared for so many soldiers, so suddenly.

"Fight, my warriors, fight!" Crow Feather screamed, firing as fast as he could load the carbine.

The soldiers were soon within the camp, shooting not only at the warriors, but at women and children as well. The shots echoed off the canyon until it seemed like a thousand guns were firing.

Crow Feather spun about and saw a soldier riding toward his lodge. He fired and winged the soldier, who yanked his reins and charged his animal straight for him. The animal bore down upon Crow Feather before he could reload his carbine.

Just as the horse was upon him, the warrior jumped aside and the animal rushed by. Crow Feather ran back to his lodge. Paints the Dead realized why he was retreating, because the boy was waiting just outside the lodge with his arrows and bow.

"Take your mother and sister and run for the creek!" Crow Feather cried. "Hide until they are gone."

Crow Feather darted away to fight, hoping with every step that his family would survive.

Paints the Dead shouted at Weasel and Stone Flower. "Come with me, quick to the creek! We can hide!"

Weasel grabbed a buffalo bladder full of water and a pouch with dried buffalo meat inside. Stone Flower grabbed the doll that Paints the Dead had made for her, then hung on to Weasel's skirt.

"Hurry!" Paints the Dead cried. "We must run!"

He jumped outside, then waited for Weasel to squeeze through. He grabbed Stone Flower's hand and pulled her out.

Like jackrabbits they darted from tipi to tipi, dodging the melee of dust and smoke and shots and shouts and galloping horsemen. With every breath, they inhaled clouds of gun smoke.

A soldier rode by, shooting at Paints the Dead. He dodged and knocked Stone Flower to the ground, then shielded her for a moment until he could get up. His hand fell to his belt and he grabbed the knife Crow Feather had given him. Paints the Dead jumped up and ran again.

Then from nowhere came another soldier, galloping down upon them. The soldier fired and Stone Flower dropped like a rock. Paints the Dead tried to help. He shook her, but she didn't open her eyes.

Weasel swooped by, scooped the girl up in her arms, and continued running toward the creek.

Paints the Dead, spun around and charged after the soldier, brandishing his knife over his head. He could not catch the mounted man, but he saw a pistol on the ground, dropped his knife, and grabbed the gun. He pointed the weapon at a cavalryman who dashed by and pulled the trigger. The gun exploded with such a recoil that his childish arm swung up in the air, and he flung the gun over his head.

Seeing a cavalryman aiming at him, he fell to the ground and grabbed his knife again as the bullet flew over him. Then Paints the Dead ran toward a log where he saw a Comanche warrior firing his rifle at the attacking soldiers. Jumping over the log, he fell against the warrior.

The warrior shoved him away, and Paints the Dead recognized Speaks Loudly, the one who had killed Willow Leaf. The one who was always mean. The one Paints the Dead hated.

He slid away from Speaks Loudly, then realized he would never have a better chance to kill this terrible man. As Speaks Loudly reloaded his carbine, Paints the Dead studied his rib cage. When Speaks Loudly finished his load and propped his arm on the log to steady his aim, he exposed his ribs.

Paints the Dead charged him then, drew his knife back and swung it forward so it would penetrate the rib cage with all his momentum. The knife caught in between Speaks Loudly's ribs, and Paints the Dead flipped over on his back.

Speaks Loudly groaned, touched his side, and brought his bloody hand to his face as he looked at Paints the Dead. He had the same questioning look that Paints the Dead remembered Willow Leaf had as he bled to death.

Speaks Loudly grabbed for Paints the Dead, but the boy dodged his grasp. He jumped over him, yanked the knife from his side, and drew the sharp blade across the side of Speaks Loudly's neck. The warrior screamed and tried to grab Paints the Dead, but he missed.

A rider galloped by, leaned over in the saddle, and snatched Paints the Dead from the ground, pulling him up in the saddle.

Paints the Dead tried to twist around to stab the soldier, but his knife fell from his hand as the soldier galloped out of camp, carrying him away.

Paints the Dead screamed for help. He did not want to be ripped from his new family as he had been cut from his birth family. But the rider was strong and the boy could not fight him.

At least not at the moment.

Benoit had the bugler sound retreat, and the soldiers fought their way out of the camp and back toward the spot where they would make a defensive stand if the Comanches counterattacked.

Benoit glanced over his shoulder and saw that most of the soldiers had retreated. He raced to join them.

"Jean, Jean!" a familiar voice cried the moment he arrived.

Benoit spun around and saw that Jace had been saved. He shouted with pleasure. "Damn, it's good to see you."

All around him, soldiers returned, dismounting and tying their horses, then aiming their carbines toward the village in readiness.

Lieutenant Hapworth dashed up, holding a captured child. "Take him, take him!" he cried. "He killed one of the warriors, knifed him. He must be Mexican."

Two soldiers took the struggling boy, and as soon as they did, Hapworth slumped forward over the neck of his horse.

Only then did Benoit see the arrow in Hapworth's back. Two more soldiers grabbed him, eased him off the saddle, and laid him on his side. Hapworth looked up and grimaced. "A man can die but once," he said. Then his eyelids closed and he died.

Benoit ordered a count. One other soldier had been killed and eleven had been wounded. But they were not yet out of danger; the Comanches could still attack them.

After waiting for an hour, Benoit concluded the Comanches would not attack. He ordered the soldiers to load up the wounded and retreat up the canyon to make a camp for the night.

Crow Feather saw the soldier gallop by and grab Paints the Dead.

"Stop!" he cried.

Paints the Dead struggled against the soldier.

Crow Feather yanked an arrow from his quiver and notched the bow. He pulled back and aimed for the soldier stealing his son.

He released the arrow.

It flew straight and true, hitting the soldier in the back, but the man rode on.

All around, other soldiers were retreating. Several fired at him as they rode by, but he stood steadfast, watching the one rider, hoping he would fall from his horse.

But instead the soldier remained on his mount, as if he had not been hurt by the arrow.

Crow Feather cried out his anguish with a scream.

The attack had been sudden, and his son was stolen. Now he could only hope that Weasel and Stone Feather had survived.

He watched, hoping he might see his son running out of the brush, back toward him.

Then he saw the last soldier disappear in the distance, and still he stood watching, hoping that Paints the Dead might return.

"Paints the Dead!" he cried.

Only the sobs of women in the village answered his cry.

"Come back, my son!"

It was as he feared. Paints the Dead would not return. He had lost his son.

Then, Crow Feather wept.

11

Paints the Dead hated his captors. One man with a horribly burned face had spoken to him in Spanish, asking him where his home was and how long he'd been a captive. Paints the Dead had stared sullenly at him, refusing to respond.

As the soldiers awaited a possible attack by the Comanches, Paints the Dead studied them, trying to spot the one who had shot Stone Flower. If he found that soldier, he hoped to kill him as he had Speaks Loudly.

Occasionally one of the soldiers would offer him food or water, but he refused their entreaties, vowing to himself to take no handouts from men who would shoot at women and children.

He sat defiant and proud, knowing that the arrow that had been taken from his captor's back was one of Crow Feather's. His new father had tried to save him. That knowledge made his lip tremble. He wanted to be with Crow Feather and Weasel, and to see that Stone Flower was buried. He would avenge her death a thousand times.

For an hour Paints the Dead waited with the soldiers, who expected an attack. When the Comanche attack did not come, the soldiers mounted their horses. The disfigured man loaded Paints the Dead on the back of his horse and rode at the head of the procession. Paints the Dead knew it would be foolish to try to escape in the daylight, but he planned to slip away after dark.

The soldiers rode up the canyon until dusk, then made a cold camp. The disfigured one offered Paints the Dead some jerked beef, but he refused it. He did accept a blanket from one of the men for bedding, wrapped himself in it and waited for the darkness of night, carefully observing where the soldiers picketed their horses and where they posted guards.

After midnight, when the camp was silent, save for the snoring of the soldiers, he squirmed on his belly through the exhausted men until he reached a picket line of horses.

He spoke softly to one animal, trying to calm it so that it would not make noise. Carefully, he untied the rope and backed the horse away from the picket line.

The horse stamped and blew, whinnied. Holding the tether line to the halter, he jumped up and threw his hands over the back of the animal, then pulled himself aboard.

"Halt!" came a cry from a guard. "Who is it?"

Paints the Dead leaned forward over the horse's neck. He shook the tether rope that would serve as reins and the horse moved away from the others.

He heard running footsteps and a commotion in the camp as men jumped up and reached for their weapons.

Paints the Dead spun the horse around, then kicked its flanks with his heels. The animal darted forward. All around him horses jumped and pulled at their picket lines. He heard charging footsteps drawing nearer, as if angling to cut off his escape.

He was bent low over his mount's neck when he heard the retort of a pistol so close that the flash of the powder lit up the face of his attacker. Paints the Dead wished he had a weapon. He screamed, trying to imitate the sound of a Comanche warrior, but his scream sounded more childish than threatening. He raced away from the camp as other bullets whizzed overhead.

And then it was over, he was beyond the range of their guns, and he sat up straight on the horse's back, riding easily back downstream. He halted his mount to listen for any soldiers who might be following him. For a moment he could barely hear above his own heavy breathing. Then all he detected was silence. The cavalry were not following.

Relieved, he turned his mount toward the lodge of his father, but had ridden only a mile farther when his horse turned fidgety. Then two riders fell in beside him. Where had they come from? For a moment he was terrified, then he heard the voice of Owl Eyes.

"Is that Paints the Dead?"

"Yes," he said, "I am returning to my father."

"It is Owl Eyes and Gives Gifts," the warrior replied. "We are shadowing the bluecoats to fight them if they return."

"They are leaving and will not attack again."

"Your father will be happy to see you," Gives Gifts said. "You have become the son Weasel could never provide. He will be honored that you have returned to your Comanche family."

Paints the Dead felt pride welling up in him like the tears in his eyes. He only wished that Stone Flower would be around to be Weasel's daughter.

Owl Eyes peeled away from the two, and Gives Gifts escorted Paints the Dead back to the village. There, he heard the sobbing and wailing of families mourning their dead.

"How many did the bluecoats kill?" he asked.

"Eight," Gives Gifts replied. "Twenty-three were wounded and some of them may die."

Reaching Crow Feather's tent, Paints the Dead dismounted and tossed the tether line to Gives Gifts. His parents must be asleep, he thought, because they were not mourning the loss of Stone Flower.

"Crow Feather," Gives Gifts called, "you have a visitor returned to see you."

In a moment the flap of the tipi was flung open and Crow Feather emerged, staring up at Gives Gifts but missing Paints the Dead.

"It is me, Father," Paints the Dead said. "I have returned.

Crow Feather shouted, then scooped Paints the Dead up in his arms and carried him inside. "Weasel," he cried, "our son has come back!"

"Now our family is complete," she answered, sitting beside her bedding.

"But what about Stone Flower?" Paints the Dead asked. "Don't you mourn her?"

"No," Weasel said.

As if by magic the buffalo robe beside her sat up, then fell away from Stone Flower, her head badly bruised with a scabbed slash across the side above her left ear.

Paints the Dead squirmed out of Crow Feather's grasp. "You're alive!" he cried in disbelief.

Stone Flower smiled, then held up the crude doll he had made her. "So is my doll."

"The bullet grazed her scalp," said Weasel.

"Now that our family is whole again," Crow Feather

stated, "I vow never again to let our villages be attacked. The prairies will run red with the blood of the white man and his bluecoat warriors."

Paints the Dead lifted his fist in the air. "And I shall become a great warrior."

"And you shall become a great warrior," Crow Feather said. "My vision has been fulfilled."

The morning after the excitement, Jean Benoit took count, and all his men were accounted for, though one horse was missing. He surmised that a Comanche had slipped into camp and stolen the horse, until Alejo Ortiz reported that the captive boy was missing.

"It was him," Ortiz said. "He seemed sullen that we had taken him. He refused all offers of food and water."

"The Comanche can take hold of a boy's imagination," Tim McManus said, "'cause it's a life of adventure compared to the farming life of most Mexicans. If we went after him, he'd just escape again."

As they discussed what to do about the boy, Jason Dobbs limped up. Although Benoit had seen him yesterday after the raid, it was only briefly and on horseback. Now, as Dobbs walked, Benoit grimaced. His friend lifted his right leg higher than normal, then let it fall to the ground before moving with his left leg.

"I won't be winning any footraces anymore," Dobbs said.

"What happened?"

"The Comanches cut my Achilles tendon so I wouldn't escape."

"What about the others?"

"They were all massacred. The great sandstorm

blew us off course, and the mule with the money got away. We followed him all the way to the Pecos, recovering him just before the Comanches attacked."

"How'd you survive?"

"My watch. The alarm went off and they thought I had magic."

"Then your watch saved you twice."

Dobbs nodded. "From what Ortiz said, it was what tipped you off that I might be alive with the Comanches."

"Yes, sir. Thanks to Ortiz, I saw it in Crespin's possession."

"The bastard took it from me, and I feared the Comanches would think I'd lost my magic. I'm glad you came when you did. They ultimately would've killed me."

"I still owe you two, Jace, for saving my family."

Dobbs smiled. "The debt's paid in full, Jean."

"It'll never be paid in full," Benoit answered.

Benoit then passed the order for the men to mount up, and they started back to Fort Union, taking six days to reach the post. He reported to the post commander about the expedition and the losses, then rode with Dobbs, Ortiz, and McManus to Santa Fe.

General Arnold Smedley greeted Jean Benoit and Jason Dobbs in his office. "Welcome back from the dead, Lieutenant Dobbs."

"Thank you, sir."

Smedley motioned for the men to take a seat, and watched Dobbs as he moved awkwardly to a chair. "Now, Lieutenant Dobbs," he said, "tell me what happened to the paymaster."

Dobbs nodded and began the story, telling of the sandstorm, the mule that got away with the money, and the Comanche ambush.

"What about the Comanchero and how he got the cash?"

"The money is of no value to the Comanches. I tried to keep it because I thought I might be able to buy my way out of captivity, but when I tried, the Comanchero Crespin realized he could take the money without me. I was glad to see his body after the fight."

Smedley turned to Benoit. "Now tell me about the fight."

Benoit related all the details he could remember, including the escape of the captive Mexican boy. He reported on the deaths and injuries.

"Very well," Smedley said. "I believe I can wait for any other details until you complete your written report. As for you, Lieutenant Dobbs, I will provide an escort for you to Fort Bliss."

"Thank you, General, but one request."

"What's that?"

"Send me with someone that doesn't mind talking. The paymaster and his men were about as dour a group as I've ever ridden with, and that includes the Comanches."

Smedley laughed. "I'll see what I can do."

Benoit and Dobbs stood up and saluted, then turned for the door. As they stepped outside, Smedley called for Benoit.

"Captain, just a word with you."

Benoit lingered.

Smedley watched until Dobbs exited the office. "A man with such an infirmity can be a liability to the Army, Captain."

"But he's a doctor, sir, not a fighting man."

"True, but even so, he's a liability. I just want you to know so that you might prepare him for that possibility."

"Yes, sir."

"Day after tomorrow I'm sending a detachment of twenty-five men to Fort Fillmore. He should accompany them."

"I will speak with him, sir, but it's unfair, him getting crippled and the Army not caring to keep him."

"Life is unfair, Captain. You should know that from your encounters with Cle Couvillion. All the talk in the world won't change the Army or life."

"Yes, sir." Benoit saluted and retreated to find Dobbs.

When Jason Dobbs departed Santa Fe, Jean Benoit, Inge, and the two babies were there to see him off.

"Don't get lost this time," Benoit teased. "I don't know that I can spend all of my Army career getting you out of trouble."

Dobbs grinned. "Seems I recall patching you up after a number of scrapes."

Benoit shook his hand. "Best of luck to you, Jace. I hope our careers cross again somewhere down the line."

"A cripple like me, I might as well head home to New Hampshire."

"Don't talk like that," Inge interrupted. "You've meant too much to me and the girls, Jace, for us to even think about that." Inge leaned over and kissed him on the cheek, then handed him Ellen.

"You're a fine girl, Ellen, just like your sister," Dobbs said. "I'll miss the whole lot of you." He kissed her on the forehead and tickled her belly. The baby laughed.

He gave the girl back to her mother, then took Colleen from Benoit. "I'll be missing you, too, Colleen." He lifted her and kissed her on the head, but Colleen struggled to get away from him. "So, you don't want your Uncle Jace to mess up your curly hair, is it?" He tickled her stomach and drew a giggle. Then he handed her back to her father. "Next time I see them, they'll be walking and talking and carrying on like they run the whole U.S. Army. And they'll have their father wrapped even tighter around their fingers."

"I won't argue with that," Benoit replied. "I didn't know how great girls could be."

"Well, sir, life handed you a pair of queens in those two, and I wouldn't change a thing about them, especially their names. They'll always mean a lot to me, knowing that you cared that much."

"It was Inge's idea," Benoit said.

"Thank you, thank you both. I'll write when I get settled at Fort Bliss. Come visit me sometime."

"We may just do that."

Dobbs snapped to full attention and saluted his friend. Benoit returned the salute as precisely as he could with Colleen in his arm.

Then Dobbs turned away and limped to his horse. He mounted awkwardly, twisted in the saddle, and tipped his hat. Shortly, the command was given to proceed, and Jason Dobbs rode down the street with the other cavalrymen. They turned a corner and one by one disappeared from sight.

Benoit stood silently watching the empty street, and wondered if he would ever see his good friend again.

Inge slipped her arm through his. "I'm sorry you must see him go."

Benoit nodded. "I'm worried that the Army will release him and it will devastate him."

"Surely, the Army wouldn't do that. Would it?"

"General Smedley thinks so."

"Oh, Jean, I am so sorry to hear that."

"It's odd, isn't it?"

"What?"

"About Jace and Erich. Both lame, and no prospects of getting better."

Over the next three weeks, Jean Benoit enjoyed the time with his wife and daughters. A lot of things entered his mind that he would never have considered before their births. Was it best to maintain a career in the Army, or would it be better to quit and begin a new life that was more conducive to supporting his family? There were certainly many opportunities available in New Orleans that would make life much more comfortable for his girls.

He pondered the questions each day after he had completed his paperwork at his office and returned home for the true joyous time with his wife and daughters.

One evening, just before dark, when Inge and Benoit were feeding their daughters, there came a rap upon the door. When Benoit opened it, he was pleased to see the archbishop.

"Father Machebeuf," he said, "what a pleasant surprise. Won't you come in?"

Machebeuf nodded. "Why, yes, thank you."

The priest came inside and immediately went to Inge. "My, how your girls have grown since I accompanied them to Chimayo."

"Have you heard any news, Father, about Erich?"

"Not a word, though I have had a missive from Father Candid Zavala. He has requested to have dinner with me tomorrow night to discuss Erich's situation."

Benoit shook his head. "I take it things are not good for Erich."

"Father Zavala did not say otherwise, and given his passion for miracles, I feel certain he would have acknowledged any change in Erich's condition."

Benoit saw a tear trail down Inge's cheek.

"Father Zavala, bless his Christian heart, believes in miracles, and I so want to believe with him that God has bestowed upon that site great powers to serve the people in need, but it must be confirmed.

"The letter was unclear, and it may be that he is bringing Erich back with him. I do not know, but I think it would be beneficial to Erich, if he does come, for you to be there to show your concern. And if he does not come, you can at least hear of matters from Father Zavala himself."

"We should be glad to join you for dinner," Benoit answered.

"Please arrive by seven o'clock."

Father Machebeuf turned around and walked to the door. "I wish I had more hope for Erich," he said.

The priest let himself out, then Inge began to cry.

Benoit patted her shoulder. "We have done all we can for him."

"But who will care for him? I am tired just caring for two babies, and now to have to change and wash him will wear me out." She began to sob. "He's my brother. I should want to do it, but it wears on me, Jean, day after day, and my spirits fall. I have so enjoyed his absence with just you, me, and the girls. I've finally felt happy again."

"It's okay, Inge. We'll do something. Maybe it's time for me to get out of the Army. We can make a home in New Orleans. I can make a good living there so we can hire someone to care for him."

"No, I don't want you to give up what you've worked for, your rank especially."

"It was tainted by Couvillion months ago."

"Perhaps we should pray for a miracle," Inge said.

"We will work it out, Inge, somehow. Just don't lose faith."

"Faith in what?"

"Faith in me, Inge, your husband."

As Benoit reined up the rented buggy in front of Machebeuf's house, he nodded at Inge. "Are you up to this?"

She smiled. "I hope the girls don't fuss and embarrass us."

Benoit laughed. "Not them, not tonight."

He tied the reins and hopped out of the buggy. He took Ellen from Inge's hands, then helped his wife down with Colleen in her arms.

She caught her breath, as if prepared for the worst.

Benoit took her arm. "It will be okay." He knocked on the door, and Father Machebeuf soon answered.

"Welcome, welcome," he said. "I am glad you are here. Father Zavala has not yet arrived, though I hear he is in town."

Machebeuf ushered them in, complimenting the girls and escorting Inge and Benoit to seats. As soon as they were seated, he moved to a cabinet and removed a bottle of wine, pouring glasses for his guests and himself.

The aroma of roasting meat was strong and enticing.

Benoit knew that he would have another good meal. He had eaten with Machebeuf once before and enjoyed the delicacies provided by Senora Dominguez, his cuisiniere.

"Roast duck, is it?" Benoit asked.

"Why, yes," the priest replied. "I do hope Father Zavala arrives shortly, as timing is critical on duck. How did you know it was duck?"

"You forget I have French blood in my veins, though from New Orleans rather than France like yourself. Duck is a delicacy I remember pleasantly from my childhood."

They spoke casually for ten minutes before someone knocked on the door.

"Excellent," Machebeuf said, "if that is Father Zavala, the timing will work for the duck."

The priest moved to the door and opened it. "Father Zavala, welcome."

"I am sorry I am late, but I had to clean up from the ride so that I would be presentable."

"Come in, come in," he said, motioning for him to join them.

Zavala walked inside and removed his hat. He bowed to Inge and then Benoit.

"You remember Jean and Inge Benoit?" Machebeuf asked.

"Indeed. I have heard many good things about them from Erich, especially about Inge, who has looked after him as a mother takes care of a child."

"And how is Erich?" Inge asked.

"He is better, but perhaps we could discuss more at dinner."

"Certainly," Machebeuf answered.

"But would it be an imposition for me to invite someone else to join us? I know, Father Machebeuf, that

I did not request to have anyone else, but it was a last minute idea."

"Your guest is welcome. There is room and food enough."

Zavala stepped to the door and waved toward the street.

"I must alert Senora Dominguez to add another place," Machebeuf said.

Zavala lifted his hand. "No, Father, you should remain to greet your new guest."

"But of course," Machebeuf said, taken aback, and stepped toward the door.

Benoit heard the sound of an odd shuffling and a slight thump.

Then the form was in the door, stepping into the lamplight.

It was Erich.

He was standing, supported by crutches.

Inge screamed, startling the two babies, who started wailing.

Erich steadied himself, then offered his crutches to Father Zavala, who moved away from the door.

Erich then stepped awkwardly forward, his smile as wide as his step. He walked stiffly, first to Inge, bending and kissing her on the forehead as she sobbed, then to Benoit. He clasped Benoit's hand and shook it firmly.

"I can walk," he said.

"I see," Benoit answered.

Erich turned to Father Machebeuf, whose mouth was agape. "I believe in miracles, Father. Do you?"

Machebeuf dropped to his knees and clasped his hands in prayer. "Gracious heavenly Father, help me that my faith is as strong as the faith of the others in this room."

"I can walk, Inge, I can walk," Erich repeated. "I tire, yes, and must use the crutches some, but when I gain my strength, I will not require them."

"It is a miracle," Father Zavala said, "even if it has not been confirmed."

Machebeuf rose from the floor and retreated from the room. "I must inform Senora Dominguez that we will be having another guest for supper."

Erich moved awkwardly but determinedly toward a chair and lowered himself into it. "I haven't gotten my balance fully back," he apologized.

Inge couldn't stop crying. The two babies wailed as well, not understanding that their mother's tears were those of joy.

Inge cradled Colleen and Benoit rocked Ellen, trying to calm them.

Erich looked around the room and shook his head. "I did not mean to cause such commotion."

"Don't apologize, Erich," Inge stammered. "I am crying out of happiness. I cannot quit because I am so happy."

Erich smiled.

Father Machebeuf reentered the room. "We shall dine in five minutes," he said, then looked at Erich. "Miracle of miracles, my son, you can walk."

"Not far, but farther each day. By the end of summer I hope to be able to walk without crutches."

"And go back to the mountains as a scout?" Benoit asked.

Erich shook his head. "I have other ambitions now."

"I must write Mother as soon as I get back," Inge said. "She will be as happy as me. And now maybe Jim Ashby will quit blaming himself for your accident."

"It wasn't an accident, Inge, but God's plan," Erich said.

An elderly Hispanic woman entered the room and nodded to Father Machebeuf. He answered her with a smile. "*Gracias.*" The woman retreated. "Dinner is on the table," Machebeuf said, pointing to the dining room.

Everyone stared at Erich as he gingerly pushed himself from the chair and walked to the dining room.

"Please, Erich," Father Machebeuf said, "sit at the foot of the table where everyone can see you."

Erich moved to his seat, then waited for everyone else to claim a chair. They all sat down at the same time.

As Inge's crying softened, the two girls began to whimper.

Machebeuf bowed his head and offered thanks. "Dear God, we thank thee for the blessings you have seen fit to bestow upon us with this fine dinner and with the miracle you have worked in Erich's life. May all of your children find in their hearts the faith that has made this remarkable miracle possible. Amen."

Everyone around the table echoed, "Amen."

Machebeuf smiled. "Please, help yourself. There is roast duck and hominy and corn bread with syrup."

As his guests covered their plates, Machebeuf turned to Zavala. "Father, tell me of this miracle."

Zavala nodded and smiled. "It was Erich's faith. God challenged him with a terrible tragedy, and Erich answered the challenge. Even when his legs came back, they only came back gradually, the feeling, the control. He never lost faith."

Erich smiled. "It was Father Zavala who created the miracle."

"How so?" Machebeuf asked.

"I heard him praying for me for a solid half hour. Knowing that he would spend that much time for me and my faith strengthened my own faith."

The Chimayo priest interrupted. "But I have a confession to make, Father Machebeuf."

"What is that, Father Zavala?"

"I wasn't praying for the right reasons. I wanted this miracle so I could prove to you the value of my ministry. I have learned from it."

"And I," Erich said, "have learned the power of faith and the power of God. They can change a man and his outlook."

"That is profoundly stated," Machebeuf answered. "Many men spend lifetimes looking for answers in the wrong places instead of following God's guidance."

"My heart and my outlook have changed, for I truly know what my calling should be," Erich said. "I have decided to enter the priesthood."

Silence engulfed the table.

Benoit was shocked. He remembered Erich most from Wyoming, loving the outdoors, fighting Indians, learning the ways of the mountain man. It seemed impossible that this same man would now be set on becoming a priest.

Father Zavala was the first to speak. "There has been a transformation in Erich. He came to the Sanctuario de Chimayo broken of body and spirit. You have seen his body and how it is mending. What you cannot so well see is his spirit. But I know that his spirit is genuine."

Machebeuf nodded. "That he walks is a miracle, I admit, but of what you speak is the greater miracle."

"It is true, Father," Erich answered. "What happened was meant to be, for it is my destiny to humbly and obediently serve my God."

Benoit looked at Inge. She seemed as shocked as himself. There was no way to reconcile the former Erich with the current Erich. He was a long way from what Benoit had known or expected. He was happy his brother-in-law could walk, but he wondered at what price he had gotten back his legs.

Erich turned to his sister. "You look surprised."

Inge blushed. "I am. I just don't know what to say."

"Aren't you happy?"

"Yes, to see you walk, and Mother will be happy, too."

"But to hear of my desire to become a priest, Inge, what about that?"

"I am surprised," she managed. "It will take some time to get used to. I was worried that you would never be able to walk again, and to see that you can is shock enough, but to learn of your wish to become a priest, it is more than I expected."

Benoit broke in. "Erich, we are proud for you. Whatever work you desire is what we want for you."

"It is a long road to become a priest," Father Machebeuf said, "but if that is where God is leading you, then I will assist you along that road."

"As will I," Father Zavala said.

"You must first convert to Catholicism and learn the sacraments and the way of all Catholics to God."

Erich nodded. "I know that I have much to learn, but I am sincere. I have been clay that He has molded in my hands."

Machebeuf nodded. "We are all clay in His hands, my son."

After the meal, everyone toasted Erich with a glass of wine, and they talked about Erich and the road ahead for him.

When the the twins turned tired and fidgety, Inge said to her husband, "It is time for us to go."

Benoit arose and hugged Erich as he got wobbily to his feet. "I am proud of you, Erich."

"Thank you."

Inge kissed her brother's cheek.

"Let me kiss my nieces," he said, then leaned over and bussed each one.

Benoit shook Machebeuf's hand and thanked him for a wonderful dinner and a most unforgettable evening. "You said it was a matter of faith, Father. Do you believe in this miracle even though it hasn't been confirmed?"

Machebeuf nodded. "The physical miracle is not nearly so great as the spiritual miracle."

Benoit shrugged. "I am just glad he can walk."

"If he stays on the path to the priesthood, he will do more than walk. He will soar in the heavens, for all the good that he can do."

Benoit stepped to Father Zavala. "Thank you for what you did. You have changed his life."

Zavala smiled. "God changed him. I merely observed."

"Either way, thank you," Benoit said.

Benoit took Ellen from Erich and herded Inge to the door. She said nothing until they were loaded in the buggy and had begun to roll toward their home.

"That was a surprising dinner," Benoit said.

She grunted.

"How do you feel about it?"

"Like I have lost a brother," she said.

Benoit returned to his office the next day, distracted from his work by the recurring thought of Erich as a priest. A mail wagon arrived mid-morning, but he no longer awaited its arrival as anxiously as he had before Inge's appearance in Santa Fe. Though he expected his first letter from Jason Dobbs in a few days, his only other correspondents were his mother, brother, and sister, and they wrote infrequently now, and the damnable Cle Couvillion, who he didn't care to hear from again.

He spent the morning reviewing quartermaster reports on the feed remaining for the horses and on when new boots would be received for the men. It was boring work in contrast to the excitement of cavalry activity in the field. Of course, the eating was better with Inge available to make him lunch and dinner.

On his way out of the office, Sergeant Hamilton Phipps stopped him. "You got a letter, sir, from New Orleans."

Benoit snatched the letter from Phipps's hand, recognized his sister's handwriting and hurried out the door. Outside, he tore open the end and pulled out two sheets of paper. He read the first line silently, then feared for his mother. Then he read on and bit his lip.

Dear Jean,

This is the saddest letter I have ever had to write. Our beloved Theo is dead. I do not know many details but that we received a letter from Annapolis telling us that he was killed by an explosion of powder and shells during his final training exercise before he was to graduate.

Mama is devastated, as am I. To make matters even worse, they did not find the body, only his shoes. It seems he was blown into the ocean. No other students or crew were around at the time, so he was the only one to die and they still do not know what caused the explosion.

Mama is bewildered by it all and seems to have lost all her will to live. I am trying to boost her spirits but I don't know that that is possible.

If you would write, or better yet come home for a while, it might save her. Otherwise, I fear I will be writing you another letter shortly about her death.

I wish I had better news but I don't. I will let you know more as I find out.

Your loving sister,
Marion

Benoit closed his eyes to fight the tears. Now he knew what he must do. He would resign his commission and return to Louisiana.

12

Brigadier General Arnold Smedley read the letter of resignation then studied Captain Jean Benoit.

Benoit stood at attention before him, preferring to maintain the formality of military protocol.

"I am sorry about your brother, Captain, most sorry. If he was half the man you are, he would've been an asset to the Navy in these difficult times."

"Thank you, sir. That means a lot to me."

Smedley nodded, then held up the letter by the top two corners and slowly tore it in half.

"But, sir, that is my resignation."

"I'm not accepting it, Captain."

"Sir," Benoit pleaded, "my family needs me in New Orleans."

"Your family's needs and the Army's are two different things, Captain, so I will not accept your resignation."

"But sir—"

Smedley held up his hand for silence. Benoit stiffened.

"The Army needs good men, Captain, and your family needs you. I will not give up a good man for this reason alone. What I will do, Captain, is grant you a three-month leave, give you time to sort out your family's problems and consider if you want to end your Army career or return. After you have had a chance to move beyond your brother's death and your family's needs, then you can make a clear-headed decision. If at that point, you decide you want to leave the Army, then I will accept your resignation with regret, but not until then."

"Thank you, sir."

"As you know, Captain, it will take a couple of weeks to get this approved up line, but I will. So write your family and let them know you will be coming home shortly."

"Yes, sir."

"The advantage of you not resigning, Captain, is that I can arrange military transportation for you and your family from here to San Antonio."

"Thank you, sir."

"This will take you through El Paso, Captain. You should see Jason Dobbs when you pass through. It is unfortunate, but he will be relieved of duty at the end of the month."

"Damnation," Benoit said. "It's unfair. He's a good man."

"A good man who can't walk or run, Captain."

Benoit knew the general was right but he did not care to admit it.

"Perhaps this will take you out of reach of Cle Couvillion for a while, if not for good, Captain."

"That's a nice thought, sir, but nothing else has gotten me out of his reach. In some ways he may have even more influence with me in New Orleans."

When the wagon was loaded with their belongings and those Dobbs had left with them, Benoit nodded to the Army teamster and he climbed in the seat and drove toward the plaza where the cavalry escort was forming up.

Benoit stepped to Inge, who was saying her farewell to her brother. Erich balanced both of his nieces in his arms.

Benoit pointed to the Army ambulance that was awaiting him and his family. "It's time we started," he said.

Tears began to trickle down Inge's cheeks. She tried to hug Erich, but her two girls were in the way. She took Ellen from him and then kissed his cheek.

"I will miss you, Erich."

He smiled. "And I will miss my three girls."

"I'm glad you're walking again."

Erich smiled softly. "I am glad I now walk with God."

Benoit took Colleen from him. "You would've made a terrific scout and mountain man in Wyoming."

"I'll make a better priest."

Benoit saluted his brother-in-law. "Father Schmidt."

Erich seemed embarrassed. "I've much to learn before I become a priest."

"But you'll learn it and you'll do well."

"Thank you." Erich leaned over and kissed Colleen and Ellen, then he studied his sister. "Motherhood becomes you."

Inge began to sob. "I'm sorry, Erich, I'm sorry."

"For what, Inge, for what?"

"For resenting having to change your soiled pants and sheets."

He stepped to her and hugged her. "It's okay. It made me a better person, and never once did you show your resentment. You were always so kind and patient." He kissed her cheek. "Now you must be going."

Benoit put his arm on Inge's shoulder. "He is right, Inge, we must leave."

Inge nodded. "I will miss you."

Erich stepped away. "And I you." Then he turned away, taking his crutches from the adobe wall where he had leaned them. Without looking back, he started walking toward the church.

Benoit helped Inge into the ambulance, then handed her Colleen. In his last moment he glanced at Erich, who was barely using the crutches at all. He thought of the miracle of Erich's recovery and knew that his own brother could never recover.

He climbed in the wagon and drove toward the plaza, falling in line in the middle of the procession that started for El Paso.

As Benoit drove out of Santa Fe, he looked back over his shoulder a final time at the town. It was the place where he first saw his twin daughters and where he had met good men like Arnold Smedley and Frank Coker. It was a town where he had learned about the Hispanos. He wondered if he would ever return to Santa Fe or, once he reached New Orleans, if he would ever set foot in the West again.

Inge leaned against him and rested her head on his shoulder as her twins rested in her arms. "Are you sad?" she asked.

"Yes," Benoit answered. "I still don't believe Theo is dead."

"No," Inge responded, "not about that, because I know how you must feel. I mean about yourself. Are you sad to be leaving Santa Fe and possibly the Army?"

"Ask me in three months," he replied.

— —

Fort Bliss, Texas

After depositing Inge and the girls in temporary quarters, Jean Benoit followed directions to the post hospital. An orderly greeted him inside the building, which smelled of strong medicines and weak men.

"I'm looking for Dr. Dobbs," Benoit said.

"He's in his office," the orderly said, as if Benoit should know where it was.

"And where is that?"

The orderly pointed to the ward where a dozen beds were lined up on either side of the center aisle. "Door at the end of the ward."

Benoit turned and strode between the beds and the half-dozen men occupying them. He knocked on the door, then opened it up without waiting for an answer. As he walked in, he saw Jason Dobbs scrambling to hide a bottle of whiskey under his rolltop desk.

Dobbs looked up, his eyes wide and wild, then blinking as if he was trying to focus on Benoit.

"Jace, it's me, Jean."

"Well, I'll be damned," Dobbs said, attempting to stand up.

"You're drunk, Jace."

"Not as drunk as I intend to be." He stood on his feet and teetered for a moment. "And, what are you doing here? You come to watch them drum me out of the Army?" Dobbs lifted the bottle defiantly. "It cures the lame, it does." He stepped toward Benoit with his crippled foot. "Laugh at me like all the rest do. I must've patched a thousand wounds in the Army, saved a bunch of soldiers so they could get shot again, and I get crippled by the damn Comanches and the Army puts me out to pasture like a lame horse. It ain't right, dammit."

"I'm not talking to you until you sober up."

Dobbs staggered forward. "You're not talking to me because I'm lame. Before that everybody talked to me, everybody but damned paymaster Farragut. Talking to him was like talking to a tree. Of course, the Comanches got him before they crippled me. What are you doing here?"

"I came to see you."

"You came to see them drum me out of the Army, didn't you?"

"I came to invite you to go with me."

"Why would I want to go with you? You just came here to laugh at me like all the rest."

"I'm going to New Orleans. I may be getting out of the Army."

Dobbs eyed him severely, his gaze coming to rest on his legs. "You don't look like a cripple to me."

Benoit shook his head.

Dobbs lifted the bottle to his mouth, but before he could take a sip, Benoit batted it away.

The bottle shattered against the wall, its contents splattering on the wall, desk, and floor.

"What'd you do that for?"

"Because I don't like seeing you like this."

"What's it to you?"

"You're my friend, dammit."

"I don't have any friends anymore, not since the Comanches crippled me."

Benoit sighed. "I'm your friend, Jace, even if you are a stubborn, hard-headed New Englander."

Dobbs stared at him, then began to sob. "You came to see me, not just to laugh at me?"

"Damn, Jace, I can't stand you drunk." Benoit lunged forward and grabbed Dobbs, locking his strong arms around his chest.

"What are you doing? Put me down."

Benoit barged out of the office, half carrying, half dragging Dobbs through the ward. He stormed past the orderly and kicked open the outside door, then marched off the plank walk toward the hitching posts and a water trough.

"Put me down."

"With pleasure," Benoit said as he dumped Dobbs on the ground by the water trough, then grabbed his hair.

"Oooowwww!" Dobbs cried.

Benoit dunked his head into the trough.

Dobbs thrashed with his hands and bubbled in the water, trying to get air.

Benoit pulled him up.

He gasped for air.

Down Benoit pushed him again.

Dobbs shook his head, trying to break free, but Benoit held an iron grip.

Benoit yanked him up again.

Dobbs spewed water and curse words.

"One more time," Benoit cried as he shoved Dobbs's head back under for the third time. He bounced Dobbs's head around in the murky water.

Dobbs slapped the side of the trough, then tried to rise up on his feet.

Benoit released him.

Windmilling his arms and spewing water from his mouth and nose, he started screaming. "What are you doing?"

"I'm trying to see if cripples can swim."

Dobbs shook his head. "Cripples can do a lot of things."

"That's not how it sounded a moment ago."

"That's no cause to drown me."

"I like you better drowned than drunk."

"You'd be drunk, too, if you was being drummed out of the Army."

Dobbs stood up, then shut his eyes and opened them wide suddenly. He wobbled on his feet a moment, the result of the liquor, not the Comanche injury.

"I came to invite you to go with me to New Orleans, Jace."

"Why would I want to go there?"

"What are you going to do when the Army releases you?"

"I don't know."

"Well, you might need a partner, Jace."

"Who'd want a cripple for a partner?"

"I would."

"The Army won't let me partner with you."

"I may not be in the Army much longer."

"You'd resign for me?"

"I resigned two weeks ago, but General Smedley gave me a three-month leave instead to go to New Orleans."

"Why'd you resign?"

"My brother was killed."

"Theo? Oh, my God."

"You're the closest I got to a brother now, Jace."

Dobbs shook his head and rubbed his eyes. It seemed as if the news of Theophile's death had finally cut through the drunken haze of his mind. "I'm sorry. How did it happen?"

"Shell exploded on a ship is all I know. They never even found the body."

"I'm sorry about that, Jean. And I'm sorry you had to see me like this. Being a cripple's bad enough, but being a cripple and a drunk is too much."

"We brought your belongings, Jace."

"I don't know what to do with them."

"You're not thinking straight right now, anyway. Wait until tomorrow."

Dobbs shrugged. "I haven't thought straight since I was notified I'd be released."

"Is that when you took to the bottle?"

Dobbs nodded sheepishly. "I don't remember ever feeling lower than then. A man can get despondent over something like that."

"I don't know what to tell you to do, Jace, but I do know this. In three days my family and I will be leaving for New Orleans. We'd love to have you accompany us, if you're sober."

"I'll be sober."

Benoit nodded. "I don't want to see you again until you are, Jace."

Benoit answered the knock on the door and found Jason Dobbs standing before him, hat in hand.

"You look better than when I saw you yesterday, Jace."

Dobbs nodded. "I was fighting my demon. Getting kicked out of the Army didn't set well with me."

"Is that Jace?" Inge called from the adjacent room inside the small quarters where the Benoits were temporarily housed.

Before Benoit could answer, Inge was standing

behind him, then brushing past him to hug Dobbs vigorously.

Benoit could see Dobbs was even more embarrassed than before.

"Glad to see you, Inge."

"Come on in," Inge said, grabbing his arms and jerking him toward the door.

Dobbs balked.

"Jean may not want me in his place."

"Don't be silly," Inge said. "You're the best friend he's got in the world."

"No doubt about it," Benoit echoed.

Dobbs limped inside, where Ellen and Colleen were playing on a blanket on the wooden floor. He squatted beside them and tickled their bellies, then moved to one of four wooden chairs around the table.

"I've been thinking, Jean, about what I'd do next. Practicing medicine's better than a lot of jobs, but it wears on you. No matter how good you are, your patients all eventually die. I've tired of that, tired of so many things."

"You can make a living at it, Jace."

"Maybe, but I think I would like to write."

"Write?"

"You know, books. You've seen them, haven't you?" Dobbs teased.

"Not as many as you have, Jace, but I've seen a few."

"Maybe even try to give lectures about the West, the vile Comanche, New Mexico Territory, Wyoming, and all of that. I could even do lectures on the iniquity of slavery."

Benoit nodded. "Jace, as much as you've read and observed, you could lecture on just about anything."

"But would they pay to come to see me?"

"Sure they would," Inge interjected.

Benoit shrugged.

"They might come to see a lecture given by a man who was crippled by the Comanche, watch him hobble across the stage."

"Don't talk like that," Inge scolded. "You've got to pick up your spirits. Remember Erich? Well, he's walking now."

"It's not the same," Dobbs countered. "We didn't know what caused his paralysis. We know what caused mine, and even God can't cure a severed Achilles tendon."

"Come with us to New Orleans, Jace. You can try out your lectures there."

Dobbs grinned. "On a less discerning audience than I would find back East."

Benoit laughed. "That's the Jason Dobbs I remember. However, I wouldn't advise you talking about the evils of slavery in New Orleans, the largest slave market on the Mississippi."

Dobbs nodded. "I couldn't outrun a lynch mob."

"Tar and feathers would be more likely."

"I'd rather have the lynch mob."

"Would you come with us, Jace? Would you?" Inge asked, unable to contain her excitement.

Now Dobbs seemed more embarrassed, not for what he had done, but for the affection that Benoit and his wife had shown him. He nodded slightly.

"Is that a yes?" Benoit asked.

Dobbs grinned and nodded again, firmly this time.

When they assembled to depart El Paso three days later, Benoit studied Dobbs. It was the first time he had seen him out of uniform. He liked what he saw, and imagined himself shed of the Army uniform he'd worn since West Point.

It was so long since he'd been back home that Benoit found it hard to remember what life along the Mississippi had been like. The river, the trees, the humidity, all seemed buried in a distant part of his memory as if it was a different life. He had left New Orleans with his family intact. Now his father was gone, and his brother dead as well. His mother might likely die soon, and it did not seem right, that she most of all might soon be gone.

He heard a giggle from one of his daughters and it gave him hope. Life did go on for some. His parents had done for him what he must do for his girls. They had seen him to maturity and given him a start in life.

But life could be hard, certainly in the West, where civilization was a great concept, but not an everyday reality. At least in New Orleans there was opera and arts and schools and culture. Life there beat life on an Army post.

Benoit looked at Dobbs, who would never have to follow a stupid command again, and envied him. Benoit sat his daughters in the ambulance, then helped Inge up to the seat. Dobbs climbed awkwardly aboard. Benoit used a wheel spoke for a step and hoisted himself up in the seat beside his wife.

Only when the wagons began to roll did he truly realize he was returning home. He looked around him at the barren land that seemed the fringe of hell and realized how much he had missed New Orleans. He could show his wife and daughters the place of his birth, the spots where he played as a boy, where he went to the academy. The thoughts flooded his mind.

Perhaps he was turning his back not only on the

West, but also on the Army. Only time would tell.

As when he left New Orleans for West Point, and later for the West, he was starting anew. There was the excitement about the unknown. This time, though, he wasn't traveling alone. He had a wife, two daughters, and the best friend a man could ever have. It was more than he had started out with.

"I am glad to be going home," he said to himself as much as to any one else.

Author's Note

Comanche Trail is a work of fiction set in a historical context. Some characters, such as Joseph Machebeuf, will be recognized as historical figures, but most are fictional, though often loosely based upon actual people who lived and died in New Mexico Territory prior to the Civil War.

A historical novel such as this would not be possible without the groundwork provided by historians and scholars of the Old West. Consequently, I owe a great debt to those whose works provided background and ideas for this work. Among those writers whose works were most helpful included Nelson Lee for *Three Years Among the Comanche*; Lynn Bridgers for *Death's Deceiver: The Life of Joseph P. Machebeuf*; and Earnest Wallace and E. Adamson Hoebel for *The Comanches: Lords of the South Plains*.

Others include Ross Calvin for *Sky Determines: An Interpretation of the Southwest*; W.W.H. Davis for *El Gringo: New Mexico and Her People*; Roland F. Dickey for *New Mexico Village Arts*; T.R. Fehrenbach for

Comanches; Jane Lenz Elder and David J. Weber for *Trading in Santa Fe;* Francis L. and Roberta B. Fugate for *Roadside History of New Mexico;* Josiah Gregg for *Commerce of the Prairies;* William E. Hill for *The Santa Fe Trail: Yesterday and Today;* Max L. Moorhead for *New Mexico's Royal Road: Trade and Travel on the Chihuahua Trail;* W. W. Newcomb Jr. for *The Indians of Texas;* David Grant Noble for *Pueblos, Villages, Forts and Trails: A Guide to New Mexico's Past;* Stanley Noyes for *Los Comanches: The Horse People, 1751–1845;* John Sherman for *Santa Fe: A Pictoral History;* and Randy Steffen for *The Horse Soldier, 1776–1943.*

Without their works, this volume in the People of the Plains saga would not have been possible. As readers of this series know, the story of Jean Benoit and the other colorful characters chronicled in this and the preceding volumes drew heavily upon the imagination of Ken Englade. My thanks to him for the opportunity to carry on this saga with a few touches of my own, and to be associated with the name of one of the best of all Southwestern writers, Tony Hillerman.

I must also acknowledge with gratitude the opportunity this book has allowed for me to continue working with HarperPaperbacks Senior Editor Jessica Lichtenstein, whose deft touch on seven previous novels has certainly enhanced the finished product each time. I must also acknowledge Ethan Ellenberg, my agent, for solid advice and his many contributions to my writing career.

Finally, I must thank my wife, Harriet, whose support, encouragement, and understanding over the years have allowed me to invest the time and energy it requires to become a novelist. Whatever successes I have had would not have been possible without her love and patience.

Will Camp
Lubbock, Texas
January 1999